CONFLICTED

COAST GUARD RECON BOOK 3

LORI MATTHEWS

ABOUT THE BOOK

From the bestselling author of the Callahan Security Series.

Meet Elias Mason of the US Coast Guard's TEAM RECON. As in reconstructed. As in broken and needs fixing.

Team RECON has a new headquarters now—Miami, Florida, which also happens to be Elias's hometown. He's been avoiding his past like the plague, but there are some things you can't outrun. Like the death of his best friend, his past involvement with the local gang, and his first love, Andrea Torres.

Andrea has been on a path of vengeance for years. Now an agent with the Bureau of Alcohol, Tobacco, Firearms and Explosives, Andy is determined to take down Santiago, the main runner of guns, money, and drugs in Miami, and the man who killed her sister. Her current undercover assignment has her so close to caging Santiago, she can taste it.

To stay on top, Santiago has to turn to buying guns from the Russians and selling them to militia groups, and then train them to use the weapons. Elias and Andrea will need to bury their animosity and ignore the fiery chemistry between them to run a game of deception as insiders for Santiago. Pretending to be the couple they once were in order to bring their common enemy to justice would work if only the Russians didn't have other plans.

Conflicted

This one is for JoAnn Ficca.
Thank you so much for being a fan.

ACKNOWLEDGMENTS

I want to thank Joseph D'Elia (Lieutenant, USCG) who has the patience of a saint and answered all my questions about the Coast Guard. Then encouraged me to create my own version of reality. I couldn't have created Team RECON without his help. Any mistakes are my own.

My deepest gratitude also goes out to my editors, Corinne DeMaagd and Heidi Senesac; my cover artist, Llewellen Designs for making my story come alive: my virtual assistant, Susan Poirier and my FaceBook guru, Amanda Robinson. My personal cheer squad which I could not survive without: Janna MacGregor, Suzanne Burke, Stacey Wilk, Kimberley Ash and Tiara Inserto. My husband and my children who make my hair turn gray but also make me laugh. And to you, the reader. Your emails and posts mean the world to me. The fact that you read my stories is the greatest gift ever. Thank you.

PROLOGUE

The deck of the boat rolled beneath their feet as they struggled with the weight of their cargo. It was heavy and, more importantly, hard to get a good hold on in the pouring rain. The storm had come out of nowhere, and the two men were unprepared.

"*Le ararras los pies!*" yelled Diego, the taller of the two men.

"*Qué?*" Luis asked. He cupped his ear. The wind gusted, and the boat rolled again. Luis grabbed for the side.

Diego tried again in Spanish, but Luis shook his head. Diego swore. He motioned wildly, indicating the legs of the dead guy.

Luis nodded. He reached down to the deck and grabbed the sneaker-clad feet of the dead man while Diego tried to spread the body bag open enough for Luis to guide the feet in. But the wind pulled it out of Diego's hand. "*Mierda!*"

They'd been trying to get the body in the bag for the last ten minutes, but with the wind, the waves, and Luis puking over the side, it was hopeless.

Diego shook his head. "Fuck the bag. Wrap the chains around the body and toss it."

Luis immediately dropped the feet. He grabbed onto the side of the boat and vomited again. Diego shook his head and swore again. It was fucking amateur hour with this kid. If he wasn't the boss's cousin, Diego would have just pushed the kid overboard to put him out of his misery.

Diego picked up the top half of the body and got Luis to place the chain underneath. Then they worked together to get it wrapped around the dead man a couple of times. Diego stood up. "Okay, Luis. On the count of three, we swing him over the side. Just make sure you secure the chain." He handed Luis a massive padlock. "I gotta check the anchor. It feels like we're moving too much."

Luis took the lock. Diego stumbled toward the bow of the speed boat. Luis bent down and tried to slide the large hasp through the chain. The boat bobbed in the waves, throwing him off-balance. He fell and hit his face on the side of the boat. Cursing, he struggled up onto his hands and knees and tried again. He managed to get the lock through the first chain and was working on the second when Diego came back.

Diego tapped him on the shoulder. "The anchor is gone. We gotta go."

Luis snapped the lock shut and then grabbed the dead man's feet. Diego picked up the top part of the body. The two men swung the dead man a few times to build up momentum. "One, two—"

The boat unexpectedly pitched sideways, and a large wave crashed over the side, driving both Diego and Luis backward. The bow swung up and then crashed down again, rattling their bones. The dead guy had been balanced on the side, but when the boat dropped into the trough, he was gone.

"Good riddance," Luis muttered. He then sat down on the deck and started praying. Diego went to the controls and threw the boat into gear. The powerful engines roared above the sound of the wind and the waves, and the boat jumped forward, heading toward Miami. This had been one of the worst jobs ever. He hated working with Luis. He'd had a bad feeling about the whole thing the moment his boss mentioned it, but it wasn't like he could say "no." He was just glad it was over. He couldn't wait to get on dry land and leave all this shit behind him.

CHAPTER ONE

"Hey babe, bring me a beer," yelled Samuel Soto from in front of the TV.

Andrea Torres gritted her teeth. She'd been working undercover for what seemed like forever, and this asshole Soto would just not budge. Usually, she was good at getting men to tell her things, but Soto was very closed-mouthed. And it was getting harder and harder to find reasons she couldn't sleep with him. There was no way in hell she was having sex with that animal. No fucking way at all. Case or no case.

Andy's long, dark curly hair was hanging loose over her shoulders. Her white tank top was a tad too small so it scooped low over her chest, showing off more cleavage than she was comfortable with, and she'd covered herself as much as possible with a red plaid shirt that was open but tied at the waist. She also wore an old pair of jeans that were a fraction too tight. She longed for a pair of sweats and a big old T-shirt.

She opened the fridge and pulled out a beer. Plastering a

fake smile on her face, she walked into the other room. "Here," she said in a sweet voice.

Soto patted the sofa next to him. "*Ven siéntate a mi lado. Come sit by my side. The match is boring.*"

His friend Tommy Rosario snorted. "It's only boring 'cause your team is losing."

"You watch your mouth, Tommy. It ain't over yet," Soto growled.

He had stopped paying any attention to Andy, so she drifted back into the kitchen. It was better if she was out of sight. He paid less attention to her that way. She leaned against the counter and then thought the better of it. The house was disgusting, and who knew what was living under all the pizza boxes and leftover take-out cartons.

"So, Soto, when's it coming?"

Andy cocked her head. *Please let this be it.* She wanted this job to be over so badly it hurt. She hated being in Miami and, worse, she hated that she was doing this job under her real name. The neighborhood where she grew up already thought she was trash just like her sister, Carmen. They all said it was such a waste that Carmen had died of a drug overdose, but Andy knew it was more than a waste. It was murder and only one man was responsible for that. Now hanging out with Soto was just confirmation of everything people thought about her for years. *Guilt by association.* Andy cupped a hand over her mouth and tuned into the conversation in the next room.

"I told you, man, I'll tell you when it's time. Stop bugging me about it."

"It's just that I'm broke, man, and I need to make some cash," Tommy whined.

Soto snorted. "Stop shooting up your money, and you won't be broke."

"I know man, but you know how it is."

Soto didn't respond. The announcer had started yelling. Someone was going in to score. They were watching some soccer game. *Football, chica, how many times do I gotta tell you that?* Soto was all into soccer. Andy was pretty sure he bet on it with his bookie.

Soto's cell phone went off. Text message. She recognized the sound. Soto must have called someone because he was talking suddenly. "Yeah. When?" Silence. "Okay." Then he must have clicked off the call because he said, "That was the call. The deal is goin' down tomorrow, but we gotta do it on the water like I said. Your boy got that boat we can use?"

"He does. He does. We can grab it in the morning."

"Nah, man, the deal don't be goin' down til it's dark. Midnight. I got the coordinates. We'll pick up the boat around eight. It'll take some time to get out there."

Andy did a mental dance of joy. She just had to make it out of here tonight, and then they'll grab him tomorrow and it will be over. They could follow the boat out and then grab Soto when he was making the exchange. She would finally be done with this damn assignment, and she could get out of Miami. *Just one more day.*

She took a deep breath. "I'm gonna go," she said as she came around the corner.

"No, babe. You stay."

She smiled at Soto. "No, I gotta go see my aunt. I'll be back. Maybe I'll bring you some of her food. You know how much you like her cookin'."

Soto's eyes narrowed. "I said you stay."

Just then, the announcer started yelling on the screen and Soto's attention drifted off her. As the announcer became more excited, Andy slowly backed out of the room. She had made it around the corner and opened the back door as quietly as possible when the announcer started screaming. Soto's team scored.

Andy hit the stairs at a dead run and made it over the backyard fence in record time. She was down the alley and into her beater car before Soto had a chance to notice, or so she hoped. If he came looking for her at her aunt's, it would be a problem.

She doubted he would because her aunt had a fierce reputation in the neighborhood, and no one wanted to take her on. Esther Madera was not someone to be messed with. The whole neighborhood knew it. Andy was thankful in more ways than one that her aunt still spoke to her. Offering Andy protection without knowing the truth made Aunt Esther truly a saint. Someday, she would explain to her aunt that she was really an Alcohol, Tobacco, and Firearms agent, ATF, and a damn fucking good one. But today was not that day.

Andy parked on the street in front of her aunt's place and went in the front door. "Hey, Aunt Esther," she called out as she walked through the front room and into the dining room that was separated from the kitchen by a breakfast bar. Her aunt, who was standing in front of the stove, turned to look at Andy.

"Andrea." Her aunt looked up from making dinner, and her lips thinned. Andy didn't want to meet Esther's gaze, so she checked out the stove in front of her. Stuffed peppers by the look of things, one of Andy's favorites.

"You were over with Soto again. He is bad news, chica."

Andy finally met her gaze. It was only one more day. One more. But the sadness written on the woman's face splintered Andy's heart. She came around the counter and went to stand by her aunt. She reached out and squeezed the woman's arm. "Aunt Esther...there's more going on than I can say. I— You just have to trust me. It shouldn't be much longer now."

Her aunt's eyes narrowed as she studied her niece, but she

nodded her head once. She went back to making dinner. "You're just in time. It's one of your favorites."

Andy smiled. She really needed to call her boss and set up a meet, but the food smelled so good her stomach growled. "Let me make a quick call, and then I'll help you."

After her aunt nodded again, Andy went to her bedroom in the back corner of the little house. She made sure the windows were closed and the blinds were down. Then she pulled the bed out slightly and knelt. She removed the vent cover and pulled out a cell phone. She dialed a number she knew by heart.

"It's me," she said when the man on the other end answered. "Soto said the deal is going down tomorrow night on the water. He's getting a boat from some friend of Tommy's."

Her boss, Derek Robins, grunted. "Did he say where on the water the meet was?"

"No. Just that they'd pick the boat up around eight because it would take a while to get there. He has the coordinates, and the meet is set for midnight."

"Okay. I want you to come in tonight, and let's get everything organized for the bust. I'll send the guys to get you. They'll be there in about twenty minutes, in back of your aunt's place."

"Make it an hour."

There was silence on the other end of the phone, but then her boss mumbled, "Fine," and then clicked off the call. Andy stared at the phone for a second and then hit the erase button. She had enough shit to deal with without Robins being an ass. She'd dumped him a few months back, and he still wasn't over it. In her mind, he'd gone from Derek to Robins overnight. Now, he was just another boss. And he made it obvious he hated that.

Robins was tall with light brown hair and blue eyes that

had seemed so sincere. He was a handsome guy in a classic sort of way, and she'd been flattered when he'd asked her out. He'd told her how much he admired her skill, and she'd believed him. But dating her boss had been a stupid thing to do, and she'd known it almost immediately, although it had taken her a few months to end the relationship.

Robins was a manipulator, and he liked to be in control of everything, including her. He'd been angry when she'd broken it off. He sucked at letting go. It was only when she mentioned that the relationship could be construed as sexual harassment since he was in a position of power over her that he finally stopped pestering her about getting back together.

He still hadn't forgiven her, though.

Andy made sure the phone was clean and even went as far as dialing the number for a local cab company, as she did after every call. That way, if someone ever found the burner phone, they wouldn't find anything if they hit redial. She put the phone back into the heating vent and put the cover on. Then she moved the bed back into place.

An hour and a half later, Andy was sitting at a picnic table in a secluded part of a small park well outside of her neighborhood with the rest of the team. Robins, her boss, was sitting across from her.

Agent Jay Vale sat next to her, eating her aunt's leftovers. Jay was tall and reed-thin with thick blond hair and hazel eyes that always struck her as a little bit sad. She'd brought enough for everyone, but only Jay and Agent Riccardo Peña had helped themselves.

Peña sat next to Robins as he tucked into the peppers. He was shorter than the other men, but he had a friendly smile and sparkling brown eyes. Peña also had a lovely wife and two daughters that he talked about constantly. Andy had liked him immediately when they'd first met.

"How's Isabella?" she asked him.

His daughter Izzy had learning difficulties. She was on the autism spectrum, and she had physical issues due to being born prematurely. He doted on her. The whole family did. She was a lovely child.

Peña sighed. "She is good. She goes to see another doctor next week. Still doing her therapy sessions, and her walking is getting much better. So is her reading. But it's expensive. I don't know how much longer we can keep them up."

Her heart broke for Peña and his family. The medical system wasn't really set up to help children like Izzy. Peña paid out thousands upon thousands of dollars to get all manner of therapy for Izzy, yet her progress was slight. She reached out and touched his arm. "Tell Izzy I said 'hey.'"

He smiled. "She'll like that."

Robins glanced at her hand on Peña's arm and then back at her face. "So back to business. You have no idea where on the water they're going to meet?" Robins asked again.

She shook her head. "Soto said he had the coordinates but didn't elaborate at all."

"What do you think, boss?" Jay asked between mouthfuls.

Derek narrowed his eyes slightly. "I think following Soto tomorrow night goes without saying, but I'd feel a lot better about it if we could get a tracker on him."

Andy shook her head. "Soto isn't stupid. He checks and rechecks everything. There's nothing he's going to take with him that we can stick a tracker on without him knowing it. We'll just have to be on our toes. How many more bodies are we going to get on this?"

"Not sure yet," Robins said. "Once I get back and run it up the chain of command, I'll have a better idea, but there will be enough to do it right. Two boats, I think, plus some air support. It's supposed to be a big shipment, so we should get the okay for the additional manpower without a problem."

"You must be happy, Andy, to be done with Soto," Peña commented.

She grinned. "You have no idea. It's getting harder and harder to keep him at arm's length."

"I don't think you're done with him just yet." Robins put his palms flat on the table.

Andy's stomach knotted, and a wave of nausea rolled through her. "What do you mean?"

"If we can't track Soto, then we have to track the next best thing." Derek pointed at her chest. "You."

Jay stopped chewing, and Peña let out a muffled curse. The weight of both of their gazes settled on Andy, but she didn't take her eyes off her boss. "No. No way. I told you he's getting more demanding. His behavior is getting more erratic. If there hadn't been some European soccer game he was watching, I wouldn't have been able to get out of there tonight. I am *not* risking my life for this." She squared her shoulders. "I'm just... no."

She'd had misgivings about this assignment from the get-go, and she'd voiced them, but Robins had overridden her doubts. He said it would affect her career negatively if she didn't take it. It was only supposed to last a couple of weeks, but here they were three months in, and she was struggling to not blow her cover. She was also running out of excuses not to sleep with him.

Soto was paranoid and a bit crazy. He was also deadly as hell. It had taken her weeks to gain his trust. In the beginning he'd had a girlfriend, so he wasn't looking to make friends but then he'd dumped Angelica and things went downhill. First, Andy had used the excuse that she had "woman problems." Then she said she needed to get on birth control, and she'd gone on in detail about the types and having to get a doctor's appointment. He'd just told her to hurry up. Now she'd run out of excuses and he was horny. He hadn't wanted to let her out of his sight. Gong back in was too dangerous.

Robins retorted, "We need you on the inside. It's too easy to lose Soto on the water with no idea where he's going. We've *all* spent months on this. Not just you. We need to see it through. It's only one more day." Her boss's face was neutral, but she couldn't get past the feeling that he was punishing her. He wanted her to suffer because she dumped him. He wanted her to feel uneasy and be scared. There was a gleam in his eye she didn't trust.

"I don't think—"

"You can manage Soto." Robins dismissed her fears with a wave of his hand. "Jay, can you get the tech guys to rig up something for Andy to take with her?"

Jay glanced at Andy. "Yeah, I'll call Craig."

"Good." Robins looked down at his phone, which had started buzzing. "I gotta take this." He got up from the table and wandered toward the trees.

"You don't have to do this, Andy," Peña said as soon as their boss was out of earshot. "It's dangerous as hell. I don't know what Robins is thinking." He shook his head.

Andy sighed. "Jay, is he right? Will it be hard to follow Soto on the water?"

Jay frowned. "Yes, he's right. We'll need air support, and I already checked; the moon will be full tomorrow night. Lots of light so the air support will be able to see clearly, but they'll have to stay back otherwise they will be seen. It would be much easier if we had a tracker on Soto or the boat."

She glanced at Robins. He was still engrossed in his call. "Do you have any suggestions on how we can get a tracker on Soto or Tommy without me going back?"

Jay looked helpless, and Peña swore as he dug a cigarillo

out of his pack. "It's a bad fucking idea, Andy, and you know it."

"You're right, Peña, it is a bad idea, but I don't have a better one and neither do you, so I guess I'm stuck with it." Her palms started to sweat. She knew in the depths of her soul something bad was going to come from this. She said a short prayer that tomorrow night's adventure didn't get her killed.

CHAPTER TWO

Elias cursed as he dropped his boot on his toe. He was late, and if he didn't haul ass, his ride to work, Cain Maddox, would start blowing the horn, which would piss off Mrs. Jimenez in the next apartment over. Then she would lie in wait for him to come home and give him another lecture. It was like living in a fucking dorm or something. He would find a new place if this one wasn't so awesome in other ways.

Elias shoved his foot into the offending boot and then laced it up. Of course, he wouldn't be late if he hadn't stayed up all night playing poker. It had been a great night. The cards fell his way. Who was he kidding? He kicked ass because he was awesome at poker. He'd started playing years ago to deal with his rage over his best friend's death. Playing poker was one of the few times he could block out all the pain. Turned out he was damn good at it. Too good. It was always hard to get up and leave the table.

He stood and did up his jeans. Then he buckled his belt and threw on his short-sleeved navy T-shirt, leaving it untucked. He grabbed his gun off the nightstand and slipped it under the T-shirt into the waist band of his jeans. He was enjoying not wearing his uniform. Rear Admiral Lower Half George Bertrand had agreed with Nick Taggert, Elias's team leader, that dressing in civilian clothes made more sense, for now. Especially since their headquarters was located in an office building.

He glanced at his reflection in the full-length mirror that was across from the bed on the wall. His brown wavy hair was short the way he liked it, but there was already a pained look in his chocolate brown eyes. His right leg was hurting again. He took a second to rub the scar from the bullet wound he'd received oh-so-long ago. He'd spent too long sitting at a poker table last night, and now he was paying for it, but he'd won a lot of cash, so it wasn't all bad.

The blue-green of the ocean caught his eye. It didn't matter how many times he looked out his windows, the view never failed to impress. It was one of the very few things he missed since he'd signed on with the Coast Guard and left Miami.

He grabbed his go bag and walked across the big open space to the door. He glanced at the kitchen area in the corner. There was still a bit of coffee in the pot, but it would be cold by now. He decided to skip it. He let his gaze roam over the apartment. Was there anything else he needed? He'd been bouncing around for years, always picking up second-hand furniture and leaving it behind, only to buy again in the new place.

The couch was overstuffed and in a shade of brown that reminded him of hot chocolate. It was in the middle of the room, facing the left wall where his big-screen TV hung. Matching overstuffed chairs flanked the sofa, and a coffee table in front. On the other side of the room was a dining table and six chairs. It was done in a light wood. He'd gotten it cheap since it was a floor model, but he'd never eaten at it since there was an island by the kitchen area that had black leather stools tucked under it. He preferred to eat there.

The view through the huge glass windows overlooking Biscayne Bay had always held his attention anyway. He didn't mind that there were tankers going in and out in front of him. He liked to watch their movements. It was soothing in a way.

He'd rented this loft because he'd liked the open plan and the view, but the thing that had really sold it was the rooftop deck. Nothing better than being out under the stars and hearing the waves when he couldn't sleep in the middle of the night.

Elias glanced at his watch and cursed. He pulled open the loft door and almost plowed over Mrs. Jimenez. She glared at him.

"He hasn't even hit the horn yet," Elias said.

"Your friend is parked directly in front of the door, so now Mr. Tanez can't get dropped off. You know he can't walk far."

Elias stared at the woman. She barely came up to the middle of his chest, so she couldn't have topped five feet. She was heavyset and constantly wore loose-fitting dresses with lots of flowers on them. Her dark eyes were always glaring at him, and because he towered over her, he knew she needed a trip to the hairdresser to fix her roots.

He sighed. "Well, then I guess you'd better move so I can leave and Mr. Tanez can have his parking spot."

Mrs. Jimenez narrowed her eyes and then mumbled something about him having bad manners. Once she shuffled to the side, Elias exited his loft. He pulled the door closed and locked it. Then he nodded to Mrs. Jimenez and jogged down the stairs, wincing each time his right leg took his weight. He hit the bottom floor a minute later and opened the main door.

Mr. Tanez was just coming up to the entryway. His gait was slow, and he leaned heavily on his cane, but his bright brown eyes twinkled. His white hair was cut close to his scalp, and he wore a polo shirt with a pair of plaid shorts. His spindly legs stuck out like sticks on a snowman. Elias gritted his teeth but couldn't seem to stop himself from apologizing to the old man. "Mr. Tanez, sorry if we blocked your spot."

Mr. Tanez looked up at Elias. "It's fine." He waved his hand. "Mrs. Jimenez, she's nosy, and you won't tell her anything. You tell her what she wants to know, and she'll be nicer to you."

Elias frowned. "But it's none of her business."

"No, but it will make your life easier." He shook his head. "You don't want to tell her the truth, make some shit up, but tell her something so she'll stop talking about you to the rest of us."

Elias grinned. The old man had a point. "I'll give it some thought."

"Just don't make it too wild. That will set her off, too," Mr. Tanez said.

"Thanks for the advice." Elias glanced up and saw Cain pointing at his watch. He nodded. "Have a good one, Mr. Tanez."

"You, too, young man," Mr. Tanez mumbled as he made his way in the door.

Elias climbed into Cain's truck. "Sorry."

Cain pulled away from the curb. "Why do you live with a pile of old people?"

Elias laughed. "The view and the rooftop deck are worth it."

"How did you even get into that building in the first place? I thought it was seniors only."

"The owners are having some security issues. There've been some attacks on the elderly in the neighborhood. They let me have the apartment with the idea that I would help them fix their security and generally try to keep the building safe."

Cain glanced over. "They hired you for that? Obviously, they didn't do their research."

"Thanks," Elias grunted. "I'll remember that."

Twenty minutes later, Cain pulled into the parking lot at their new office. Elias shook his head slightly. None of the team liked being in an office building. It was just weird. "At least there's parking."

"If only you had a car."

"Funny," Elias said as he opened the door. "I'll get coffee." He got out and slammed the door and then headed to the food truck parked at the curb, shouting a greeting at the owner. "Morning, Carlos."

"Hey, man. How's it going?"

He nodded his head. "Going well."

Carlos already started lining up the little cups for Cuban coffee. "Your usual?"

"Yeah." Cafe Cubano was something Elias had missed. The Cuban espresso beans had a particular taste, and when sugar was added, well, it was better than any other caffeine drink going. He always brought eight little cups up to the office with him each morning. The guys had adjusted to it and now had come to expect it. They were even starting to order it on their own.

He scanned the street. An SUV was parked down the block with two men in it. "The SUV down the block…" Elias started.

"The one with the two men in it?" Carlos asked without looking up from making the coffee.

"Yeah. They been here long?"

Carlos started pouring the dark, rich liquid into the small to-go cups. "They arrived about an hour ago. Not sure what they're watching, something in your building. But dude, you got a lot of shady stuff going on in your building."

Elias smiled slowly. Carlos was not wrong. He dug some bills out of his pocket and dropped them on the counter. Carlos finished putting the cups in two to-go cup holders and picked up the cash. It was the price of the coffee plus a hefty tip.

Elias cocked an eyebrow at Carlos. "You'll let me know if…?" He didn't finish the sentence. He didn't have to. Carlos was already nodding. "You got my cell?" Elias confirmed, and Carlos nodded again. The two men clasped hands, and then Elias picked up the two trays. "Have a good one."

He walked away from the food truck and headed over to the office building. He hated having both hands full, but he didn't feel there was any immediate danger. Besides, he'd drop the coffee and get his gun in a heartbeat if necessary. It would just be a waste of good coffee.

Elias entered the building and took the elevator up to the fourth floor. Once the doors slid open, he walked across the hallway to a plain brown door. A small sign on the wall next to the door read *American Atlantic Sales Company*. Below that was a doorbell. Elias hit the bell with his elbow and waited.

Axel Cantor opened the door and grinned when he saw the coffee. "My man. I have been waiting for this." His blue eyes shone with appreciation for the drinks. He flicked his blond hair out of his eyes and said, "After you," ushering Elias into the room.

Elias entered and immediately turned right and then went around the cubicle walls that were facing the door. He set the coffee down on the first desk. "Those two are mine," he told the other guys as they all got up and came forward.

The office space was just that, office space, and it wasn't ideal for their situation, no matter what the upper echelon at Homeland thought. It was a big, open square space with floor-to-ceiling windows on two walls. When they'd first arrived in the new space, it had been organized into little cubicles. Nick Taggert, their team leader, immediately got them to work changing it. Now the cubicle walls lined the outside, leaving a small hallway between them and the windows.

Inside the square there were a bunch of desks in rows. Every man had claimed one for himself, and there were plenty of empty ones in between. On the right wall was a row of metal cabinets that stored all kinds of extra equipment, including ammunition. There were no guns, though. Security wasn't tight enough yet that anyone felt comfortable leaving weapons overnight.

Axe sat down at his desk in the front row. Finn Walsh sat in the row behind, but two desks over. His brown hair was lightening from the sunshine, and his light blue eyes looked a little less haunted since they'd made the move to Miami six weeks ago.

Finn had his zoo of origami animals set up on the desk next to him.

"Not sure if Cuban coffee is a good thing for you. I thought the whole point of the origami was for you to relax. Two shots of those, and you'll be bouncing off the walls," Axe declared.

"No one asked you," Finn retorted as he downed his first shot. "It just helps me make them faster."

Axe burst out laughing.

Cain took the desk in the corner of the back row. Typical for him. He liked his space, and everyone left him to it. Elias walked over and handed two cups to Cain, who was adjusting his black hair into a man bun. He was the only guy who could get away with being in the Coast Guard and having long hair. No one fucked with Cain, not even the top brass. It just wasn't worth the hell he could rain down.

Nick grabbed his two cups and went to the first desk in the first row. His brown hair was a little longer than regulation length, but not out of control like the others. He did, however, have stubble on his jawline. They all bucked the system in their own way. He picked up one of the small cups and downed the coffee shot.

"Tag, man, there's a black SUV on the street about half a block down. There are two men inside. Carlos says they arrived a little more than an hour ago, but they're keeping an eye on this building."

"The men are wearing suits," Cain said as he sipped his coffee. "Feds of some kind, by the look of things."

"Yeah," Nick said, "I saw them on the way in. Makes me a wee nervous. I think we give them a bit of time to settle in, and then if they don't disappear before lunch, we can go out and rattle their cage."

"Any news on the new office space?" Elias asked.

"Nope." Nick shook his head. "The lovely folks at Homeland seem to think this is an ideal location for us."

Axe frowned. "They are aware that our headquarters in Panama blew up, and the boat we were working out of in the Middle East burnt to the waterline, aren't they? Not that we're going to have a repeat of those two incidents..." he said with a grin and then sobered up. "But seriously, there are other people here. Someone could get hurt."

Nick leaned his butt on the surface of an adjacent desk. "I pointed that out to Admiral Bertrand, but there's only so much he can do. Hopefully, we'll be able to eventually find something. Cain, how's the security system coming?"

Cain shrugged. "It's as good as I can get it without building a whole new panel in the electrical room. This place isn't wired right for that type of thing. I can rewire, but it will draw attention."

"Let's avoid any attention. Keep the extra guns in the

storage unit for now. We'll see about bringing them over if things don't get sorted out with some new office digs."

Elias finished his first coffee and walked over to the garbage can in the corner by the window. As he dropped the cup in, he checked out the SUV below. No movement. From this angle, it was hard to tell if anyone was inside, but he was guessing that if the men had gotten out, Carlos would have called him. He idly wondered where on Carlos's list he was in terms of calls. Carlos was too street smart for Elias to be the only one paying him for information.

Elias went back to his desk and started his second coffee. Carlos was right about shady characters in the building. It was only six floors, with an average of four offices per floor, but most of them were just like this office. A solid brown door with a plaque and a name next to it. The names were not familiar, and if he looked them up, Elias was sure that half of them wouldn't exist. Homeland owned the building, so the guys had assumed the other tenants were clandestine government organizations as well, but with the SUV out front, Elias wondered if they were wrong about that.

Nick put his hands on his hips. "So, the ATF requested backup for some op that's happening out on the water tonight. Since we're in town, the local Coast Guard boys decided to invite us along. I'm getting the impression they don't love the ATF guy in charge, and they want some backup in case everything turns to shit."

"Nice! Been a while since we had some action." Finn stood up and stretched his right arm, as though trying to loosen up his shoulder. "I could use some fun."

There were general noises of agreement, but Elias remained silent. He had an uneasy feeling in the pit of his stomach. Something was off. His grandmother used to say she could smell trouble on the wind. He just knew that something was brewing, and it wasn't good.

CHAPTER THREE

"Where did you go last night?" Soto demanded for the umpteenth time as he gripped Andy's arm and twisted it.

Andy gritted her teeth. "I told you I went to see my aunt. We had dinner, and she asked me to take some food over to Mrs. Gonzales. I took her some stuffed peppers and sat and chatted with her for a while. That's it."

"I went to your aunt's place. She said you were out. If you were at the neighbor's, why didn't she tell me?" Soto demanded, his stale breath hot on her face. "She said she didn't know."

"Soto, man," Tommy said as he glanced around the Blue Iguana dance bar, "people are watching, man."

"I don't give a fuck," Soto snarled. "I'm a Street Ace. Ain't nobody gonna say anything to me. We run this joint." But he glanced around and dropped Andy's arm. He adjusted his black leather jacket. Then he grabbed her arm again but a little less conspicuously.

Tommy looked scared, his eyes darting around the bar area as he twisted the front of his black T-shirt in his hands.

They were seated at a table not far from the bar. The place was fairly empty, and no one was on the dance floor yet. It was early. Soto and Tommy had come in for dinner, as Andy knew they would.

"My aunt probably didn't want you to go over and scare Mrs. Gonzales. You know she gets confused real easy." Andy had managed to avoid Soto last night and for most of the day today, but she still had to either plant the tracker on him or Tommy or go with them on the boat. So, here she was getting her arm wrenched from her shoulder by the paranoid asshole.

"You're hurting me," she said between clenched teeth. She'd worn jeans, a white tank top with a navy T-shirt over it, and a gray hoodie. Soto liked her to show off her assets so she usually wore tight, little tank tops or T-shirts to please him, but she knew the boat would be cold and she was hoping to deter him from wanting to have sex with her. She had a nice figure, and letting her boobs hang out wouldn't help her cause. She couldn't wait til this job was over so she could go back to her normal clothes, a nice blouse and blazer with dress pants or jeans. So much more comfortable.

"I'll fuckin' hurt you if you're seeing someone else." Soto got right in her face. "You hear me, bitch! You are mine, and you're gonna stay that way. We gotta long boat ride ahead of us tonight, and we're gonna make the most of it."

He shoved her, but finally released her arm for good this time. "Go get me a beer."

Andy stood up and approached the bar. She tried to get her equilibrium back, but it was hard. The desire to smash Soto's nose into his face was strong. She would never put up with this kind of shit in real life, and it pained her greatly to have to do it in the name of a job.

Antonio, the bartender, came over and stood in front of her.

"Three beers," Andy said.

Antonio nodded. He reached behind him and grabbed the bottles out of the fridge. He turned around and placed them on the counter. "You okay?" he asked in a low voice.

She nodded once.

"You know Soto is an animal. You could do much better, Andrea."

"I hear you." She'd grown up with Antonio. They'd known each other since they were little. "I'm okay, Antonio, but thanks for looking out for me." She reached in her pocket and pulled out the cash for the beer. She always had to pay. Soto was also a cheap bastard.

"Soto might be a Street Ace, but he's not well-liked. Tying yourself to him might not be such a great idea in more ways than one."

Andy glanced up at Antonio. She had to make a split-second decision about the future of her op. If it didn't work out tonight, she needed other options. "I'm not tied to him. He's not my boyfriend, despite what he thinks. I'm trying to get in, Antonio. I want to make some real money. I thought Soto might be able to help, but it turns out he's all talk."

Antonio grimaced. "He's got a big mouth. He's also got a mean streak a mile wide. You just watch yourself. I'll let you know if I hear of any…opportunities."

"I appreciate that, Antonio." She smiled at her friend as she picked up the beers and headed back to the table. Soto was glaring at her.

"What the fuck were you talking about with Antonio?" he demanded.

Andy tightly squeezed the beer bottles in her hands. "The fucking weather, Soto." She slammed the beers down on the table and sat down hard on the chair.

"Don't you get—"

"Soto," barked a tall, bald man from across the dance floor. "Come here."

Soto glared at her and then stood up. He walked across the room. No one said no to Ignacio. He was Santiago's right-hand man, and Santiago was the top of the food chain in these parts. He started out as a Street Ace back when Andy was a kid. He was the cause of all her troubles. She hated Santiago with a fierceness that took her breath away. He was also the reason she left Miami and became an ATF agent.

During her absence, he'd climbed to the top of the Street Aces and then beyond. Technically, he'll always be a Street Ace but he didn't bother with gang life anymore. He'd gone beyond that. He was a major player in drugs and guns in Miami. He was the man that made things happen. Ignacio was, by extension, the man in charge. When he said jump, a Street Ace asked, "How high?"

Rumbles about some of the gang not liking that Santiago had gotten out, but he threw enough business their way and offered them just enough protection that no one really did more than grumble.

Except for Soto.

Soto was ambitious. He was stirring the pot. He wanted a bigger piece of the pie, and this deal was his way up. Ignacio was giving him his shot. If Soto didn't mess this up, he could rise up the food chain.

The thing was, Soto was going to fuck up the deal. He was too aggressive for his own good. Andy knew Soto would have something planned. She had no idea what it was, but her gut said he wasn't going to just do the deal and hand over the guns to Ignacio. He was going to make some play.

It was why she insisted the team grab the guns instead of letting Soto keep going. She'd pushed it with Robins, and he'd finally agreed that if they could get Soto, they could get him to turn on others and maybe get all the way to Ignacio. From him, they could get Santiago.

In her heart of hearts, she knew they'd be lucky to get Ignacio, and there was no way they had a shot at Santiago, but she couldn't safely stay under with Soto. So, it was now or never.

"Andrea"—Tommy glanced at Soto and then back at her —"I think it's better if you stay here tonight." Tommy had been a bit sweet on her from the minute she'd met him. Possibly because she'd always been nice to him. He was a druggie, but he was a nice kid, or at least that's how she saw him. Not too smart, but not a real threat either.

She glanced at Soto. He looked like he was having some sort of argument with Ignacio. Not good. "Soto seems a bit...intense tonight." She kept her voice low. "Is he worried about the deal not happening?"

Tommy frowned. "No. It's going to happen but...he's made some other plans and"—Tommy shot another look across the dance floor—"I don't think... I mean, it might not go so well. It could be dangerous. I don't want you to get hurt."

She smiled at Tommy. "Thanks for looking out for me."

Tommy's face lit up at her smile and kind words. It made her stomach churn. She hated this part of undercover work. Mostly it was scumbags and lowlifes she dealt with, but every once in a while, she met someone that she genuinely felt for, and that made it hard.

Tommy took a sip of beer. "Soto is going to double-cross Ignacio. He's got another buyer lined up for the guns. He says he can get more from the new buyer, and he wants to take control of the Street Aces. He says the gang is too up Santiago's ass and they aren't doing what's best for them. He wants to be the new head Street Ace."

"Jesus," she mumbled. "Does Tomás know?" Tomás had

been the head of the Street Aces for the last seven years. He was close with Santiago. There was no way he'd let Soto take over without a fight.

Tommy shook his head. "Don't think so. Soto has about half the guys on his side. He's…promised them a lot if they back him."

"He can't deliver on it, can he, Tommy?" When Tommy shook his head, Andy asked, "What the fuck is he thinking?" Her stomach was in knots. Soto was about to start a war with one of the biggest criminals in Miami. He was going to get crushed into dust. Just as she glanced over, Ignacio handed Soto a duffel bag. Soto just lifted the strap over his shoulder, like he knew better than to open it right there. That had to be the money for tonight's deal.

"He's gone…insane, Andrea." Tommy shook his head, worry written all over his face. "I tried to get him to see that maybe this isn't the best idea, but I think he's on something. I mean, I saw him poppin' some kind of pills, but I got no idea what it is. It's not like a street drug. It's some kind of prescription thing."

It all clicked. The aggression, the paranoia, the intense workouts he'd been doing and the fact that he hadn't actually forced her to have sex with him yet. He couldn't get it up. Anabolic steroids. *Fuck.* She had to warn Robins and the guys. They needed to call off tonight. God only knew what the hell was going to happen. It was too dangerous.

"Tommy, can you get your friend with the boat to say we can't use it? Maybe we can stop this mess before it starts."

Tommy shook his head. "I tried, but Soto offered him double, and now we're going for sure." Tommy's eyes were bright. The kid was scared out of his mind. "I tried to get Soto to see reason, but he just threatened me, and then my mom. He said he'd kill my mom if I didn't go with him tonight."

Andy closed her eyes for a brief second. This was a fucking disaster. She opened her eyes again. "Okay, Tommy, I'm gonna go—"

"Go where? You're not going anywhere." Soto stood next to the table and glared down at her.

Andy's heart sank. "I'm gonna go to the bathroom."

She stood up, but Soto grabbed her arm. "You can go later. We're leaving now."

"But I—"

"Now," he snarled, pulling her up from the chair and dragging her toward the door of the bar. She shot a look at Antonio, and he nodded slightly. She wanted out of Soto's reach. Antonio got the message. She wasn't sure this deal was going to happen, so she needed another way into the gang if this all fell apart.

Soto shook her by the arm once more. He'd totally lost it, and she had no way to contact her team.

"Soto, maybe let Andrea go. I think you're hurting her." Tommy was walking along behind them.

Soto whirled around, dragging Andy with him. "I don't give a fuck! What the fuck do you care?"

"The whole bar is looking at you, and Ignacio doesn't look happy." Tommy glanced over at Ignacio and then back at Soto.

Ignacio looked royally pissed as far as Andy could tell, and so did a lot of the other guys in the bar. *They know.* Holy shit, they knew that Soto was going to make a play for the guns and the head of the gang. No one was saying anything, but it was the way they were all watching Soto. No one usually paid that much attention to him, but now there wasn't an eye in the room that wasn't on him.

She could *not* get on that boat. She'd be signing her own death warrant if she did.

Soto dragged her out of the bar with Tommy at their

heels. He moved across the parking lot and pulled open the passenger door of his black Dodge Challenger. He lifted the front seat and started to push Andy into the back.

"Soto, I don't want to go with you. I don't think—"

He smashed his palm across her face. She saw stars as he pushed her into the back seat.

"You don't think bitch!" He shoved the seat back down. "Drive!" he screamed at Tommy, who got in the driver side to do what he was told. Soto dropped the duffel bag in the passenger seat well and sat down. Tommy backed out of the parking lot and then headed toward the marina.

Andy lay across the backseat. Her cheek stung where Soto had slapped her but, mostly, she lay there because she needed to figure out a plan. She was stuck with this crazy fuck, and she had to be able to signal her team that she was in trouble.

She had the Apple tag on her. It was what they agreed they would use as a tracker. She had it on her key chain. It was small, and Soto shouldn't take any notice of it, but he'd gone off the deep end so there was no predicting what he would or wouldn't care about.

She sat up and looked over the center console. Soto had his gun out and in his lap. She met Tommy's eyes in the rearview mirror. His grew wide. She must look worse than she anticipated. Soto had clipped her good. She would have a nice bruise on her cheek and probably a black eye.

Tommy started to say something, but she shook her head, so he closed his mouth again. Who knew what Soto's reaction would be? Twenty minutes later, they pulled into the marina. Tommy parked the car, and Soto got out. He kept his gun in his hand.

For a minute, Andy thought he'd forgotten about her. He started to close the car door with her still in the backseat. She didn't make a sound. Tommy got out and closed his door. He didn't say a word either.

"Where's your boy?" Soto demanded.

Tommy lifted his chin. "Over there by the fishing boat."

"You moron. Which fishing boat? It's a fucking marina!"

Tommy leaned on the car. "It's the one at the end of the walkway. *The Lucky Lady*."

"What kind of boat is she?" Soto seemed to be calming down since he didn't yell the question.

"How the fuck should I know?" Tommy replied.

Andy couldn't see Soto's face. Just his chest and his gun. He was tapping the side of his gun with his pointer finger. She assumed he was looking around. He wasn't saying anything, and neither was Tommy.

Finally, Soto said, "Okay, it looks good. Let's go."

He bent down and grabbed the duffel bag and then straightened. Then he went and got something from the trunk. When he came back into view, he had a backpack on one shoulder. He hit the latch for the seat and flipped it up. Andy swore silently as she crawled out of the car. Soto slammed the car door and started across the parking lot to the gated entrance to the boat area.

Andy hadn't moved. She was trying to figure out where her team was. She needed to signal them that she was in trouble. They'd agreed if she wanted to call it off, she'd take her long dark hair and put it up in a ponytail. She had grabbed her hair to put it up when Soto turned around and pointed the gun at her.

"Faster," he growled. Then he smiled and came back to stand next to her. He stroked her cheek. "We wouldn't want you to miss the boat. We're gonna have some fun on the way, aren't we, babe? Yes, ma'am. I've been looking forward to this." She pushed his hand away, but he brought the gun up and pointed it in her face. "Yes, this is going to be fun."

He grabbed her arm and pulled her toward the gate. Tommy was already there and opened it for them. He shot her an apologetic look. She didn't say anything. There was no point. She stepped inside and then waited until Soto took the lead. She walked along beside Tommy and behind Soto. She had options. She could hit the water or hit Soto, but they weren't alone. There were people on some of the boats, and Tommy was there. Soto would start shooting and there was no way she couldn't guarantee that someone wouldn't get hurt.

She pulled her hair into a ponytail and put it into a hair tie. She glanced around but didn't see any movement. They came to a stop beside the boat. It was a fifty-footer, with an assortment of fishing poles hanging off the back. It had a main deck, and another one above: the boat could be driven from either location.

There were a couple cabins down the stairs from the main deck. Tommy had said that was where the bathroom and two bedrooms were. Andy wanted to avoid being down there at all costs.

The deck itself had some cushions over storage around the outside of the deck. The cushions were dark blue. They didn't look the cleanest but, overall, the boat looked pretty good. Better than she'd anticipated. Brayden Langford came out and stood on the deck. He was wearing a blue Hawaiian shirt and a pair of beige shorts. He was in his bare feet. "Hello, all."

"Brayden." Tommy offered a hand, and they did a shoulder bump.

"Soto." Brayden offered his hand to do the same thing, but Soto ignored him and walked on board. "We gotta go," was all he said.

"Yeah, yeah, of course. Just let me show you a few things,

and then I'll be out of your way." Brayden started forward, but Soto brought up his gun.

"Whoa." Brayden stopped and put his hands up. "Soto, man, what the fuck?"

Soto stared at him. "I said we gotta go. We're late. You need to leave."

Brayden looked uncertain. He glanced at Tommy, who shrugged, and then back at Soto. He purposely avoided looking at Andy. She must really look bad. Brayden Langford was a low-level bookie. How he managed to have a boat like this was anyone's guess, but again, he was a pretty harmless guy. Soto pulling a gun would be enough to totally freak him out.

"Okay then." He dug in his pocket and pulled out the keys. "Here. She's all gassed up and ready to go. Please take good care of her, and I'll see you when you get back. Around two a.m., right?"

Soto just nodded and then turned back and entered the salon. The lights were on so they could see it was nicely appointed with light carpet, beige sofas on opposite walls, and a coffee table in front of the sofa on the right. Soto was standing inside with his shoes on. He dropped the duffel bag on the sofa and the backpack next to it.

Back on deck, Brayden glanced at Andy standing beside him and then at Tommy, who was standing on her left. Brayden seemed very unsure of himself. He frowned. "Uh, Soto man, your shoes. You need to take them off, man. You can't wear shoes on my carpet."

Soto turned and raised the gun. Brayden brought his hands up again and swallowed. When Brayden started backing up, Soto turned around. "Whatever, man," Brayden muttered. "Better you than me, Tommy. That guy's insane. Just make sure he brings my boat back in one piece."

Tommy grimaced in apology before Brayden got off the boat.

Soto came back out on deck. "Tommy, get your ass up there and drive this thing." He pointed to the deck above. Tommy swallowed hard but went up the stairs. A second later, the engines rolled over.

Andy looked around. Where the hell was her team? She'd put up her hair. It was the signal she wanted to call it off. Why weren't they coming? *Fucking Robins.* Was he hanging her out to dry? Did he really hate her that much for dumping him? Could he really be that unprofessional? That was way out there. If an agent wanted to call off an op, it was called off. They were the one in the field. They knew better than anyone if the operation would work. She was calling time on theirs. *Where the fuck were her people?*

Pete untied the lines and threw them onto the boat. Tommy throttled up, and they pulled away from the dock. Andy considered jumping overboard and swimming for it, but Soto would probably shoot at her. She'd seen kids on a couple other boats. Stunned, she stood motionless on the deck as Brayden and the marina receded behind her. Her team hadn't come. Now she was stuck on the boat with Soto. She'd be lucky if the only thing that happened was her being raped. She shuddered as the tension in her shoulders escalated painfully. The chances of her getting out of this alive were getting smaller and smaller as the marina disappeared from sight.

CHAPTER FOUR

E lias stood on the deck of the Coast Guard cutter and donned his gear. He was wearing black tactical pants with a black shirt. He finished by putting on his bullet proof vest and then loaded up his weapons and the rest of his gear. They weren't sure what this operation was going to look like. He got a seriously bad vibe from Robins, the guy in charge. There were too many unknowns to suit Elias. From conversations between some of the other team members, Elias had the distinct impression they weren't thrilled with their boss either.

"I don't like this," Cain muttered as he pulled on his gear. "There's something wrong with this whole thing."

"Agreed. I think we should pull the plug." Elias looked around for Nick. He was talking to the captain of the cutter. Elias raised his chin, and Nick nodded.

Axe came to stand beside the two men. "I got a bad feeling about this."

"Join the club," Elias grumbled. "This is going to turn into a shit show."

"Agreed," Nick said as he came to join them. "I just told

Captain Myers we were not comfortable with this operation and our spidey-senses don't tingle unless something is off."

"What did he say?" Finn asked as he compulsively checked his weapon for the third time.

Nick frowned. "He said we don't have a choice. Apparently, Robins has an inside man, an Andy someone, and we have to do this in order to extricate him."

"Shit," Cain mumbled.

"Yeah," Nick agreed. "So, we're going to have to be ready. You guys all good to go? If we have to board the vessel, Cain, I want you and Elias up front. The rest of you boys know what to do, but follow their lead. Be ready for anything. We have air support, but they're gonna be hanging back a bit since the moon is so bright. They don't want to be spotted."

"Do we know where this is taking place yet?" Finn asked as he secured the straps of his bulletproof vest.

Nick shook his head. "We've been following some sort of tracking device. They said the meet should happen at midnight. We're thirty minutes out. The helo is already doing higher altitude sweeps of the area, trying to see if they can locate any boats. We're waiting to hear back from them now."

Elias lifted his chin at the other boat. "Do they even know what the fuck they're doing?"

"The ATF has some experience with this, but... I wouldn't necessarily say they know what they're doing. I'd feel a lot better if we were dealing with the DEA." Nick checked his own gun and stuck it in his leg holster.

"Me fucking too," Cain grumbled. "This is amateur hour, and we could all get our asses shot off. Look lively, girls, 'cause this is going to be a wild one." There were grunts of agreement as everyone finished getting ready.

Fifteen minutes later, there was a flurry of activity on the bridge. The captain waved, and Nick went up to see what was going on. He was back in minutes. "They've located the other vessel. We think it's the sellers. A large speed boat with some 'big ass engines' quote unquote. There are bags on deck. They must be the weapons. They are coming in from the southeast. The ATF boat has already swung out and will come in from the northeast."

"Well, that's just fucking great," Elias snarled. "Do they know not to shoot at anything because we'll be on the opposite side?" They were coming in from the west. "If I get shot by some dumb ass ATF agent, I'm going to shoot back."

Nick grimaced. "Yeah. They've been told to watch what they're doing but, guys, this just feels all kinds of wrong. So be on your toes and watch your six."

The guys all did their final checks and then stood on deck waiting to move over to the rigid-hulled inflatable boat that was trailing along behind the cutter.

Elias took a deep breath. He hated going into an op that he didn't plan. He glanced at Cain, and the other man shook his head. He was thinking the same thing. They all were. It was what made them a good team. They knew what was on each other's minds. At the moment no one was feeling good about this op.

The cutter floated into position, just west of the meet, and waited. There wasn't anything else they could do but wait. "Do we even know what weapons these guys are buying?" Elias asked.

Nick shook his head. "Guns. The ATF agent in charge, Robins, said assault rifles and possibly some handguns, but there were no specifics."

"Why come all the way out here to do the exchange?"

"On the water is as good a spot as any—better even. Fewer people around to see what's going on." Nick adjusted his bulletproof vest.

Elias shrugged. "I get that, but why way the fuck out

here? We're a good hour offshore. They'd only really have to go a mile or two to make the exchange without anyone paying attention. Why go this far?"

Nick cocked his head. "You make a good point. Doesn't really make much sense."

"And another thing, who's the seller?" Elias adjusted his leg holster.

"I've been wondering that myself," Nick commented.

Finn moved over next to Nick. "Being this far out, those guns could be coming from anywhere in the Caribbean."

"Or beyond," Cain grumbled. "Those are international waters, and we're out in the shipping lanes. The sellers could drop it off the side of a cargo ship."

"Shit, they don't have to dive to get this stuff, right?" Axe asked. "They're just doing an exchange. We're not set up for diving."

"As far as I know from Robins, this is an exchange, but you make a good point, Axe. Maybe we should have someone ready to go in the water." Nick looked at Elias and Cain. They had been Maritime Security Response Team members before they'd gotten hurt and were reassigned to Team RECON. They'd often trained with the Navy SEALs, so they were ideal for this sort of situation. "Any takers?"

Elias ground his teeth but nodded. He didn't really feel like getting wet, but it was better for them to be prepared. He started taking off his gear.

Nick reached out and touched his shoulder. "Wait, we didn't bring anything with us, and I'm not sure this cutter has the level of gear you'd need." He turned, walked across the deck, and then disappeared around the corner.

"Are you sure you want to go in?" Cain asked. He glanced at Elias's leg.

Aw, shit. He'd volunteered without thinking about his leg. It wasn't hurting at the moment, but if he had to do a lot of swimming, it would throb like a son of a bitch later. "Yeah, I'm good." It was just something he was going to have to get used to. The scar tissue pulled and made the area ache. That's the reason his doctor had given him. It just hurt a lot more than Elias had imagined it would.

Nick came back around the corner. "They've got tanks and wet suits, but they don't have the right weapons. I'm not sending you in without working guns. We didn't bring ours, and we don't have anything to keep the water out of what we have brought. It was an oversight on my part." He swore. "We need a better set up. Having the equipment in the storage locker just isn't working, and I'm not putting it in that office building. Too dangerous."

Elias started to speak, "I—"

Axe touched his earbud. "The other boat is about ten minutes out."

The men clicked on their comms. They went to the side of the cutter to get ready to make the transfer to the rigid-hulled inflatable boat. A seaman, under the watchful eye of his superior officer, had driven the boat to the rendezvous coordinates for them. Training for the future was important in the Coast Guard but it had to take a back seat when there was a mission at steak.

The RHIB was brought along side and the guys boarded. Finn took over the controls and the crew that had driven it out went back aboard the cutter. It was time for business. The bad feeling in Elias's gut worsened by the minute, a tight cramping feeling that had nothing to do with the waves.

"You're gonna do what I say, bitch. I'm not playin'!" Soto leaned over her and put the gun to her head. They were standing on the main deck and Soto had her backed up against the glass door to the salon.

She had managed to avoid Soto most of the ride out. She'd told him she felt like she was gonna puke, and Tommy had said he needed help driving the boat. Neither was true, but it kept Soto at bay the whole way to the rendezvous point. It didn't hurt that they were close to an hour behind schedule, and the waves were bigger than anticipated.

But now they were there and waiting. Soto was on her for what he felt was his due. "Get below and take off your clothes," Soto barked.

Andy fisted her hands. If she went below, chances were excellent she'd be killed. The rape was just a given. She wasn't going down without a fight, but she had to at least try and defuse the situation. "But the sellers are supposed to be here soon. You don't want them to be able to sneak up on you."

"Don't you worry your little head, *puta*. Tommy will look out while you take care of me."

"I still don't feel good. I don't wanna puke on you."

He pressed the gun into her temple. "You puke, you die."

"But Soto," she moaned, trying to make herself sound sicker than she was, "I can't help it if I puke." The rolling motion of the boat was actually making her feel queasy, but the adrenaline was helping to keep it in check. She looked around the deck for a weapon, but there was nothing close at hand. Being pinned to the glass door didn't give her any leverage either.

"I don't care. Take your clothes off. I'll fuck you right here." He moved back a step to give her room to take off her clothes.

She hesitated. She tried to remind herself that she was there to get justice for her sister but getting Santiago seemed like a pipedream. First she had to survive dealing with Soto and the odds on that were getting longer by the minute.

"Now!" he yelled and waved the gun. Soto was excited. He was dancing around, and his eyes were flitting all over the place. He was high, she realized. *Great.* On top of being messed up on anabolic steroids, he was stoned. Coke, if she had to guess. He was probably worried he couldn't get it up.

She reached up and started untying the knot she'd made in the ties of her hoodie. She'd done it on purpose, hoping it would buy her time should this moment come. The thing was, time wasn't helping. She had no access to a weapon.

"C'mon, faster." He shook his head. "Forget the top. Just take off your fucking jeans."

Fuck! Now what was she supposed to do? If she pretended to puke, would he kill her? Her stomach rolled. The vomiting might not have to be pretend. Where the fuck was her back up? If she got out of this—no, when she got out of this—she was going to kill Robins.

She moved her hands to her belt and started to undo it.

"Soto," Tommy called, "they're here."

Soto stuck his head around the side of the boat and came back. "Later, bitch. We'll celebrate in style after I do this deal." He turned and walked over to sit on the built-in sofa on the side of the deck.

Andy slumped against the door. She wanted to go inside and get away from everything, but that would only be a temporary fix. She needed a weapon. She looked back at the kitchen. A knife? It wasn't the best against a gun, but beggars couldn't be choosers. She slowly started to open the door.

"No. You stay right there." Soto pointed his gun at her again. "I want you where I can see you at all times." Tommy came down the ladder from above and moved across the deck to stand beside her.

The engines of the other boat were audible across the waves now. She stepped away from the door and craned her neck. The other boat was one of those sleek powerboats that she'd seen on Miami Vice reruns. Some sort of a power boat, she thought they were called. It pulled up alongside their fishing boat.

Two men were on deck, one behind the controls and another guy sitting on the built-in seats. "*Hola,*" the second guy called.

Soto nodded.

The guy stood up and spoke in rapid-fire Spanish. Andy grew up speaking Spanish to some degree. Her mother was white from Des Moines, but her father was Cuban. He made sure she could speak to him and his family in Spanish. She'd used it over the years since she'd left Miami, but not as much, so she was a bit rusty when she'd started with Soto. It had come back mostly, but if people spoke too fast, she didn't get all of it.

"*Trajiste el dinero?*" Did you bring the money?

"*Sí. Trajiste las armas?*" Yes. Did you bring the guns?

Soto was acting all cool, but his knee bounced a mile a minute and his eyes were darting everywhere. The driver of the other boat noticed and so did the passenger. They exchanged a look. This was going to go downhill fucking fast. She wrapped her hand around her ponytail one more time. Where the hell was her backup? She moved a bit more forward so she could be seen.

Jesus, Robins, you need to come now. This was a clusterfuck.

CHAPTER FIVE

"I count three—that's three on deck of the fishing boat. Confirm," Axe said into his earbud as he looked through binoculars.

"Confirmed. Three on deck," the voice on the other end said. "One of them is a woman, and she keeps playing with her hair. I don't know if that's important, but you said to give you details."

Elias grinned as he shifted on the RHIB. He liked the seaman who had been given the job as their observer. He seemed like a competent, nice kid. It wasn't a job for an amateur, but again, they had to train the next generation. He was feeding them data on what he could see from his vantage point on the bridge of the cutter.

Elias glanced over at Axe, who smiled. "Confirmed. The woman is playing with her hair.

Elias squinted, but he could barely make out the boats, let alone how many on deck.

"I count two. No, make that three on the powerboat," the seaman said.

"Location of the three?" Axe demanded. "I only see two."

"One behind the controls, one on the seat on the far side of the boat, and one on the stairs between the driver and the passenger."

"Is he armed?" Axe asked.

"I can't tell from here, sir. His hands aren't visible. I mean, unknown."

Axe flashed a quick grin at the young seaman's correction. "Roger that." He turned toward Elias and the guys. "The buyers on the fishing boat can't see the guy on the stairs. You guys heard it. He has to have a gun. Otherwise, why have him there?"

Nick grabbed the radio from the seaman. "Coyote One, this is Two,"

"Go for One," a voice said.

Nick hit the talk button. "There's a third man on the small craft. He is armed."

There was silence, and then a new voice came on. "Say again, Coyote One?"

"There's a third guy on the small craft, and he is armed," Nick repeated.

"Roger that."

They all waited, but the voice didn't say anything else. Nick tried again. "Coyote One, please advise on how to proceed."

"We'll let you know."

Axe ground out, "Is he for fucking real? He's got a guy undercover with the sellers, one who is lying in wait to shoot, and he wants to *let us know*?"

Nick's face hardened. "It's his operation and his guy. If this goes south, it was all his call. There's nothing we can do."

They all stood silently on the deck. This was bullshit, and they knew it. Elias put his hand out to Axe for the binoculars. He passed them over. Elias held them up to his face and made some adjustments. Two men and a woman on the fishing boat. He glanced at the powerboat. Three men. None of this looked good.

"Come on board," Soto said from his seat on the cushions. His arm rested on the edge of the boat like he had all the time in the world.

The driver frowned. "No. You throw us the money; we give you the guns." The man who spoke was shorter and rounder than the other passenger and wore a gray nylon jacket. He had short dark hair and a beard, but it was hard to see any actual facial features in this light.

Soto stood up. He still had a gun in his hand. The two men stared at him, but then they each brought out a handgun. Soto grinned. "Now we're all good, man. No worries." He took a step closer to the other boat.

From her angle, Andy couldn't see much. The powerboat was bobbing on the waves, shifting until it was almost perpendicular to their boat. The driver gave it a little gas and maneuvered so it swung back alongside. At this time of night, away from the the lights on shore, visibility was limited. The dark void of the vast ocean caused nerves to crawl under Andy's skin. Luckily, the moon was bright, but without that, it would have been total blackness.

Soto lifted his chin. "Let's see the guns."

The seated passenger said, "Let's see the money." He appeared to be taller than the driver, his long legs stretched out in front of him, and he wore a short-sleeved, dark colored T-shirt. He was clean shaven, including his head.

Soto turned to her and pointed. *Great.* Now, suddenly, she had to be a part of this game. She went into the salon and grabbed the duffel bag off the sofa. She glanced at it as she picked it up. There were bits of paper caught in the zipper. Why would there be paper in the zipper? Then it clicked. The backpack was gone. Her heart dropped to her feet.

When they'd first left the marina and she was pretending to be sick, Soto had gone into the salon. He'd been by the sofa but had kept his back to her. She stayed out of his line of vision on purpose. She didn't want to encourage him, but he must have made the switch then. He walked into the kitchen after that and then had come back outside.

She hurried back out onto the deck. Soto was going to try to rip these guys off with fake wads of paper. She knew it in her bones. There would still be cash in the bag, enough to make it look good in the low light, but when they got back home and opened the bag, they would find out that they'd been had. Soto would get the guns and have the money he needed to take over the Street Aces.

Andy handed the duffel to Soto. Then she moved back so she was at the far corner of deck where it met the salon. When the shooting started, she had a better chance if she went into the water at this point, provided her team were actually going to rescue her. Could she depend on Robins? Maybe not. Maybe she'd have to hug the outside wall of the salon and hope for the best.

"Let's see the guns,'" Soto demanded.

The bald man reached down to the deck to presumably open a bag or crate or something. She was too far away to see, but an evil grin spread over Soto's face, so it must have been what they'd agreed on.

"Now you," the driver said and scratched his beard.

Andy tensed. If he caught sight of the fake money, it was all over for Soto for sure, and maybe her and Tommy. *Tommy.* She wanted to warn him, but then remembered he already knew. Soto had stashed the fake money in the back of his car. Soto would have made Tommy do the leg work to create the fake money. He sure as hell wouldn't do it himself.

So be it. Tommy was on his own. She couldn't help him now anyway.

Soto unzipped the duffel, but he held it so it scrunched up a bit in the middle.

"I can't see," the bald man said.

Soto opened the bag a bit more and tilted it into the light. The guy grunted and nodded. Soto zipped the bag back up. The man knelt down and did something on the floor of the boat. Then he brought up two duffels the size of hockey bags and started to hand them to Tommy, but the boats were too far apart. The driver goosed the engines again and brought the boats together.

Tommy reached for the bags and fell back on his ass under the weight. The two men laughed uproariously at Tommy, who struggled to his feet and then reached for the next two bags, one at a time. Once all four bags were on board, Soto tossed the duffel bag.

The driver waved and then revved the engines, preparing to steer the powerboat away. Andy glanced around. Where the fuck was Robins?

———

"What the fuck is he waiting for?" Axe demanded.

Nick shook his head. He tried the radio once more. "Coyote One, it's time to round up the rabbits, over." Nothing. He frowned.

Axe stared at his boss. "The exchange has been made. If we don't move now, the sellers get away."

Nick looked around the deck at his men. "If we go now, then it's our heads for fucking up an ATF op."

Cain snorted. "The ATF doesn't have jurisdiction out here. We do. That's why we're here."

"If they have line of sight, they can follow into international waters and make arrests," Nick supplied.

"It could be argued they don't have line of sight since they're so fucking far away, but I doubt we'd win." Axe shook his head. "It's their guy on the inside. Why don't they want to get him out safely?" Finn asked.

Everyone refocused on the two boats a short distance away. The powerboat's engines revved up, and then abruptly cut out.

Elias tensed. The sound of gun shots cracked over the waves.

Nick hit his ear bud and told Finn to go. The RHIB took off at a high rate of speed coming in from the southwest. The cutter was off to their port side. It was coming but it wasn't as fast as the RHIB. The cutter hit the spotlights, turning them onto the two other boats. "This is the US Coast Guard. Drop your weapons!"

More shots were fired, and one of the men went down on the deck of the fishing boat. A man on the power boat stood with something on his shoulder.

Holy shit! With instincts born from training, Elias identified what the man on the boat was holding, just as Axe screamed.

"RPG!"

The RHIB ate up the ground between it and the two boats. They had a clear path. The ATF were coming in from the northeast which was ahead and off their port side. They were coming in from the southwest and the fishing boat and the power boat were between them.

Elias shouldered his rifle. They'd all braced themselves and were in assault position. Within seconds they would be close enough to fire. All eyes were on the guy with the rocket launcher. That asshole struggled to maintain his footing because of the waves.

Elias took a deep breath, waited two beats, and then took the shot. The guy with the rocket launcher went down in a red mist. The tall guy who was firing at the fishing boat now switched his aim to the RHIB, but it was too late, and he went down in a hail of gunfire, as did the bearded driver.

The firing stopped as the RHIB pulled alongside the fishing boat. The cutter cut her engines and floated behind them. Elias jumped on board, followed by Cain and the rest of the team.

One of the men on the fishing boat, a guy wearing a leather jacket, had a half dozen bullet holes in his chest, lying in the middle of the deck. Another guy in a black T-shirt was still alive but barely. Axe was doing his best to stem the flow of blood from the guy's stomach, but he looked up and shook his head. No way that guy was making it.

The ATF boat pulled alongside, and a couple of men jumped off. "What the fuck do you people think you're doing?" Robins asked.

Elias just ignored him. "Which one of these guys is yours?"

"Neither."

Wait...what? "I thought you said you had a guy on board."

"No." He shook his head. "I said I had a person on board." He looked around. "Andy?" Robins yelled. He walked over to the side of the boat and searched the water.

"There's no one in the water. No one went over the side." Elias moved toward the dead guy in the jacket.

"How do you know?"

"'Cause I got eyes, asshole. I watched the boats the entire time, and no one went over the side."

"Elias." Nick gave him a look.

"He's not wrong," Cain said as he unzipped one of the bags.

"So then where the fuck is Andy?"

"Here," a voice said. A female voice. Elias turned to see Axe come out of the salon with a woman behind him.

When Axe stepped out of the way, Elias came face-to-face with the missing Andy. "Son of a bitch."

CHAPTER SIX

Elias stopped dead and so did his heart. Not a beat. Not for at least thirty seconds. All the air disappeared from his lungs. He was frozen in time and space. Andrea Torres was standing in front of him, the girl who had ripped his heart out of his chest and pissed all over it. The one female on earth who had ever made him cry.

"Elias?" Her voice sounded so calm. He was falling apart inside, torn between two emotions. He wanted to destroy her, and he wanted to crush her into his arms at the same time. How could she be calm?

Cain hit him in the shoulder, and the spell was broken. His lungs started functioning. He took a deep breath. "Andrea," he said, then pivoted, walked across the deck of the boat, and climbed aboard the RHIB. He didn't even turn and look at her. He couldn't. He didn't trust himself. He had guns, and he was so damn tempted to use them.

Finn had stayed on the RHIB. He took one look at Elias and then glanced past him at the fishing boat.

Elias was not alright. He was so fucking not good it wasn't funny. He wanted to yell and rage, but he just stood there with his back to the other boat and stared out at the water.

The boat rocked under the weight of someone coming on board. Nick's face appeared in front of his. "What the fuck is wrong?" he snarled and then seeing Elias's face, he immediately backed off. "Are you okay?"

Elias just shook his head. He couldn't get the words out. Couldn't get them past his lips. The hatred was so fucking intense, but so was the longing. He'd thought he'd left that part of his life behind, but damn, he'd been wrong. Seeing her for two seconds made him want her all over again.

"Elias, man, what's wrong?"

Elias just looked out at the water, but he gripped his weapon so hard the metal bit into his skin.

Nick's eyes narrowed.

"If you fucking hug me, I will put you down right here," Elias growled. Nick had hugged him unexpectedly one day when he couldn't seem to talk about his injury. It had startled him so much he immediately spilled his guts about it.

A smiled tugged at the corners of Nick's mouth. "At least you're still able to talk. Want to tell me what the hell is going on?"

Elias took a deep breath. He had to say something; he owed Nick that much. Hell, he owed the whole team for everything he'd put them through with his gambling and his ornery nature. "That woman is the reason I am the way I am. My best friend was killed because of her and she walked away scot-free. She is the devil. Do not trust her."

Nick looked over Elias's shoulder and then back at him. "Got it. I'll need details later, but let's get this wrapped up and we'll get out of here." Nick disappeared from view, and the boat rocked, telling Elias that Nick had gotten off again.

Elias stared out at the ocean. He took a few deep breaths and tried to get his focus back. He was still on the job. He couldn't let his teammates down. There was work to be done. It was just such a fucking shock to see Andrea. He'd heard she'd left not long after he did. Of all the people he'd expected to run into every damn day that he was now back in his hometown, she was not one of them. He took one more deep breath and turned around.

"You, okay?" Finn asked.

"No. But I'm good enough to finish this mess and get back to the cutter." Elias shut down all thoughts of what happened years ago. He forced it all back into the box in his mind that he ruthlessly kept under lock and key. Squaring his shoulders, he fought to focus.

He studied what was happening on the deck of the fishing boat. Nick appeared to be arguing with Robins about something. Axe and Cain had finished searching the vessel and had come back to stand beside Nick. Andrea stood opposite Nick with her back to the salon. One of her ATF colleagues stood guard on her left. Elias had the immediate impression that he was trying to protect her. He kept shooting glances at Robins. He must be their boss, but they weren't too pleased with him by the looks they aimed at him.

"No, we are not going to do that. No way." Nick's voice carried across to Elias. Cain and Axe were on board to back up Nick. Elias didn't need to be there, and he was trying to convince himself that staying on the RHIB was the best choice, but his curiosity was getting the better of him. Not to mention his ego. He'd essentially run away when he'd seen Andrea. Not because he was afraid of *her*, but because he was afraid of what he might do to her. Now he had to prove to himself more than anyone else that he could face her and not react.

"I want to go back on board," Elias said.

Finn cocked an eyebrow. "Are you sure?"

Elias nodded once, and Finn goosed the engine and

brought the RHIB up close. Elias stepped onto the fishing boat and then moved to stand next to Cain.

"You cannot leave the powerboat out here with dead bodies on it," Nick fumed. "That's the dumbest idea I've ever heard."

Robins scowled. "I didn't say we'd leave it out here. We just can't have you or us tow it in at the moment. People will be watching. Andy is undercover, and if we come in towing these boats, the whole operation will be blown. That's months of work."

"I don't give a shit how long this has been going on. You cannot leave these boats out here."

Andrea pushed a stray tendril of hair behind her ear. "Look, I can drive this boat back, but if we leave the bodies on board, it's gonna cause major issues. The people I'm dealing with will want to get rid of them, and I won't be able to stop them. It's not like the Street Aces will listen to me."

Elias's breath caught in his throat again. *Andrea was working a case involving the Street Aces?* Was she really out to bring them down, or was she working with Santiago to help him stay out of trouble with the law? He didn't trust her. Not one bit.

Nick shook his head. "This is a crime scene. I get that you don't want to fuck up your case, but you cannot just drive away with the boat."

Robins rolled his eyes. "What the hell do you know about it? Go back to rescuing disabled boats."

Nick took a step forward and almost bumping his chest into Robins'. "Listen, asshole, you're going to do this right, or we'll tow this boat right into downtown Miami and hold a fucking press conference."

Robins glared. "Fine. What do you suggest? We need this boat to keep Andy in the game."

Andy? Seriously? Andrea Torres looked like a lot of

things, but "Andy" wasn't one of them. Her hair was pulled back, but it was curling with the humidity. Her big green eyes made her look young and innocent. She had full, naturally red lips. Her full figure hadn't changed any, and Elias remembered every inch of it like it was yesterday. Some things were just never forgotten. No matter how hard he tried.

Nick glanced at Axe who stepped forward. "We bring the boat into shore, but far away from where you think people will be watching. You let it be processed. Then in a couple of hours"—Axe pointed at Andrea—"she can drive it back to wherever you want."

"What about the speedboat? We need that to be found at sea," Robins said.

"Why?" Axe demanded.

Andrea cleared her throat. "Because I'm going to go back and tell one of the biggest gun and drug dealers in Miami that I killed these guys to save myself, and I need to bring him the money and guns. Santiago isn't going to believe me right off, so I'm going to need proof. Finding the powerboat out here with bodies in it will go a long way toward backing my story."

Elias narrowed his eyes. "You're going after Santiago?"

Andrea looked up at him and nodded. "He graduated from being the head of the Street Aces. He's now one of, if not *the*, top dealer in Miami. These are his guns. We're trying to bring him and his crew down."

Santiago, the man that had killed his best friend. Elias suddenly wanted in. No. That wasn't right. He wanted to take over. He wanted Santiago so much he could taste it, but he didn't trust Andrea no matter how good she looked or how much his fingers itched to bury themselves in her hair. Andrea was the devil, and if he let the devil in again, he was certain he wouldn't survive.

"So, you see, we really need this boat out here with the bodies in it," Robins said.

"Yeah, well, that's not going to happen," Elias said flatly. "You're not leaving bodies in a powerboat out here to rot in the sun. God knows who will find them. Hell, the thing could sink, and they'd never be found. What you want isn't possible."

"Who the fuck are you to come in here and tell me what's going to happen in my operation?" Robins demanded.

"We're the guys who just saved your agent's ass while you took your sweet fuckin' time getting here!" Elias snarled.

"You fucking jumped the gun. We almost lost the whole deal because you went charging in," Robins roared.

Nick put a hand up to calm Robins down. "Your agent was in trouble, and you were a little slow to lead the charge, so we did the appropriate thing and attempted to apprehend the criminals as soon as they started shooting. It would have been nice to know that they had rocket-propelled grenades, by the way. You risked all our lives by keeping that nugget to yourself."

"We didn't know," the tall guy next to Andrea said.

Robins whipped around. "Shut up, Jay."

But, apparently, Jay had had enough because he continued, "We didn't know how many guns there would be, and we weren't even sure who the sellers were either. It was a bit of a crapshoot, and it shouldn't have gone down the way it did." He aimed a steely-eyes glare at Robins.

"Jay, we'll discuss this later."

Jay ignored his boss. "We should have gone in immediately. Andy's hair was up. That was the signal. It's a miracle she wasn't hurt."

Robins drew a deep breath and exhaled out his nose slowly. It seemed to Elias he was a bit overly dramatic and not so professional right now.

Chopping his hand in the air with his words, Robins said, "We couldn't go in until Soto handed over the money. We needed the exchange to happen. We went as soon as it did. End of story." He turned back to Nick. "Now your job here is finished. You can head out, and we'll take care of the rest."

Nick shook his head. "No. This is what we're going to do." Robins opened his mouth, but Nick raised both hands this time and said, "Just listen to me. We're gonna take the fishing boat in like we said, and you can have your people process it. Then Ms…"

"Torres," Elias supplied.

"Ms. Torres can drive it to wherever you want. We, as in them"—he pointed to the Coast Guard cutter bobbing in the waves behind them—"will wait a few hours and then tow the powerboat into shore. The captain will call the local police, and they can process the boat. Once your operation is over, you can reach out to the local cops and tell them what happened on the powerboat. That should give you what you need; a legitimate source finding the bodies."

Robins glared at Nick, but then grudgingly agreed. "Fine. That will work. I'll call our people and tell them where to meet us to process the fishing boat."

Nick said, "Let me speak with Captain Myers. He's going to want to know where you're going and probably have someone meet you to be sure things are done properly."

Robins started to protest but must have thought the better of it because he shut his mouth and nodded.

"Good." Nick turned to Elias, Axe, and Cain. He gestured toward the RHIB with his head, and they all turned and started off the boat.

"Elias," Andrea called.

Elias cursed silently but turned back around. He didn't say a word, just stared at her.

"I…I just wanted to…" Her voice died out.

Elias continued to stare for a few seconds longer and then turned and went back to the RHIB. He had nothing to say to Andrea Torres.

He helped the guys to get organized, but his thoughts were still on Andrea. At last, Nick boarded. "I spoke with Myers. We're gonna head back on the RHIB and he's going to take care of towing the powerboat in," Everyone nodded and Nick gave Finn the signal. He dropped the boat into gear, and they turned away from the boats and started back toward Miami.

Elias knew he was going to have to explain to the guys about Andrea, but at this moment, he didn't know what to say. His brain seemed on a steady repeat of *what the actual fuck?* He had to work doubly hard to process what had just happened. What he really wanted was to go find a poker game and lose himself in the cards for a few hours, but he knew Nick wasn't going to let that happen. He closed his eyes.

Two hours later, they'd changed out of their gear and were at their desks in the office. Elias's leg hurt like a bitch. He rubbed it through his jeans. His navy T-shirt was thin, and he realized for the first time in a while, he was actually cold. Axe had cranked the thermostat to the frozen tundra setting. He liked it cool. Elias shivered.

It was the middle of the night, and everyone wanted to be home in bed, but they were a team, and they were there to support him. Elias just didn't know how to begin. He looked up and met Nick's gaze. *Shit.*

Elias cleared his throat, and everyone turned to look at him. "I guess I owe you all an apology for earlier. I was…gut-punched, I guess you could say. I didn't expect to see Andrea on that boat. I had heard she'd moved to L.A."

He glanced around the room. No one seemed pissed off at him. They were all just waiting for an explanation.

He swallowed and then began. "I didn't grow up in New York like I said. I spent a lot of summers there with my mom's family, but I actually grew up here in Miami. My mom is Cuban and my dad, he's just some white guy that blew into town for a few years and then left again. You know I have a sister, so it was just the three of us, but I have a pile of cousins, like more than you can imagine, both here and in New York.

"Anyway, Andrea and I were…together before I joined the Coast Guard. We met in high school and stayed together after. I thought—well, it doesn't matter what I thought—but we were together. Andrea and I, and my best friend Mateo, all hung out together. We were like the three musketeers. We were…a family of sorts." He smiled slightly at the memory.

"Mateo had a…wild streak. He liked to mix it up sometimes. I spent a lot of time keeping him out of trouble, but he was a good guy. He was the brother I never had. Anyway, Mateo, Mattie to us, got involved with the Street Aces. It took me a while to catch on since he'd kept it hidden from me. Said he had a sick cousin in Fort Lauderdale he had to help out with. I believed him because that was the sort of thing he'd do.

"By the time I found out, it was too late. He was part of the gang. He wanted Andrea and me to join, but we weren't interested. We still all hung out, though, so Andrea and I kinda got pulled in by association. We were never actual gang members, but we knew everyone, and they knew us."

Elias took a gulp from the water bottle he had on his desk. This was so fucking hard. He hadn't talked about Mateo for years. "Mattie was smart, like super fucking smart, especially with numbers. He could do shit in his head faster than I could with a calculator. He was also ambitious as hell.

He wanted to move up in the gang. He wanted to be at the top, and everyone knew it. Hell, he wanted to go beyond the gang and run Miami. He could have done it, too. Such a fucking waste. If he'd just stayed legit…"

Elias cleared his throat. "Anyway, Mattie figured out that someone was skimming off the money coming in. I don't know the details really, just that the numbers weren't adding up.

"Santiago was also a Street Ace back then. He joined long before Mattie. He was also ambitious, but he wasn't as smart as Mattie. They were enemies within the gang. When Mattie pointed out there was money missing to the head of the gang, a guy called Paco, Paco said to find out who was stealing it. Mattie figured out it was Santiago, but before he could do anything, Santiago went to Paco and blamed Mattie, and then he…" Elias's breath caught in his chest. "And then Santiago killed Mattie before anyone could question it."

Elias suddenly realized that he was gripping the arms of his chair so tightly his knuckles were white. He flexed his fingers.

"Where does Andrea come into this?" Nick asked.

"She knew. She knew that Santiago was skimming the money. She'd actually seen him do it. She knew where his stash was, and she knew he was going to kill Mattie, but she didn't say anything. Not one fucking word." Sadness and anger swarmed up his chest. He shook his head to clear the poisonous emotions. "I knew something was up. I pushed her to tell me, and I finally got her to spill, but it was too late. By the time I got to the ambush that Santiago had set up, Mattie had already been shot. He died in my arms." Elias blinked to stop the tears that had snuck up on him. He chugged the rest of the water from the bottle on his desk.

"The day we buried Mattie, I joined the Coast Guard, and I haven't been back to Miami until now."

"Elias, man. I'm so sorry. That's rough," Axe said in a quiet voice. "I can totally see why you freaked when you saw Andrea. That must have been mind-blowing."

"Yeah. It was surreal."

"That explains a whole lot," Nick stated. "I'm sorry it's been such a rough transition to Miami for you. This mess tonight didn't help, but moving forward we need to know this stuff, Elias. When personal shit interferes with work, it affects all of us. And this goes for everyone in this room. We're a team, and we function best when we know what's going on and we can have each other's backs."

"I know," Elias admitted, "and I'm sorry for not telling you sooner. It's just a bit…tough to talk about. Mattie was… trouble and probably a bad influence, but he was still my best friend. His death and Andrea's…involvement has been hard to…live with."

Nick nodded. "Now we all know, and we're on your side on this."

"Thanks, Tag. I started playing poker right after Mattie's death. It was the only time I could shut out the rage and helplessness. Anyway, since I do okay at it, a while back I started donating a lot of my winnings to anti-gang non-profit organizations. I always do it in Mattie's name." He scrubbed his hands down his face. "Anyway, I thought you should know that bit too. Andrea, Mattie, the whole mess, is what got me into poker and poker is what's helping some people get out of the life."

"I'm glad you're doing something positive with the money," Nick said. "That's a great way to honor Mateo." He yawned and stretched his arms over his head. "Let's call it a night. I want everyone back here by noon tomorrow. We'll start fresh then."

Everyone stood up. Axe came around to Elias and shook his hand. They did a shoulder bump. Finn was next, and then Cain.

"Elias," Cain said, "you need anything, you let me know." Then he turned and walked out. Cain had lost his whole team, so Elias knew he understood the shock and the guilt. It was one of the things that had bonded the two of them immediately after they'd met. Elias recognized the pain and anger that Cain felt. It was good to know the guys had his back.

Nick waited at the door to the office. "Go see your mom."

"It's four a.m., she'll be asleep."

"Elias, go see your mom. Someone who knows you just saw you. How long do you think you can go without someone else seeing you and telling your mom? How hurt will she be if she finds out you are in town and you didn't go see her first thing?"

Guilt sucker-punched him and his breath seized. His mother would be crushed. Then she would get angry and yell at him. Then she would go silent. The silence was the worst.

"Okay. I'll go see her and talk to my sister, too. I'm not going over there tonight. She's got three kids. She'll kill me if I wake them up."

Nick grinned as he opened the door and urged Elias out of the office. "No need to do that. Just see your mom."

Elias nodded.

They rode the elevator down to the lobby and walked out the front door. "'Night, Elias," Nick said. "Thanks for telling us the truth."

"Sorry it took so long." He grimaced.

"Better late than never," Nick called over his shoulder as he walked to his vehicle.

Suddenly, it occurred to Elias that he didn't have a ride.

He'd sold his old SUV before he moved to Miami and hadn't gotten around to buying a new one.

An engine roared behind him and he looked up. Cain pulled up in front of him. He didn't say anything, but he didn't have to. Cain was that kind of guy. They all were. There when he needed them, sometimes before he even realized he had a problem.

Elias climbed into the pickup and gave Cain the address of his mom's house before he changed his mind. He leaned his head back on the headrest. This day had gone from bad to catastrophic. He massaged his leg. The bad feeling he'd had earlier hadn't gone away. It had gotten worse. There was a shit storm coming, and there wasn't a damn thing he could do about it.

CHAPTER SEVEN

Andy stood back and watched the techs work. She shivered in her hoodie. Not that it was cold, but she just couldn't seem to get warm.

Peña touched her arm and offered her a steaming cup of coffee. "I thought you could use this."

"Thanks," she said and smiled at him.

"I want to apologize to you for what happened tonight. It never should have gone down that way. *Never*. Robins... I just don't know what was going on with him. We saw your ponytail. It was the signal. We told him it was time to go in, but he said we had to wait for the exchange. He said it was too much of a risk if we went in early. We wouldn't have enough to convict anyone. I tried to convince him, but he wouldn't budge."

Andy took a sip of coffee. "It's okay. I know it was Robins. I'll have to deal with him later, after all this is sorted. What's done is done at this point." She frowned. "Why weren't you guys at the marina? I thought we agreed you would be there just in case I needed help before I got on the boat."

"We did agree," Jay said as he came to stand beside her at the top of the dock. Two techs continued to process the fishing boat. "Robins decided it would take too long to go to the marina and then back to get our boat. He said he was worried we wouldn't be out there in time for the exchange." Jay shook his head. "We did argue with him, but you know what he's like."

"I do." Andy frowned. There was no doubt in her mind that the guys had fought for her. They were good agents and good people, but they were also not stupid. If Robins turned on either one of them, their career would be over. They'd done their best to support her, but their best hadn't been good enough. She'd been left on her own and almost gotten killed because of it.

She took another sip of coffee. Exhaustion rolled over her. Adrenaline had flooded her body when the bullets started flying, and it had finally evaporated, leaving her with aching bones and a serious urge to purge her guts. She just wanted to sleep. But it wasn't over. She needed to go back and see Ignacio and tell him her version of what happened. She sure as hell wasn't going to tell him the truth.

Once the passenger in the powerboat had realized the money was fake, the shooting had started, just like she'd predicted. She'd thought for sure she was dead when a third guy came out of nowhere and opened fire. She'd only just managed to get inside the salon and hide behind the counter in the galley before the place was shot up. There'd been no chance to hide on the outside of the salon wall. She knew Soto was dead, but she'd hoped Tommy had found cover somehow. A vain hope it turned out.

The RPG had been a shock. She'd seen it through the windows. Then the Coast Guard had swooped in, and everything stopped. They'd saved her life. Robins had been late.

He'd left her out there on purpose. She knew it in her bones, but she'd never be able to prove it.

Robins was right about the exchange, and Soto hadn't given them the money until the very last possible moment, so he was covered. She could argue that Robins broke protocol by not showing up at the marina and leaving her in serious danger, but he would argue it was more important to be out at the exchange point, and how was he to know she was in trouble? At most, he'd get a slap on the wrist, if anything, and she would look whiny to her bosses.

Still, if the Coast Guard hadn't shown up, there wasn't a doubt in her mind she'd be dead. Those guys wouldn't have let her live. They'd have grabbed their guns back and probably tossed the place for the money. They'd have killed her on sight. So, she owed the Coast Guard her life. She owed Elias.

Elias.

She'd damn near passed out when she saw him. It was like he'd stepped out of her dreams. He looked the same. No, that wasn't true. He looked older, handsomer. He'd filled out. His wide shoulders seemed to be even wider, and his chest was definitely more developed. She had no doubt he was solid muscle under all that gear.

His dark curly hair was still thick, and those dark eyes that haunted her dreams were still as soul-piercing as they ever were. His square jaw and model-worthy looks were the stuff of legend in the neighborhood. She hadn't heard he was back, which was shocking.

Elias Mason was one of the hottest men she'd ever seen, and time hadn't changed that at all. If the neighborhood knew he was back, it would be all atwitter about it. She idly wondered how he'd managed to keep such a low profile.

"Andy, we need to discuss your approach to Ignacio," Robins barked as he charged toward where she was standing.

She looked up at him. "I've got it, thanks. I don't need to discuss it." She kept her voice clipped. She was pissed, and she wanted him to know it.

He frowned. "Well, that may be, but I need to know what your plan is."

"Why? So you can ignore it and do your own thing?" Anger burned in her veins.

"What's that supposed to mean?" Robins demanded.

She whirled around and squared off with her boss. "You left me in a deadly situation *with no backup*!"

"I told you we had to wait for—"

"Bullshit!" she yelled. "You were supposed to be at the marina. Soto started beating on me, and you were nowhere to be seen. You left me to fend him off on my own with no choice but to get on the fucking boat with him because he held me at gunpoint. Don't try and sell me some shit about how going to the marina would take too long. You and I both know what this is about. You sold me out because you're pissed at me, and it almost got me killed!"

She drew in a ragged breath. She hadn't meant to yell all that at her boss, but she'd been thinking it, and it had been a hell of a night, no thanks to him, so he deserved it.

Robins' face lost all its color, and then his cheeks flushed. He opened his mouth and then closed it again. He looked around to see who heard but, obviously, everyone who was in the area had heard her yell at him and they were staring. "This is not the time or place to discuss this. Obviously, you are upset. It's been a difficult night—"

"No, shit! I almost had my ass shot off because you left me hanging, so fuck yeah, it was a difficult night! And it's not over 'cause I gotta go sell to one of the top gangsters in Miami that I—alone—just killed a pile of guys, so why don't you just fuck right off and leave me alone."

Robins stared at her, his face bright red. She knew he wanted to yell at her and take her to task for insubordination, but Jay and Peña were standing there with her. They knew the truth, and she knew Robins was afraid of what would happen if they backed her up instead of him. "Fine. You need to calm down. I'll come back when the techs are finished, and we'll discuss the next steps." He turned on his heel and went back up the dock.

Andy turned back around and stared at the techs until they resumed what they were doing. "I'm sure I'm going to pay for that, but man, that felt hella good."

Jay grinned. "He had it coming."

Peña sighed. "Just remember, he's still your lifeline. There's only so much Jay and I can do. You keep pushing him like that, and it won't end well for any of us."

Andy wanted to argue with Peña, but she knew he was right. She would pay dearly for her outburst. It was all Elias's fault. Seeing him had thrown her for a loop. She just hadn't expected it, and now she was all jangling nerves. She'd always dreamed of getting a chance to explain everything that happened back then, but Elias had left so abruptly, she never thought it would happen. Now he was here in Miami, and she'd seen him. She might just get that chance. She wasn't sure if that was a good thing or not.

She gulped her coffee. Either way, she needed to put Elias out of her head. She had a job to do, and it would require all her concentration and skill to get it done and done right. If she screwed this up, she'd be dead for sure.

"I need to hash this out. Are you guys okay with that?"

Both Jay and Peña nodded.

"Okay, I need to convince Ignacio that I killed everyone and drove the boat back. Any ideas on how I can do that?"

Jay shook his blond head. "You only have to convince

him that you survived while the others didn't. You don't have to take credit for shooting all of them."

"What do you mean?" Andy asked.

"Tell the truth. Soto tried to shortchange the buyers with fake paper and only a fraction of the cash. The buyers caught him and started shooting. You were smart enough to keep your head down, so you didn't get killed. Once the shooting stopped you came out to see what happened and they were all dead."

Andy frowned. "I don't know, Jay. I'm not sure that sounds believable. Things were crazy out there. The guy almost shot off an RPG. What happened to that anyway?"

Peña shoved his hands in his pockets. "I heard the Coast Guard confiscated it. They said they were going to hand it over to the Navy and let them deal with it. I don't think their head guy, Taggert, trusts Robins. I think he was afraid Robins would let it go to a gang."

"He's not wrong," Andy said. "At least someone is on the ball." Andy swore silently. "I don't mean you two. You know it's about Robins. I know you guys did your best." She gave them a half-hearted smile. It didn't change the fact that now she didn't know if she could trust her backup. Robins had hung her out to dry. Would he do it again?

"I guess your version is the best I'm going to get, Jay. Let's hope Ignacio buys it." Andy stifled a yawn. She was exhausted, and her day wasn't over yet.

Robins came back down the dock as the crime scene guys were finishing up. He ordered Jay and Peña to get busy. "Take the two bodies to West Palm Beach and put them in the morgue up there. Call their head medical examiner and explain the situation. We don't want word to get out that these guys are in the morgue. That would blow Andy's cover,"

"Andy, what is your plan?" he asked in a formal voice.

As much as she should do, she just couldn't bring herself to respond in a professional way. The man had almost gotten her killed. She cleared her throat and fisted her hands. *Yelling wasn't going to help,* she reminded herself. "Jay can tell you." It was the best she could come up with.

She couldn't even look at Robins without wanting to punch him, so she avoided eye contact as she climbed aboard the boat. "I'm going now since the techs are finished. I'll hose down the boat at the other end to get rid of fingerprint dust smudges and the other stuff the crime scene people left behind." She looked at Peña. "Where are the guns?"

He glanced over his shoulder. "The guys are just finishing cataloging them. I'll bring them back." He walked up the dock.

"And the money?" she asked Jay.

"I'll go get it." He turned and jogged along the dock.

"What will you tell Ignacio?" Robins asked.

Andy took a deep breath and finally met his gaze. "Whatever I can think of that will make him believe me."

Robins frowned. "I would like more of a plan. I don't like you going out there unprepared."

"That's rich, coming from you," she snarled.

"Look, it's been a rough night, I get that, so I let you run your mouth before. But you are out of line. Don't push it," Robins snapped.

Andy took a step forward so they were inches apart. "Don't you ever threaten me. I know what you did. So do they." She pointed at Jay and Peña. "And I know why you did it. You were supposed to back me up, and you didn't. You're pissed because I dumped you." She hauled in a breath. "Know this; if you try and hang me out to dry again, I'm going to take you down for sexual harassment, Special Agent Robins."

Andy knew she'd practically signed her own termination papers, but she decided it was better to have her cards on the table than try to hide them. She was calling his bluff, and he knew it.

Robins glared at her but didn't say a word as Jay and Peña rejoined them. Andy helped the two men load the money and the guns into the boat. "I'll reach out once I meet with Ignacio. I'm going to head directly over to him as soon as I wash down the boat unless he directs me to do otherwise."

"Understood," Robins hissed.

Jay and Peña looked at each other and then at Andy. Jay cocked an eyebrow, but Andy just shook her head. It wasn't the time or the place to bring out her dirty laundry.

"Uh, okay, well, we'll be at the meet. You know, hidden but watching," Jay said.

She nodded. "Can you get the boat lines?"

Jay untied the ropes as Andy went up to the fly bridge and started the engines. A few minutes later, she was cruising out of the secluded inlet they'd been hiding the boat in and started down the coast. At the slower pace she set, she'd arrive at the marina in about forty-five minutes.

She took some deep breaths and tried to let the night air calm her down. It would be sunrise soon. Another beautiful sunny day in south Florida. She rolled her shoulders and tried not to yawn. She needed sleep. Real sleep. Being at her aunt's house meant she didn't relax fully. She would love to be in her own apartment back in L.A. Even flying out of town and staying in a hotel somewhere would be a help. But until this was behind her, sleep was not something she was going to get much of, for sure.

She swallowed hard as she steered the boat through the calm waters. No matter what Jay said or what Peña might think, Robins was going to screw her over in some way, shape, or form. Hell, she'd practically dared him to let her get killed. She'd been stupid about it. She'd called his bluff, and at the time it had seemed like the right decision. But now she had her doubts. All she really knew was no one was going to come running if she called. She was well and truly on her own. Not the best place to be when heading in for a chat with one of the top bad guys in Miami.

CHAPTER EIGHT

Elias stood on the small front stoop of his mother's house. She'd painted the structure since he'd left. The house was now a cheery yellow with white trim. She'd planted a little garden out front, and a genuine white picket fence surrounded the whole yard. She'd even had the garage door redone so it no longer had the dent in it from the time he'd backed into it when he was first learning to drive. His mother had always taken pride in owning her own home, no matter how small it was, and he'd loved her for it.

Sofia Mason had been a tough but fair mom. She'd raised Elias and his sister Maria all on her own. Her work as an office manager required her to hone her skills and she'd used her business senses to keep her kids organized, too. The Coast Guard had not been such a huge change in some ways. The thought made Elias smile.

He wiped his palms on his jeans and tried to calm his galloping heart. He wasn't sure why he was so nervous. He'd seen his mom a number of times since he'd left. His sister, too, and her kids. But it was always in New York with other family around. It meant that his mother couldn't ask him questions or get into anything serious. It kept him from having to have difficult conversations with her, the ones that he knew she wanted to have.

He glanced over his shoulder at the empty street. He'd had a lot of good times on this street and some not so good ones. He faced the door once again and knocked. It was almost dawn. His mother would not be pleased to be woken at this hour. She liked to sleep until seven. Maybe it was better if he waited until she was up. No need to wake her this way. He stepped back from the door just as the inside metal door swung open and the outside light turned on.

"Elias, *mi hijo,* is that you?"

His throat closed over, and he had to swallow the lump that suddenly grew there. He cleared his throat. "Yes, Mama, it's me."

His mother opened the door and stared up at her son. When she opened her arms, he stepped forward into her warm hug. "Oh, Elias, *mi hijo,* it is so good to see you." Her words were muffled because her face was buried against his chest. His mother was barely over five feet tall. He bent down and picked her up in a hug. Then he walked them through the door to the living room area.

"Put me down," his mother chided him, but still gave him another squeeze.

Elias set her down on the floor. "It's good to see you, Mama."

He examined his mother in the low light that came from the kitchen. Her black hair had more gray in it than he remembered, and there were a few more wrinkles around her eyes and mouth, but other than that, she looked the same as she always did and, for that, he was eternally grateful.

His mother stepped back and swatted him on the arm.

"What are you doing here at this hour?" She smiled, but it quickly changed to a frown. "You aren't in trouble, are you?"

Elias chuckled. "No, Mama. I'm not in trouble. I moved back to Miami, and I wanted to come see you."

A furrow appeared between her brows. "At this hour?" She made a clucking sound. "You ran into someone, and you were afraid they would tell me you were back before you came to see me."

Elias graced her with a sheepish smile. "Well, er…"

"Never mind," his mother said. "Come." She pointed at the kitchen. "We have coffee, and you tell me what is going on. Are you still in the Coast Guard?" she asked as she walked around the counter and grabbed the pot from the coffee maker. "Where are you living? Have you met a nice girl yet? How is your leg?" She filled her old Mr. Coffee machine with water and coffee grounds. "You should go see your cousin, Lucia. She is a doctor in Hialeah. She's very good. She can help you with your leg. I'll call her." She started toward the phone, but then abruptly turned and went back to the coffee maker. "I'll call her when she wakes up."

Elias sat down at the kitchen table. He didn't even remember Cousin Lucia but if his mom wanted to call her, whatever. He couldn't get the smile off his face. No matter how many difficult conversations were going to happen, he was happy to be home. "I'll fill you in later, but everything is fine, and my leg is okay."

His mom sat down across from him. "So, who did you see?"

He hesitated. He wasn't sure how much he should tell his mother. Technically, he should say nothing, but he'd put her through too much already to start lying to her now. "I bumped into Andrea."

Sofia gave a knowing nod. "I thought it might be her.

She's been back for a few months. She's not hanging out with the best crowd, *mi hijo.* Her aunt is very worried about her."

"Yes, I know." He wasn't going to provide details unless absolutely necessary.

His mother studied his face. "There is something going on. Something you aren't telling me about Andrea. You aren't very good at lying or hiding things from me. You never were."

Elias blinked. He was a damn good liar, and his poker face could not be beat. "I—"

"Don't bother to deny it. I can see it in your face. You are worried about her. Andrea."

"No. I don't care about Andrea, and who she hangs out with is not my concern."

His mother sighed. "You may say you do not care, but I see how your face changes when you speak of her. You still care about that girl." She held up her hands. "I know you think you don't, but you listen to your mama. I know you still care. We've never talked about it, *mi hijo,* but I know you blame her for Mateo's death. It wasn't her fault. There is more to the story than you know."

"What are you talking about?" Elias demanded.

She shook her head. "It is not for me to say. You must ask Andrea." She got up and poured two cups of coffee. She put a mug down in front of her son. "I know you loved Mateo like a brother, but he was not a good influence on you. I'm sorry he died, but it was for the best."

Elias sucked in air like he'd been gut-punched. "How can you say that?"

"Because it's true. Mateo was good to you, but not so good to other people. He was dragging you and Andrea down into gang life." His mother's eyes drilled into him. "I spent too many years sacrificing so you and your sister would not join a gang. So you would go to college and make something of yourselves. Mateo was pulling you down. His death set you free."

He stared at his mother. This was not how he thought this conversation would go. The anger in her eyes was real. She'd hid it from him for all these years, but now the truth was coming out. He was shocked. "I thought you liked Mateo. You treated him like he was my brother."

"I did that for you, Elias, because you needed him. You had no father, and your uncles... You just didn't connect with them. You and Mateo were family, but I told him that if he brought you down with him, he would have to deal with me."

"Mama, are you serious? You threatened Mateo?"

"It didn't help. He just pulled you in deeper." She took a sip of her coffee. She was preparing to tell him something he wasn't going to like. She always made this face when bad news was coming. "If Mateo hadn't been killed, I had made arrangements to ship you up to New York to live with your cousins. Your uncles agreed to come get you."

Elias leaned back in his seat. *Holy shit.* He'd had no idea. None. He'd always thought his mother liked Mateo, just like he did. That she was planning an intervention for him was crazy. He was dumbfounded. "I don't know what to say."

She nodded. "I know. It surprises you but, Elias, you were heading down a dark path. Mateo's death saved you. The Coast Guard saved you. You have become the man I always knew you could be. I am forever grateful for that."

The lump was back. Elias took a slug of his coffee and promptly burned his mouth. "You never made me come back here because you knew it would be difficult for me."

"I was just pleased that you found a career that you love, and you are happy. So, tell me, why are you back?" his mother stared at him, her dark eyes full of curiosity.

"My team got transferred to Miami. I'll be working here for the foreseeable future."

His mother beamed. "Oh, *mi hijo,* my heart is so very happy that you are back. Now," she said, moving his coffee away from him, "you are exhausted. You need sleep. Go in and go to bed. We'll talk more when you get up."

"Mama, I can go to my own—"

"Don't disappoint me. Go. Your room is ready for you. Sleep. We'll talk more later." She stood up and came around the table. She kissed him on the cheek and gave him a quick hug. Then she straightened and went down the hallway to her bedroom. He heard her sniffles as she walked away.

He stared at the table for a minute. He was so totally gobsmacked by what his mother said, he couldn't quite comprehend it. She had never liked Mateo. It was earth-shattering.

When he closed his eyes, exhaustion leaked out of every pore of his body. If this was the way conversations were going to go with his mother, maybe it was better they didn't have any. He didn't think he could take anymore shocks like this one. He just wasn't up to it.

He got to his feet and walked down the hallway to his bedroom, the last door on the right, across from his mother's room. When he opened the door, everything was exactly as he'd left it. On the walls, there were still the posters of the bands he'd listened to, and his favorite books were still on his bookcase. The bedspread was the same, and so was the lamp on the nightstand. He looked to his right. There were even some clothes still hanging in the closet. He had a weird sense of stepping back in time.

He closed the door behind him and walked over to the bed. He sat down and slowly took off his boots. Then he stood up and got undressed. It was all too much to process.

Andrea.

His mother.

His room.

He just needed sleep, then he'd deal with everything. Once he had some decent sleep and, possibly, several pots of coffee. Maybe even a poker game or two. Eventually, he'd be equipped to deal with all the shit that just had gone down. Or, at least, he hoped he could because, currently, he couldn't get his head around it.

Five hours later, a loud bang woke Elias out of a deep sleep. He sat bolt upright in bed and looked around bewildered. *Where was he?* It took a couple of seconds for it to click. *His old room.* There was another loud crash and some yelling. Elias was out of bed and out of the room in seconds, only to come face-to-face with his sister and her three kids.

"Elias," she squealed as she threw her arms around him. He blinked and hugged her back as her youngest, Sebastian, let out an ear-piercing scream. He might be only two but *damn*, he had the lungs of a full-grown man.

"Why aren't they in school?" He was sure it was Wednesday unless he'd slept several days away, which sounded like a good plan considering the way he felt.

"Good to see you, too!" Maria said as she let him go and swatted his arm. "The older two have an in-service day. The teachers are doing a bunch of meetings."

Elias grunted as Nicolas, the middle one, hit him in the leg with a plastic bat. He said a silent prayer of gratitude that Nic hadn't hit his gunshot wound. It would be agonizing. No sooner had the thought occurred to him when Nic brought the bat back and swung for all he was worth. Elias caught the plastic bat in one hand with a loud whack. Nic's eyes got big as he stared up at his uncle. Elias glared at him, and the little tyke promptly burst into tears.

"Elias, you ass, he's only four. You scared him!" Maria scolded.

Scared him? Nic was damn lucky Elias hadn't throttled him.

"Your scar looks like a bull eye to him. It's also ugly. You should have someone take a look at that. I know a great plastic surgeon. I can give you the number."

Martin, his oldest nephew, sniggered and stuck his tongue out at his uncle.

Elias shook his head. Seriously. Kids, plastic surgeons, it was just way too much to deal with without caffeine.

"Nice underwear," a voice commented. He glanced into the living room. His cousin Cara sat on the couch, bouncing a baby on her knee while a toddler played at her feet. "Expecting company?"

Elias looked down. He was wearing black boxer briefs that left little to the imagination. His cousin commenting on them was too much. He turned, walked back into his room, and slammed the door. The howl of the baby ratcheted up again. Now it was all coming back to him. Besides the Mateo mess, the other major reason he never ventured back to Miami was too much family. They were all up in each other's business constantly. Hell, they all lived only a few streets apart. It was…suffocating to say the least.

He grabbed his clothes and headed to the bathroom where he had to remove a toddler, a teddy bear, and two stuffed elephants before he could get the door closed and locked. He leaned against it and let out a long sigh. He'd gotten some sleep, but it hadn't been enough. Not only that, but he also had a headache and, most importantly, he was seriously hungry.

He took a ten-minute shower, during which four different people pounded on the door, yelling at him for locking it because they needed to get in for something or other. His sister, his cousin, his mother, and apparently his other cousin, Stephanie, who had been in the backyard, were now all mad at him for occupying the sole bathroom in the house and locking the door. He grinned. It truly was the little things in life.

He got out, dried off, and was dressed in minutes. He unlocked the door only to be hit in the legs by a toddler this time. He picked up his cousin's son, Ernesto, and set him back down facing the opposite direction so the toddler would run in the other direction. Then he took a deep breath and ventured into the fray. He made it as far as the kitchen before Maria was after him. "So, how long have you been in town if you're showing up here at four-thirty in the morning to tell Mama you're here?"

"A couple of weeks," he mumbled and then waited for the onslaught, but none came. He met Maria's gaze. She was studying him. "What?" he asked.

"How's the leg?" she offered.

"Not too bad as long as someone doesn't hit it with a bat." He smirked as he reached the coffee maker. Damn, the pot was empty. "And no, I don't want your plastic surgeon's number."

Maria rolled her eyes at him. "Always so dramatic."

His mother came in and handed the baby to Maria. "I'll make you some coffee and breakfast. Sit."

He sat. The need for coffee and food was strong, and he had no way out of there, anyway. He would text Cain after breakfast and see if he could get a lift back to his apartment.

Maria sat down across from him after putting Sebastian down on the floor. "You know Andrea is back."

"I heard." He willed his mother not to say anything. He didn't want to get into anything with his sister. After everything his mother said during their conversation, he didn't think he could handle it if his sister came out with some other bombshell. Maria fussed with Sebastian in the kitchen, but the living room had gotten suspiciously quiet. Elias asked, "Where are the other kids?"

"Cartoons," Maria said.

"Here." His mother put a hot cup of coffee down in front of him, and then a couple of minutes later, a plate of eggs with rice and beans.

Elias dug in with gusto. His mama was an awesome cook. Nothing was ever as good as her home cooking. He relished every bite.

"She's been hanging out with some unsavory people."

Elias nodded but didn't comment.

"She went to see Ignacio this morning and told him some wild story about Soto and Tommy being killed during a gun buy because they tried to rip off the sellers. According to her, everyone ended up dead."

He took a sip of coffee. "How do you know this?"

"Rodrigo's cousin is in the Street Aces. Stupid kid." She shook her head. "He told Rodrigo this morning at the garage."

Elias tried to steer the conversation away from Andrea. He really didn't even want to think about her, let alone discuss her. "How is your husband? How's the garage? Did he open the third one?"

"Rodrigo is fine. Yes, he opened the third one a bit north of here, but the one around the corner is still his baby. He loves it. He prefers to work there than the other two."

"It's good he has good help to look after the other two," his mother said. She caught Elias's eye. She was trying to help.

Maria still stared at him across the table.

"What?" he demanded as he ate the last bite of food off his plate.

"Was it you?"

He frowned. "Was it me what?"

"Did you help Andrea kill those men?"

He froze. "What?" he croaked.

Maria's chin jutted out. "I know how much you loved Andrea. She's back, and suddenly you're back. She's been hanging with the wrong crowd. Soto has been beating on her, and suddenly Soto is dead. Was it you? Did you help Andrea kill those men?"

"Maria!" their mother screeched. "How could you ask such a thing?"

She shrugged. "It's awful coincidental that he's suddenly back in town when his ex needs some help. Plus, you said it yourself, he hasn't been the same since he got shot. Is he even working for the Coast Guard anymore?"

Elias met his mother's gaze. There was an opportunity here, a chance for him to get on the inside and help take down Santiago. A chance for justice for Mateo, but he'd have to work with Andrea. His gut churned. Suddenly, breakfast wasn't sitting comfortably in his gut.

Did people in the neighborhood really think he was one of the bad guys? His sister was thinking it, so others must think it, too. His cover would hold. The question was, what would happen to his family when all this was over? Would the Street Aces come after them? He needed to speak to Nick and the rest of the team.

"You're not denying it," Maria stated.

"I'm not going to talk about it. There's a difference." Elias finished his coffee, and his mother quickly poured him another cup.

"Well, if it was you, you need to step up. Your girlfriend is out there on her own, and word on the street is she's meeting with Santiago tonight. If he doesn't believe her, she's a dead woman."

Elias's heart thumped as his adrenaline kicked in. "Why wouldn't Santiago believe her?"

"Because everyone knows Soto and Tommy couldn't hit the broad side of a barn if they were ten feet from it. There's no way they killed the other guys on their own. Someone had to help. Andrea should be dead but she's alive and you're here."

He needed to go. Now. He stood up. "Thanks for breakfast, Mama." He kissed his mother on her cheek. "Can I borrow your car?"

She shook her head and pointed to the key rack on the wall. "Your truck is here. Take that."

"Mama, it hasn't been driven in years. It won't start."

Maria stood up. "Rodrigo has been taking care of it. It runs fine."

Elias stared at his sister. If her husband had taken care of Elias's truck all the years he'd been gone, it was because Maria had asked him. He'd never really thought about how his leaving had affected her or how his life choices influenced hers.

He walked around the table and gave her a big hug. Then he kissed her on the cheek and whispered, "Thanks, Short Stuff." She smiled at his use of the nickname he'd given her growing up.

She grabbed his arm. "Be careful. I want you around for a long time, okay? I need help with Mama." She winked at him but squeezed his arm. He got the message. *Don't go getting yourself killed. Mama wouldn't survive it.*

He nodded at her.

He walked across the kitchen and grabbed the keys to his truck from the peg. He opened the side door and went into the garage, closing the door after him. The sounds from the kitchen diminished.

His truck was in the second bay. The first had his mother's white Toyota. It had been twelve years since he'd seen his truck. Lots had changed since then, but it still brought a smile to his lips. He'd had the old pickup painted black, but he'd added running boards that he'd kept in wood. He'd had it lowered so it was not that far off the ground. He'd saved forever to modify it the way he'd wanted. Mattie had given him the last few hundred he'd needed to fix the engine, making it perfect.

The truck was spotless. Rodrigo had done a great job of keeping it clean and shiny. He looked in the window. The inside was clean as well. He opened the door and slid in. The scent of Andrea's perfume was the first thing that hit him. She used to wear some citrusy scent. An ache started in his chest. He longed for those carefree days when they drove around in his truck, making big plans about where they'd live and what they'd do.

He closed his eyes and took a deep breath. They used to drive down to the beach and have sex in the back of the truck under the stars. He kept a blanket and some pillows behind the seats, so it was more comfortable. They'd thought they had the world by the tail back then. They were young and foolish, and he missed those days more than he thought possible.

He opened his eyes and stuck the key in the ignition. He turned it, and the engine roared to life. He smiled. There was movement in his peripheral vision. He looked over at the door and saw his sister standing there. He gave her a big smile. She waved back, but she was frowning. She was worried about him. He hated that, but if it meant that he had a chance at bringing Santiago down, she was going to have to worry a bit longer.

Maria hit the button for the garage door, and it lifted behind him. He waved his thanks and backed the truck out. Twenty minutes later, he was pulling into the parking lot beside his office. He texted the guys to come ASAP and went to get coffee from Carlos.

He had the beginnings of a plan in his head. Would they be allowed to work it was another question altogether. Santiago was not their case. Yet. Bertrand had given them latitude before. Elias could only hope he'd do it again and that the flexibility didn't get him killed.

CHAPTER NINE

Andy rested her head on her arms and tried to get some sleep. Since her talk with Ignacio, she wasn't allowed to leave the bar. He didn't believe her story and didn't want to take the chance on her running if she was allowed to go to her aunt's place. She'd told him that she wasn't going to run. She had nowhere to go, but he didn't believe her. What he didn't say was that her aunt's fierce reputation scared some of the Street Aces. If she called out all the mothers and grandmothers, the guys would have no defense and Andy could do whatever she wanted.

So, she was exhausted and stuck in the bar. She dozed a little here and there, but it wasn't exactly relaxing. She moved her head slightly and tried to get more comfortable.

"Come on." Antonio tapped her on her shoulder.

She sat up. "I'm not allowed to leave."

"I know. You're not leaving. We're just going in the back room. Come on." Antonio led the way. She stood and followed him down the hallway next to the bar and through a door marked *Private*.

The office was dark. The only light came from a small

lamp that was on the corner of the desk and a small window that was high up behind the desk, which sat in the middle of the opposite wall from the door. It was a big wooden affair with lots of papers on it and a laptop. There were two wooden chairs in front of it.

On the right side of the room, just beyond the door, were a couple of filing cabinets. On the left side was a long, dark brown leather couch that had a throw pillow with a palm tree on it in each corner.

"Grab some sleep there. There's a blanket on the back. It's clean. I washed it myself a couple of days ago. The pillows, too."

She gave him a brief smile. "Thanks, Antonio." She hesitated before moving slowly toward the sofa. She wanted to sleep but was afraid to let her guard down. The last thing she needed was to be attacked. She was running on empty and wouldn't have the strength to fight off an aggressor.

"What's wrong?" Antonio asked. It must have clicked for him because he said, "Don't worry. I won't let anyone back here. You're safe."

She sat down on the sofa and almost wept with relief. She was desperate for sleep at this point. "Thank you, Antonio. I mean it. I really appreciate this."

Antonio smiled. "I know." He heaved a breath out before he said, "Look, I don't know what happened out there, but telling Ignacio the truth would go a long way to making things good. The fact that you have the money and the guns and you're willing to give both to Ignacio says a lot. They like loyalty. You just have to tell them the truth about what happened."

She started to speak, but Antonio was out the door without a backward glance. She heard the key in the lock. Her heart dropped to her feet. When he'd said he wouldn't let anyone back here, she hadn't thought that meant he was going to lock her in. *Stupid.* She was so damn tired she was making rookie mistakes.

She stretched out on the sofa, but her mind was racing again. She wanted to bring Santiago down so badly, she could taste it, but it wouldn't change the past. Carmen was gone. Avenging her sister's death had seemed all noble and righteous when she'd started this operation but now, here, locked in this room, it just seemed a fool's errand.

She cupped her hands over her face and took a deep breath. It was too late to have second thoughts. There was nothing to do for it now but sleep. Maybe, just maybe, by the time she woke up, Ignacio would be back, and this part of the hell would be over.

The sound of a key scraping in the lock woke her, and Andy sat up a little too fast. She was woozy. She leaned back on the sofa as the door opened. Antonio entered, carrying a tray. "I thought you might like some food."

"That would be great. A shower and a change of clothes would be fantastic. Any chance Ignacio is back yet?"

He shook his head. "Sorry. To be honest, he won't be back before tonight is my guess."

"Great," she groaned.

"Why don't you eat something. It will make you feel better. I brought you your favorite. A cheeseburger with extra pickles and no onions, and some fries. There's also coffee." He set the tray down on the desk and then handed her the plate.

"Thanks, Antonio." She took a bite of the burger and winced. She'd forgotten about the split lip Soto had given her, but she was hungry, so she ignored the pain and continued eating. The burger tasted really good. She smiled up at Antonio. He grinned back as he sat behind the desk.

She studied him from under her lashes. He was wearing jeans and a white button-down dress shirt. His light brown hair was neatly trimmed, but his brown eyes were always a little bloodshot. She assumed contact lenses were the cause. He'd always been friendly when they were kids, but they weren't really friends. As far as she could tell, he didn't appear to have any real friends, but he seemed to be on good terms with everyone.

He was tall and slightly muscular, which seemed to be enough to discourage anyone from challenging him in the bar, but he kept to himself when the gang was hanging out on the premises. He didn't seem to like them much.

"Why do you work here?" she asked suddenly.

Antonio looked up from the laptop screen he'd been studying. "It's a job, and it pays well. The tips are good on the weekends."

"Yes, but why do you work here? You aren't a Street Ace, and you don't seem to want to be one…"

Antonio drew in a long breath. "I guess I could work anywhere, but this is where the neighborhood hangs out. I'm comfortable here. Everyone knows me and leaves me alone."

She frowned, but then it dawned on her. Protection. The neighborhood protected him. He was gay. She'd always known that growing up. She didn't care, but she was willing to bet there were people who weren't as unconcerned, and it probably wasn't pretty.

Antonio leaned back in the chair. "Why did you come back?"

She took a bite of her burger to stall. She finally swallowed. "It was time, I guess. I liked L.A. but missed home." As she said it, she knew it was actually true. "My plan didn't involve this." She gestured around the room. "I thought I would come back and get a real job. In L.A., I worked as an office manager. I just assumed I would do the same here, but there wasn't much available. Well, not that paid decently. I don't want to live with my aunt forever." She frowned. "Old habits." She nibbled a fry. She hated lying to Antonio, but it was her cover story, so she had to stick to it.

Antonio's cell vibrated on the desk. He grabbed it and answered, "Yes, she's right here." Andy looked up at him. He glanced at his watch. "Okay." A slight pause, then, "Okay, yeah, I'll make sure. Yeah." He clicked off the call.

"What?" she said.

"That was Ignacio. He said you are going to meet with Santiago tonight at ten at his place."

She glanced at her watch. It was already five p.m. She'd had about five hours sleep. She could stand a few more if she was going to be stuck here. "Am I still jailed here, or can I go home and grab a shower?"

Antonio shook his head. "Sorry, no going home."

Her shoulders sagged. She really wanted a shower and a chance to decompress in the privacy of her own room. Talking to Jay and Peña would also be good. Who knew what Robins had them doing, or even if they were doing anything to back her up.

"You can, however, come to my place and grab a shower. I even have some clothes you can change into. My sister left them the last time she was in town."

"That would be awesome!" It wasn't perfect, but she'd take it. "How is Lola, anyway? Is she still liking Las Vegas?"

"Yeah, she's loving it. She keeps trying to get me to move out there."

"Why not? They have lots of bars out there and lots of people. Might be a nice change."

"It's a thought." Antonio smiled. "You ready to go?"

"Absolutely," she said as she grabbed her dishes and stood

up. Antonio walked around the desk and opened the door. She followed him down the hallway and out into the bar. One of the other bartenders, Hector, was there. She set her dishes on the counter and gave him a wave. He nodded, his gaze still on her as she turned to leave. She hoped Antonio wasn't going to get in trouble for this. As much as she needed to make contact with the outside world, she didn't want him to pay the price for it.

They went out the front door and crossed the parking lot to Antonio's convertible Audi. He unlocked the doors, and they climbed in. "You aren't going to get in trouble for this, are you?"

He shook his head. "Ignacio doesn't want you showing up to Santiago's looking like something the cat threw up."

"Thanks!" she said as she playfully whacked his arm.

He laughed as he pulled out of the parking lot. "Honey, you do look a sight. I think I might have some makeup to disguise that black eye and bruised lip."

She'd forgotten all about her face. When Soto hit her, it had hurt, but her adrenaline had kicked in and she'd forgotten about it until she'd bit into the burger. She flipped down the visor and opened the mirror. "Oh, shit. You weren't wrong. I look awful." Her right cheek was red, and the skin under her right eye was definitely bruised. Her lip was cut. She was going to need some serious makeup to cover up this mess. "I don't think a bit of makeup is going to do it. Any chance we can stop at the CVS and get some stuff?"

Antonio glanced over at her. "Sure, we can stop. Santiago throws a lot of parties. There will be a lot of people there tonight. You do not want to do anything that might embarrass him. We'll get you looking okay so he'll be pleased to see you."

"Is he…?" What was the word she was looking for? "As volatile as he used to be?" Santiago had a hair-trigger temper and used to take it out on the guys around him. No one wanted to be the one that set him off. They'd be in for a beatdown.

Antonio navigated into the drugstore's lot and parked the car. He put his hand on her arm. "He's worse. He's scary as hell. When I said don't do anything to embarrass him, I wasn't joking. He's killed people who made him look bad. Tread very lightly around him, Andrea. He'll kill you in an instant if he feels like it."

Her gut rolled, and the cheeseburger soured in her stomach. Just what she needed…a lunatic with a quick temper. "Thanks for telling me. Forewarned is forearmed, as they say."

They got out of the car and entered the pharmacy. Twenty minutes later, they were back on their way again with a brand-new bag full of makeup essentials. "Thanks for stopping, Antonio."

He gave her a brief smile as he entered the parking garage beneath his building. It was a high-rise condo in a nicer area of Miami. How could he afford a place like this on his bartender's salary? A small frisson of fear snaked across her skin.

After exiting the car, they rode the elevator up to the eighteenth floor. Antonio opened the door to his apartment and ushered her in.

The first thing that hit her was the view from the sliding doors out to the balcony. She was drawn to it and walked over to stand in front of the glass. "Oh, my god, the view is incredible! You can see all the way up and down Miami Beach." There was a cruise ship sailing in the distance.

Andy turned and looked at the apartment. There was a kitchen area on the right with a dining table, and then the rest of the room was a sitting area and bathroom on the left. A curved staircase led up to a loft. Floor-to-ceiling windows created dramatic lighting throughout the space. The place was all modern with white furniture and a light brown wooden floor, like the color of oak. The kitchen was also done in white with marble countertops. The white walls were broken up by artwork, which were a riot of colors. It was a nice effect.

"Antonio, your place is beautiful." She smiled at him, hoping to hide the fear that was building in the pit of her stomach.

"Thank you." He strolled into the kitchen. "Water?" He opened the Sub-Zero fridge and held up a bottle. She nodded. He brought the water over to her. "I know you're wondering how I can afford this place, or if I *can* afford it, why do I work at the Blue Iguana?"

She offered him a tentative smile then took a sip of water. She turned so she was facing him with the open bottle in her hand. If he did anything, she could douse him with water as a distraction before she hit him. She wasn't going to get many chances with Antonio. He was in decent shape and larger than she was.

"My partner Jasper owns the bar. He…has an agreement with Santiago about the Street Aces hanging out there. I work behind the bar to keep an eye on the place. The neighborhood knows who I am, and no one bothers with me. It means Jasper knows what's going on and how to best maneuver around Santiago. See, Jasper owns a few different businesses around Miami. He's come up against Santiago on a few occasions. It's better to be on Santiago's good side."

Andy grimaced. "That's for sure. So, your partner is into some not-so-legal things, and you working the bar means he has the inside scoop on what's happening with Santiago and how best to avoid him."

Antonio smiled. "Our way of helping to keep the peace."

"So that's why you stay."

"Yes, Jasper is why I stay."

"Does he live here with you?"

He shook his head. "We don't have that kind of relationship. It's…"

"Complicated?" she supplied.

"Yes." He smiled. "Complicated is a fitting description."

The knots in her stomach started to unwind a bit. "Does Santiago know of your relationship with Jasper?"

Antonio moved his head back and forth. "He knows we know each other, but he doesn't know the…extent of our relationship."

She cocked an eyebrow. "How do you hide this place?"

He smiled. "Do you remember my old Aunt Mary?"

Andy frowned. "The one with all the cats?"

"Yes. She died a few years ago and left me some money. I may have let people believe it was more money than it actually was, and then I told them I spent my entire inheritance to buy this place so now I have work at the club to pay the bills."

"Clever. No one bothers to look too closely." She took a sip of water.

"If they ever did, I would be found out, but in the end, it wouldn't be to Santiago's advantage to harm me in any way. Jasper is not without…resources."

"Good to know."

"So, how about that shower? I'd offer you something stronger to drink, but my guess is you're going to want your wits about you tonight."

She nodded. He had no idea.

CHAPTER TEN

E lias walked into the office and set a bunch of bags on the back table. "Sorry I got everyone down here a bit early but I brought coffee and pastries to make it up to you."

"Don't mind if I do," Axe said as he tried to stifle a yawn. He walked over to the table and started rummaging through the bags.

"If there are cheese danish, they're mine," Finn called as he got up from his desk.

Cain, who was the closest to the table, reached over and grabbed a coffee. "Why are we here?"

"Yes, good question." Nick stood up and moved to the back table, grabbing an apple turnover.

Elias stood at the front of the room with a Cuban coffee in hand. "I heard through the grapevine that Andrea went to Ignacio with some story, and he doesn't believe her. He's keeping her at the dive bar they run called the Blue Iguana until tonight when she meets with Santiago. If he doesn't believe her, she's dead."

"Whoa, that's rough," Finn commented as he sat down with his coffee and danish.

"I am assuming she has the ATF team as backup to get her out of the situation." Nick sat down at his desk after placing his food and drink next to his computer.

"I don't know and, honestly, that's not what's important." He swallowed. Okay, maybe that wasn't true. He didn't necessarily want her dead. He just wanted her to pay. "The thing is, as of early this morning, no one knows who the sellers were or where they came from. I know it's an ATF case, but they're concentrating on bringing down the gang and Santiago. It's our job to follow up on who the sellers were. We need to figure out who is bringing in guns. Robins said they didn't know, and there was no identification on those men."

"Nice spin. Is that what you want me to use when selling whatever your scheme is to Bertrand?" Nick asked casually and then sipped his coffee.

Elias grinned. "Busted. But yeah, it's true. Drug, gun, human trafficking interdiction—it's all us."

"What do you really want? To bring down Santiago? That's the ATF or the DEAs job."

Elias took a deep breath. He had to play this right, or he would be shut down immediately. "What if I said I could get on the inside and close to Santiago quickly? He has to know who the sellers were. They had RPGs. That's not run-of-the-mill stuff. We need to know where that's coming from."

"Why would Santiago let you in?" Axe ripped off a bite of his second danish. "I mean he has to know you hate him." He tossed the morsel in the air and caught it in his mouth.

"He will think he has something on me. Plus keep your enemies close and all that."

"You've thought this through, but what makes you think he'll believe you?" Nick cocked his head. "What aren't you telling us?"

"So, last night or early this morning, I went to my

mom's. I crashed for a few hours, and when I woke up, a lot of my family was there. My sister told me about Andrea and Ignacio and how he didn't believe Andrea could've managed everything that happened on her own. Tommy and Soto were bad shots. My sister asked me if *I* killed Soto and Tommy. The neighborhood thinks I was there and backed up Andrea."

"Jesus. Your own sister?" Finn shook his head. "That's cold."

Elias shrugged. "Not really. Andrea and I… We were a forever kind of couple back then. Everyone thought we'd get married. Andrea moves back, and a few months later, I just happen to show up around the time this whole mess goes down? It's too much of a coincidence for them to buy. They think Andrea and I are back together but keeping it on the down-low."

"So, you want to go in as the gunman behind the shootings. Tell Santiago it was you who did the heavy lifting during the exchange." Cain nodded. "Could work."

Nick grunted. "Maybe." He chewed the last bite of his danish. "But why do you think they will believe you?"

"Hey, if his own sister thinks it's possible," Finn responded, "it shouldn't be a hard sell."

Elias agreed. "My thought exactly. Santiago will want to check out my story. He'll have one of his goons break into my place, and he'll find the rifle I used to take out the guy with the RPG. He'll think he has me dead to rights. He can always drop the gun with the cops and have me arrested for murder. If one of you guys can sit on my place or check the security feed, then we can know for sure when it happens.

"Everyone knows I got shot. I didn't go into detail with my family about being in Panama. Just that I was benched, more or less. I have avoided everyone since being back in Miami. I can sell it that I'm still benched and unhappy about it." He looked out the window. "I may have said as much during a poker game or two since I got back into town."

Nick narrowed his eyes. "I see."

"If Santiago asks around, that's what he's going to hear. He'll believe my story because I have the skill set to pull it off, and they all think I still love Andrea. He'll also have the rifle he thinks he can blackmail me with."

"So, you get in. Then what?" Axe asked.

"Then I find out who is supplying the guns. Normally, this stuff comes from Mexico, but why the hell would they meet so far offshore? What if there's a new player in the game? Someone we don't know about. It would be better for us to find out now, rather than when the next shipment of RPGs makes it through."

"Damn straight," Finn agreed.

"And if Santiago just happens to go down in the mean-time, it's all good, right?" Nick asked. "I'm not so sure about this Elias."

"Run it by Bertrand. If he says no, then I'm out. If he goes for it, then we start planning." It was a gamble, but Elias was counting on Bertrand wanting to find out about those guns. It would be another point for him if his team managed to figure out the new source of guns that were showing up in Miami before ATF or anyone else.

It was also a big fucking risk. Santiago could decide to kill him at any time. There was also the question of his family. What if Santiago decided to use them to get revenge? It was a possibility. But his family was well-liked and had a certain status in the community. Gunning them down would bring repercussions for Santiago and the Street Aces. It could cause a lot of problems for the gang.

Things people had seen or knew of could come out suddenly. He'd seen it happen when he was growing up. If the gang pushed too hard and killed the wrong person, regular citizens turned on them. He only hoped that Santiago would be aware of the consequences and make the best choice. Really, he hoped Santiago would be dead and it wouldn't be a problem anymore.

Nick got up from his desk and tapped his cell phone screen. "I'll be back," he said and left the office space.

"Elias," Cain said, "you sure you want to do this?"

He hesitated for a second. "I want Santiago, yeah, and I think we really do need to find out where the hell those guns and RPGs came from so, I guess, yes, I want to do this."

"This op might come with a heavy price," Axe pointed out. "You're going to have to keep it together in the face of the man that killed your best friend. That's a big fucking ask."

Elias nodded. "You're not wrong there. But…I just can't let this opportunity slide by. A chance to bring down Santiago and stop more guns from coming in. Two birds, one stone."

"Not to mention possibly saving your ex. I don't care how much you hate her now. It's gotta make you a bit nervous that her life is on the line. Her people weren't so keen on saving her ass last night. She may not have the backup she needs."

Finn had nailed it in one. Elias hated her for what she did, but being in the truck today had brought back so many memories. She'd been important to him once. He didn't want to see her dead. Of course, that was assuming she wasn't helping Santiago in some way. Maybe the whole thing was a setup so she could bring Santiago the guns and return his money. If that were the case, he would enjoy bringing her down as much as Santiago. It was a win-win either way for him. Andrea was just a distraction really. Santiago was the main event.

Nick stepped out his office, shutting the door behind

him. He came around the dividers and took up his place at the front of the room. "Bertrand is busy. He'll get back to me."

Elias sighed and slouched in his chair. He hated waiting.

"In the meantime, we've got a murder to look into," Nick said as he picked up a file from his desk. "They found a dead body by an abandoned boat on South Beach. The local cops figured someone tried to dispose of a body a couple of days ago during the storm."

"Why do they assume that?" Finn asked.

Nick took a sip of his second coffee. "Because, apparently, the boat was found half-swamped. It looks like it took a hell of a battering, according to the report, and the body was found wrapped in chains. The report says whoever wrapped the guy up didn't do a stellar job, and the chains started to unravel a bit. They think a part of the chain on the dead guy must have gotten hooked onto the anchor chain when the body was dumped off the boat, and they ended up dragging it all the way back to shore. I guess the body is in bad shape as well."

"So why do we care about this?" Elias finished his second coffee and eyed a third. He always bought two extra just in case a couple of the guys had a hard night and needed a bonus pick-me-up shot. Of course, "one of the guys" was usually him.

"We care because the dead body is that of one Mark Daniel Waters, former Seaman in the USCG. Or, at least, the local cops want us to care. They don't have any leads on the case and are stretched too thin to bother spending much time on it. They figure it's another drug hit. They could spend months on it and never get anywhere." Nick dropped the file onto his desk. "They called the local Coasties, who then were told to give it to us."

Axe leaned back in his chair. "Why do they think it's a drug thing? Like why not gambling or an angry spouse?"

"How many angry spouses wrap their husband up in chains and dump him over the side of a boat during a storm?" Finn asked with a grin.

Axe shrugged. "It's Miami. Things seem to be more… extreme down there."

"You are not wrong," Finn agreed as he finished an origami baby elephant. "Did you see the woman on the news that hit her husband with the car and then backed up and drove over him again? Insane!"

"It's got to be the heat. Don't you think?" Axe asked.

"Probably. But back to the case at hand." Nick straightened. "They think it's drugs because he started working as muscle for a local gang a few months ago. The Street Aces." He turned to Elias. "Seems your old friends are still causing trouble, even with Santiago moving up to drug kingpin, or at least that's what Robins called him last night."

Even though they'd just been talking about Santiago, Elias's blood ran cold at the mention of the name. It was like PTSD or something. Any mention of the name had his adrenaline kicking in.

"Bertrand wants us to take a look since the kid used to be one of us. There's more to the story, but he's not saying anything else." Nick shrugged. "So even though this is not our usual thing, we're going to poke around a bit. Axe, you and Finn go talk to his live-in girlfriend. She reported him missing. See if you can get anything out of her. Elias, take Cain and head to the morgue and get some face time with the Medical Examiner. See if there's anything new there or anything that isn't in the file. The file is thin, so there must be something missing.

"I'm going to go chat with the detectives assigned to the case and see what they have to say. As always, gentlemen, keep a low profile. This isn't our normal thing, but it's a nice trial run to see how things are going to go down here. Bertrand and the top brass will be watching, so let's not fuck this up."

Stunned, Elias remained in his seat. He'd known it was only a matter of time before he'd have to deal with the past; he just didn't think it would be so soon. Nor did he think it would be at work. Shit. This was his nightmare coming true. How was he going to navigate his way through this without fucking things up?

Elias and Cain walked down the hall into the morgue. They came to a stop in front of some sort of reception desk. There was a young woman behind the desk, wearing a white blouse and a tan skirt. Her medium brown hair was pulled back into a bun. She was staring at the computer screen in front of her.

"We're here to speak with a Dr. Carr," Elias stated with authority.

The woman at the desk looked up at him. "Do you have an appointment?"

"No, but—"

"Then it's impossible. You'll have to come back." She went back to staring at the screen.

Elias ground his teeth. "If you would let me finish. We're here to speak to Dr. Carr about a body he recently pulled out of the ocean. Mark Daniel Waters."

She took her time, but eventually looked up again. "Are you family of Mr. Water's?"

"No. We're—"

"Then, as I said, you'll have to come back after you've made an appointment."

Elias glanced at Cain and cocked an eyebrow. What the

fuck was wrong with this woman? How many people demanded to get into the morgue every day that she was this over the top about keeping them out?

"We are with the Coast Guard. Mr. Waters, a former serviceman with the Coast Guard, was murdered. The police have asked us to look into it."

Axe was technically the only one that had experience in the law enforcement area of the Coast Guard. None of the rest of them were part of the Coast Guard Investigative Service, but Admiral Bertrand had given them a lot of leeway within this new team. If he wanted them to investigate a purported crime, they had the authority to do so.

The woman let out an exaggerated sigh and pointedly glanced at their civilian clothes. "You two are supposed to be investigating a death? I want to see your badges."

Elias tried to remain calm and friendly, but he was finding it harder by the moment. "We don't carry badges, but we do have IDs. Like I said, we're with the Coast Guard. The body was found off the coast. The guy was a former member of the Coast Guard. We've been asked to take a look at his death."

The woman eyed Elias and Cain. She sighed again. "Let me see some identification." Both men pulled out their Coast Guard IDs. She studied each one and then picked up the phone. She hit a button and then said, "There are two men here who claim they are with the Coast Guard. Something about—"

After a brief pause, she met Elias's gaze and glared at him. "Yes, sir. Of course, sir." The woman hung up the phone. "If you'll follow me, please."

She got up from her desk and started down the hallway to her right. Elias and Cain followed. She stopped at an office doorway and indicated they should enter. The room was fairly small, but the back wall of it was windowed. There was a desk filled with files and a desktop computer and two visitor chairs. Elias and Cain moved into the office and sat down.

"Dr. Carr will be with you momentarily." She turned and stalked out.

The sound of her heels clicking on the floor died out. "Who pissed in her cornflakes?" Cain asked, and Elias grinned. Sometimes Cain nailed it, no question.

A minute later, a tall, slender man bustled in. His blond hair was thinning, and he wore wire-rimmed glasses. He had on a white lab coat. "Sorry to keep you gentlemen waiting," he said as he offered his hand.

Elias offered his name and shook the man's hand.

Cain followed suit. "Dr. Carr, we're here about Mark Daniel Waters. We were wondering if you could give us some details of his death."

Dr. Carr smiled as he sat down. "Yes, your boss called ahead to let me know you were coming." He started clicking around, using his mouse. "I do hope Clementine wasn't too difficult. She tends to be a bit…overzealous."

Clementine? Lemontine seemed more appropriate, but Elias didn't say a word. He just let it go.

"We have a copy of the report from the detectives, but it seemed…thin." Elias didn't want to piss the man off, but the autopsy report seemed kind of meager.

"Yes. Here it is." Dr. Carr clicked one last time and then skimmed the information on the screen. "Right. I remember this now." He looked over the computer screen at them. "I realize it was only last week but, sadly, it was a busy weekend here." He went back to his screen. "The man was drowned and then his body was wrapped in chains. I see a note here that it was during that big storm, and the body ended up getting dragged through the water behind the boat. Not the best way to get rid of a body."

Cain said, "I would have thought dumping a body out in the ocean would be an effective method of disposal."

Dr. Carr's face lit up. "You would think that, wouldn't you? In this case, it all went horribly wrong. Whoever wrapped the chains didn't do a good job, and then having him tangled up in their own anchor chain…well, it was a comedy of errors really. But in normal circumstances—if I can say that"—the doctor grinned—"if you were going to dispose of a body in water, you should be aware that, over time, the flesh will rot away and be eaten by aquatic life. The connective tissue will also disappear, making the bones come apart. Depending on how the weights are added, it can make the body surface faster than one might expect. For example, if you weigh down the feet in cement, then once the connective tissue dissolves, the legs separate from the feet, and the body surfaces.

"There were several errors made in this case. Not only were the chains not fastened correctly, but there also weren't enough of them to actually sink the body. This is an interesting point. The water in the lungs was fresh water so he didn't drown in the ocean when they threw him overboard. He was dead before he hit the water."

"So, he drowned in fresh water, not salt water?" Elias confirmed.

Dr. Carr nodded. "Yes."

"Would it be possible for you to tell what kind of fresh water he drowned in? I mean, like a lake or a shower or something like that?"

"Yes, he drowned in a swimming pool."

Cain's eyes narrowed. "How can you be so sure?"

Dr. Carr turned the computer screen so they could see it better. "See here? That's a list of chemicals found in the water that was in his lungs. I can tell by looking at it he drowned in a swimming pool. Those chemicals are what are used to keep a pool clean."

"Huh. If we find a pool that we think he may have drowned in, could we bring you a water sample and see if you can match it?"

Dr. Carr cocked his head. "You could, but I sincerely doubt it would be conclusive. The chemical makeup of a pool changes daily based on weather patterns and usage. It's never the same from one day to the next. I can check and see if there's anything about this water sample that really stands out, but my guess is you won't find your killer or crime scene from the water sample."

Elias sighed to himself. He'd been excited that the doctor knew it was pool water. Turned out that wasn't good enough. "Is there anything else in the report that jumps out at you? We didn't see any mention of pool water in our report."

"You wouldn't. You have a copy of the preliminary report. There are still tests outstanding. As they come in, we fill in more details on the report. Once the final tests come back, we'll issue a final report."

"Is there anything else in your report that we wouldn't have seen yet?" Cain asked. His voice was deceptively calm, but Elias knew him well enough to know he was slightly annoyed.

"Let's see..." The doctor scanned the report. "Here. There was a substance found in a cut that was on his head. It was sent out for analysis but came back quickly. It's gold foil."

"Gold foil? You mean like tin foil that's gold in color?" Elias asked.

Dr. Carr shook his head. "No, I mean gold leaf. You know, they use it in elaborate decor. There are some hotels that use it down by the beach. Some restaurants use it in desserts."

"So, someone hit him with something that has gold leaf on it?"

The doctor did some more clicking around. "Hmmm. More like he hit his head on something that was covered in gold leaf, if I had to guess from the impression in his skull."

"Is there anything else, Dr. Carr, that stands out to you?" Elias asked.

He shook his head. "No, but as I said, we don't have all the test results back yet."

Cain stood. "Could we get a copy of the report as it is now?"

The doctor looked like he was going to refuse, but one look at Cain's face must have changed his mind. With a sigh, he clicked another couple of times, and the printer started spitting out pages. Dr. Carr grabbed the pages off the printer and stuck them in a file folder. "Here you go, gentleman. I'll be in touch with my final findings when all the tests come back."

Elias stood as well. "Do you know when that will be?"

"Probably six weeks or so. The labs take a while."

Elias swallowed his disappointment. Patience wasn't one of his strong suits. He offered his hand. "Thanks for speaking with us." Dr. Carr shook hands with both men, and then they left.

Back in Cain's SUV, Elias read through the report. "What do you think he could have hit his head on?"

"No clue."

"Do you think that's why he drowned?"

Cain shrugged.

Elias rubbed his thigh and yawned. He needed sleep, and he needed to rest his leg. He also needed food. "How about lunch?"

Cain glanced over at him. "You're exhausted, and your leg is hurting. You need to get some sleep if you're going to go undercover because you won't sleep right once you do. Too hard to relax."

Elias nodded.

"You sure you want to do this? Work undercover with your ex to go after the guy that killed your best friend—it's not gonna be a walk in the park. Like, not even close. You need to be on top of your game and, brother, you are not there."

Elias stayed silent. He knew Cain was right, but he also knew he wasn't going to change his mind.

Twenty minutes later, they pulled into the parking lot beside their building. Elias hadn't bothered replying, and Cain hadn't said another word. There was nothing he could say.

The SUV Elias had noted the day before, the one with the men in it, was still down the block. Elias got out of the truck and started across the parking lot. Cain was behind him. They entered the building, but instead of taking the elevator or the stairs to their floor, Elias continued through the lobby to the back door.

"Elias," Cain said, "it's not a good idea."

Elias shrugged. "Gonna do it anyway." His blood was up, and he was tired and pissed off and needed to let off steam. He hated waiting, and going to a poker game was out, so this was the next best thing.

Cain shook his head but followed his teammate through the lobby and out the back door. Elias knew he would and felt a tiny bit bad about that. It was Cain's fatal flaw. He would follow any of his team members anywhere anytime. Not because he was a follower—Cain was a born leader—but because he would never leave one of his friends unprotected. No matter how much he yelled at Elias, he would always be there when Elias needed support. Elias took full advantage of it, but only because he knew he would do the same for Cain. He would follow his partner straight to the gates of hell.

The two men wound their way behind the buildings to the end of the block. Then they turned left until they came to the street corner. They stayed behind a building until a car approached. Elias timed it so they crossed the street when the car blocked the view of the guys in the SUV.

They moved swiftly up the block until they were only a few cars away from the SUV. Cain stayed on the sidewalk, and Elias went out onto the street. They approached the vehicle so they arrived at the driver's window and passenger window simultaneously.

Elias tapped on the glass with his gun. "Open the fuck up."

The man inside glared at him, or at least Elias assumed he did. He was wearing mirrored sunglasses and a gray suit. A Fed, for sure.

The window went down. "Walk away," the man growled.

Elias, not feeling the least bit intimidated, just smiled. "Not until you tell me what the fuck you and your partner are doing surveilling that building."

The second guy stared at Elias and then turned toward Cain who, by now, had his gun resting on his chest. "Just show them, Bob."

The driver cursed and then started to move. Elias stuck his gun next to the man's head. "Move slowly."

The man reached into his inside pocket and slowly pulled out a wallet. He offered it to Elias. Elias took it and flipped it open, never taking his eyes off the driver. "Cain," he said.

"Yo," Cain responded and stepped up so his gun was level with the man in the passenger seat.

Elias nodded toward Cain. "He will shoot if you try anything."

The driver put his hands back on the wheel, but said

nothing. Elias glanced down at the ID in his hand. Robert Stedman. Homeland Security. Elias clenched his jaw. He put the wallet on the hood of the SUV and pulled out his cell. He kept his gun aimed at the driver.

"Tag, our friends in the SUV are from Homeland. What do you want me to do with them?"

"Jesus Fucking Christ, Elias," Nick growled. He took a deep breath. "Let me make a call." He hung up.

Elias stood there, gun raised, and waited for his team leader to call back. It was not the best to be holding two men at gun point in the middle of the street, going on high noon, but it was Miami, so they had a fifty-fifty shot of anyone actually calling the cops.

His cell rang. "Tag," Elias answered.

"Let them go but tell them to fuck right off. If we see them again, we won't be so fucking friendly."

"Will do." He hung up. "My boss said to tell you to fuck right off. That's a direct quote. I don't know why you'd be spying on your own team, but you're wasting your time and ours. And"—he looked at both men—"you suck at it. If we see you again, it won't be such a pleasant conversation."

He nodded to Cain, and they both stepped away from the SUV and crossed the street. They went back into the building and up to the fourth floor.

"You just couldn't leave it alone?" Nick snarled as soon as they walked into the office. Cain started to open his mouth, but Nick interrupted, "Shut up, Cain. I know it was Elias dragging you into this shit." He glared at Elias and then shook his head. "Smarten up. I'm only letting you off easy on this one because of what's going on. Pull that kind of bullshit maneuver again, and I will bench you."

"Understood," Elias gritted out and then went and then stomped toward his desk.

"So," Nick said as he rested his butt on his desk, "those assholes in the SUV were Homeland sent to check up on us."

"Shit," Axe mumbled. "I suppose they're all gonna be pissed at us back in Washington."

"On the contrary." Nick grinned. "I just got off the phone with Bertrand, and he is delighted. They assumed they could watch us and not be seen. The fact we lit them up this morning is impressing the top brass. Apparently, there are those who are not convinced of our abilities."

"Is that why they are making us work a murder case? It's not our usual thing. The investigations unit should handle this one," Finn said as he rolled his injured shoulder.

"Bertrand finally 'fessed up that Mark Waters was actually someone's nephew, and they asked him if we could take a look as a personal favor. He didn't say who asked, but it's got to be someone big for Bertrand to bother, so we're stuck with it."

Elias wanted to ask if Bertrand had given the go-ahead for his plan, but he knew Nick was making him wait on purpose. He needed to cool his heels. It was fair, considering what he'd done but Andrea was going to meet with Santiago soon. That was his way in. He needed to be at the meet and the longer it took to get permission the less likely it was that he would get there in time.

"Finn, what did you and Axe find out from the girlfriend?"

"She's pregnant," he said, "about seven months." Finn shook his head.

"Shit," Nick sighed.

"Yeah," agreed Axe. "She says Waters only got involved in the gang stuff because they were expecting, and he wanted to put aside some cash to take care of the kid. They don't live in the best neighborhood. He wanted to move them up to the Panhandle, and they needed a chunk of cash to do it."

Elias's gut churned. This guy was just trying to do right by his family, and he ended up paying the ultimate price for it. Granted, he could have found a legal way to do it, but he wouldn't have made the same amount of money in the same timeframe.

"The girlfriend is moving in with her mom in the next couple of days," Finn said. "I encouraged her to go today. We don't know what happened. I thought it might be better if she wasn't by herself at their apartment."

"Smart thinking," Nick said. "What else? Did the girlfriend…? What's her name?"

"Mandy Paulson," Axe supplied.

"Does Mandy have any idea what happened? Did Waters have any kind of inkling something was up? Did he make an enemy already?"

Finn shook his head. "She said Waters kept her out of the loop on everything. She did say he'd been acting a bit weird. He told her that they might have to leave town sooner than expected, but he thought they had a couple of weeks. She pressed him on it, but he clammed up. Told her it was better if she didn't know."

"So, what are we thinking? Axe? You've got the most law enforcement experience. What does your gut say?"

Axe cocked his head. "I think Waters got in over his head, for sure. After talking to Mandy and taking a look around their place, my feel on Waters was that he's *that* guy. You know, the one who sometimes makes the wrong choice but always with the best intentions. I'm sure he got kicked out of the Coast Guard rather than quitting, for doing something stupid, nothing major, but stupid enough they had to let him go but made it look like he left.

"Getting a job as a bouncer at a gang club is stupid. Everyone knows it's stupid, but Mark Waters didn't know it was stupid. He just thought he could handle it." Axe frowned.

Finn added, "Mandy said Waters had cleaned up his act a lot once they found out she was pregnant. He even applied to go back to school online. He did some computer classes before and was good at it, but he hacked into a professor's laptop as a joke, and it got him kicked out of school." He picked up a pencil and started doodling on a piece of paper on his desk. "Do you think he might have done something…?"

"Stupid?" Axe said.

"Yeah, stupid and gotten into a computer he shouldn't have?" Finn asked.

Nick leaned back, crossing his ankles out in front of him. "Certainly sounds like it."

Elias absently rubbed his leg. "Do you think Waters was the type to see something bad was about to go down and step in and try and stop it?"

Finn shook his head. "I think if he saw something like that, he was smart enough to not get involved, but stupid enough to mention it to someone."

"So, you think he's basically a good guy but makes the occasional poor choice," Nick confirmed.

Both Axe and Finn nodded.

"Well, I spoke to the detectives that caught the case, Ben Thompson and Eduardo Sanchez. I asked what they thought, and they said it was some gang shit that went wrong. Figured Waters got himself mixed up in drugs or something and ended up getting killed for it. They don't put much stock in the girlfriend claiming he didn't do drugs. They aren't going to put much effort into it. One druggie offs another, and they're doing the world a favor."

Elias fisted his hands. It was the attitude he'd run into when he was growing up. He was part Cuban, so the authorities figured he had to be bad news. He was hanging out with gang kids, so he had to be in the gang and doing drugs. People, cops especially, made way too many assumptions for his liking. Then again, if he were being honest, after everything he'd seen, he naturally made assumptions now, too.

"Axe, Finn, do you guys think Waters was involved in drugs?"

Axe and Finn looked at each other. Axe shrugged. "If he was into drugs, then it was because he made a poor decision to get involved in selling them. I would be surprised if he was a user. He had a lot of gym equipment in the front room of the apartment, and Mandy said he ate clean. Drank kale and spinach protein shakes for breakfast. Doesn't sound like a drug addict to me."

"We spoke to Dr. Carr, the medical examiner assigned to the case. Waters did not drown in the ocean," Elias said. "He had water in his lungs but according to Dr. Carr, it was pool water."

"That's interesting," Finn commented.

"He also had a foreign substance on a cut on his head. The doc said it looks like he banged his head on something with gold leaf and then drowned."

Nick stood up. "Do you think it could have been an accident and someone panicked?"

Cain grunted. "He went to work at the club and wound up in chains attached to a boat. This wasn't an accident. He did something, and someone wanted him dead."

Elias shrugged. "It's all just speculation at this point anyway. All we know is Waters drowned in a swimming pool and then was tossed off a boat out at sea. We're going to have to dig for the rest of the story. If that's what Bertrand wants."

"Yes, it is," Nick stated. He looked at Elias. "He also wants you to go ahead with your plan. He thinks it's a good idea to know where the guns are coming from, but it also means you might find out more about Mark Waters' murder since he worked at the Blue Iguana, which is a Street Aces hang out. Bertrand feels you will have a better chance at finding out the truth about what happened to him if you are on the inside."

Yes. Elias was elated. A chance to bring down Santiago and get justice for Mattie. He'd forgotten all about Waters, but that wasn't fair to the dead man. Everyone deserved justice.

"But, and this is a big-ass 'but,' you have to tell us what's going on. If things look like they're going bad, I'm pulling you out ASAP. Undercover is not our usual thing. You have to listen to what I say and no grandstanding."

"Agreed."

"I'm fucking serious, Elias. There's no room to maneuver here. If you don't listen or go against orders, you will be out, and not just from the op, but from the team and the Coast Guard. Bertrand's words."

Elias gave a curt nod. He understood, but he also knew that if he didn't do this, he'd never get better. Not just his leg, but his whole mental state. He'd let Mattie down. No matter how he looked at it, or how much time had passed, he just couldn't let it go.

If Andrea had said something sooner, he could have saved Mattie. He knew it in his bones. He could never have a do-over, but the next best thing was to bring down Santiago. And Andrea. He couldn't forgive her. If she was mixed up with Santiago in an illegal way, she'd go down too. He had no qualms about that. He may not want to see her dead, but he wouldn't cry any tears if she ended up behind bars.

"I understand, Tag. I will follow orders." He looked at the other guys in the room. "Now I need your help. We have to plan this out. I need to figure out how to approach Ignacio and how to get Andrea to back up my story."

"You're also going to need a cover story as to how you and Andrea reconnected," Axe added.

"Yeah, and what you're doing in Miami if not seeing your family." Finn gestured to the table. "I think we're going to need more food if we hope to get this done."

Elias grinned. "I'll make a call."

CHAPTER ELEVEN

ndy checked her look in the mirror on the visor in Antonio's car as they pulled up in front of a set of large iron gates. Star Island was *the* most exclusive neighborhood in Miami. There were only thirty-something homes, and someone literally had to die before a new person could move in. These places almost never went up for sale.

The gate opened, and Andy's heartbeat increased. She wiped her palms on the little black slip dress she was wearing, *little* being the operative word. Antonio's sister, Lola, was shorter than Andy, so the dark shift would hang down closer to Lola's knees. On Andy, it hit a little north of mid-thigh. She had to be careful when she sat down. Thankfully, Lola had big feet for her size and Andy had no problem sliding into the sky-high stilettos that matched the dress. Wearing them all night might be a problem, however.

The drive was cobblestones. Gardens of tropical flowers boldly accented the dark, leafy greenery. The front yard was ablaze with all kinds of up-lighting. The bursts of color provided a stark contrast to the massive white house done in a Mediterranean style.

"Jesus Christ," she muttered, "how big is this place?"

Antonio grinned. "Thirty-thousand square feet."

"My apartment in L.A. was twelve hundred. How many people live here?"

"Just Santiago."

"You've got to be shitting me. He stays here by himself?" There was just no way. Star Island was gated and had its own security, but she couldn't imagine Santiago stayed here on his own.

"No, he has round the clock security but they don't live in the house with him. They live in the guest house, and they work in shifts. But there are always some hangers-on with him. Beautiful women, that sort of thing, but he is the only one who actually lives here."

Antonio stopped the car, and two massive men approached them. They each opened a door, and Andy and Antonio got out. The guards then patted them down.

Andy glared at the guy. She didn't care how big he was. If he got too touchy feely, she was going to punch him. Lucky for him, he remained professional. It wasn't like she had anywhere she could hide anything. The dress barely covered her assets as it was.

They went up the steps to the large wooden hand-carved front door that opened as they approached. Stepping inside, Andy immediately saw the appeal of the house. Like Antonio's condo, the whole back wall of the great room was floor to ceiling glass and overlooked a pool surrounded by lush lawns. But the most appealing view was of the Biscayne Bay. There was a dock, where Santiago most likely moored his yacht. She didn't need to see it to know he had one. Everyone who had a dock on Biscayne Bay had a yacht to match. The house and the surrounding area were magical, and it had to be worth north of sixty million. Drug dealer, star athlete, and movie star money. Money, she did not have nor ever would.

The floors were white marble with hints of warm brown. The furniture was white with rounded edges and colorful throw pillows. The tables were made of wood and most likely hand carved like the doors. She had no doubt the house had every amenity imaginable. Santiago wanted the world to know he'd arrived.

"Are you ready?" Antonio asked in a quiet voice. There were a few people scattered around the room, all dressed to the nines in every designer imaginable, but the real crowd was outside. That's where Santiago would be holding court.

She glanced in the ornate full-length gold-framed mirror that hung on the wall to her left. She'd done a good job with the makeup in covering the bruises on her face. Her hair hung down her back in loose waves that would curl more in the humidity as the night wore on. The black dress made her eyes look darker than her normal brown, so she looked more mysterious, or at least that was what she'd been told in the past when she'd worn black. The short dress, in combination with the stilettos, made her legs look miles long. She was five-feet-six in stocking feet. Now she had to be about five-ten, and most of it seemed to be legs.

She turned to Antonio. "Let's do this." If she was going to go down tonight, at least she looked fabulous. There were worse times to go.

Antonio led her across the room and outside. Salsa music was playing, and there was a small dance floor off to the right of the pool. The pool itself was enormous and there was the typical undulating glow, powered by LED lights in the walls. There was an intricate design on the bottom. It took her a second to recognize that it was actually a cursive *S* and looked like it was written in gold. There were some Grecian statues around that had touches of gold as well.

A few women in tiny bikinis played in the water and floated along the sides, talking to men who were fully dressed. One woman reached up and pulled the guy who'd crouched down on the side into the water with her. There was a lot of screaming and splashing and great peals of laughter. The guy came up sputtering and then kissed the woman who'd pulled him in.

Angry and Antonio wound their way through the crowd until they were around the far side of the pool. A pavilion of sorts rose on the left, decorated with sunbeds and loungers, but there was also a long conference-style table with a dozen or more chairs around it. Santiago was sitting at the end of the table. And she'd guessed right. He was holding court.

There was a man standing in front of him, wearing light-colored pants and a white button-down. He seemed to be pleading with Santiago. Santiago's face remained impassive, but his fingers were playing with a lighter.

Santiago himself was dressed in black. A black button-down shirt and black suit pants, probably Armani, or some other high-end designer. He wore his salt and pepper hair shaved close to the scalp. And he still had his goatee after all these years, but unlike his hair, it was black as ink, no gray streaks. She suspected that was the work of a careful dye job.

Her heart raced and fear snaked its way through her belly. She hadn't seen him since that night all those years ago. She could still smell his breath from when he threatened to kill her. Still hear the steel in his voice. And despite being a well-trained federal agent, just seeing him made her want to run. She sucked in a shaky breath, more like the scared young girl she'd been all those years ago—in over her head.

"Looks like he's busy," Antonio said and then glanced at her. "Maybe a drink isn't such a bad idea." He took her by the elbow and guided her to the bar. He leaned over and said something to the bartender, but she couldn't hear it. The music was louder here, and the constantly pounding beat was echoed in a ferocious throb behind her eyes.

Antonio handed her a drink.

"What is it?" she asked.

"Bourbon."

She nodded and took a big gulp. It burned all the way down but then spread warmth through her belly. It felt good. She'd gone cold inside, and the warmth was much needed. "Now what do we do?"

"We wait until he's free, and we pray that whoever that guy is, he doesn't piss Santiago off before you get a chance to talk with him. If he's annoyed, things will not…go well."

That's what she was afraid of. There was no way her backup was anywhere near here. They probably had no idea where she was, and even if they knew, they couldn't get onto the island without clearing security. They wouldn't even try anyway since it would tip their hand. She was all alone in a crowd of hundreds of people, and her fate rested with one man. A man she loathed more than anyone else on earth.

"Are you sure you've got everything?" Axe asked for the third time but in a soft voice. Sound carried at night on the water.

"I'm sure, man," Elias reassured him. "I've got my suit on. Got my shoes right here in the waterproof bag along with socks and a towel. My wallet and keys and stuff are in there, too, along with a knife."

"I would feel much better about this if you could take a gun and an ear bud," Finn commented as he helped Elias adjust his dry suit and pull the top part over his head. Then he zipped it closed.

Elias adjusted the neoprene around his face. "Thanks for the help."

Finn nodded. "He's ready," he called.

Cain started the engine. Nick climbed onto the boat.

"Cain's going to drop you not too far out in the bay. Stay under until you're close. The clouds are hiding the moonlight tonight but there's lots of light pollution. You don't want to be seen by someone glancing out their window. Santiago's place is the one lit up like it's Christmas. Just follow the noise."

Elias said. "Will do."

"Here." Nick handed him a flashlight. "You might need this. How are you going to signal us if you need help?"

Elias shrugged. "I'll think of something. It should be fine. He won't do anything at the party. Just keep eyes on me, and if he takes me anywhere at gunpoint, make sure you follow."

"Goes without saying," Nick said. "Finn and I will be in the second boat. Axe will be with Cain in this one. We'll have eyes on you."

"I gotcha, boo," Axe called and then made kissy noises.

Cain sniggered, and Elias rolled his eyes. It was good, though, and he appreciated the effort to keep it light. He'd never really done undercover stuff. It was a bit more daunting than he'd anticipated. He took a deep breath and blew it out. This was it. His chance to get justice for Mattie. He wasn't going to fuck up this op.

"Let's do it." He gave the thumbs up signal. Nick stepped back onto the dock, and he and Finn threw the ropes over onto the powerboat. Axe grabbed the ropes and started to coil them as Cain took off. Elias lowered himself onto a seat. He was already overheating in the dry suit and just wanted to get there.

Cain took the boat out and around the islands. Ten minutes later, they were in Biscayne Bay. Cain slowed the boat until they floated along at a sedate pace. Finn and Nick were farther down the bay, but both boats had a good view of Santiago's house.

"You ready?" Axe asked.

When Elias nodded, Cain handed him a rebreather that gave him thirty minutes of air. He wouldn't need that much, but it was good to have. The boat ran parallel to the shore, so Elias sat on the far edge of the boat away from the island and tied the waterproof bag around his leg. The last thing he wanted was to be spotted by one of Santiago's security guys before he even got off the boat.

"Good luck," Axe said.

Cain gave him a nod.

He gave them both a thumbs up and fell backward into the water. He took a minute to orient himself and then started swimming for shore. He had calculated the swim under water would take about 20 minutes, depending on the current. He checked his diver's watch and then surfaced slowly.

He planned right. He arrived next door to the party. He studied the large, dark house in front of him. It had a pool and a grassy yard between the house and the water. More importantly, the mansion had a few palm trees encircled by bushes along the property line and they were in the shadows, making a nice place for cover. He watched for a few minutes, but nothing moved. He started forward, careful to keep just his head, covered in the black dry suit, out of the water.

The fact that Santiago's house was on an island was a plus as far as Elias was concerned. He could hit the water and be gone in a flash thanks to all his training. If things turned ugly, the team knew he'd aim for the bay.

Elias swam up to the dock in front of the dark house. The party at Santiago's was going full tilt, and he hoped that he wasn't too late. He didn't think Santiago would meet with Andrea at the Blue Iguana, but he hadn't counted on it being at Santiago's own house. Elias hoped that his cousin's nephew was right about the meeting place. If the nephew got it wrong, Andrea could wind up dead. A small jolt of fear hit him, but he shook it off. Why should he care if she died? Well, he needed her to get in with Santiago, but other than that, it shouldn't matter.

But it did. *That damn truck.* If he hadn't sat in the truck, he could have kept the haunting memories of her buried. He'd worked hard to put the woman out of his mind, and he wasn't going to let her take up any more real estate than absolutely necessary.

He paused for another minute or so, but nothing moved. Making his way over to the stand of trees took him a couple of minutes. He moved slowly, stuck to the shadows as much as possible, and watched his surroundings. The deep-water anchorage at the end of the property meant he didn't have to walk out onto a beach but rather pull himself up on a retaining wall and then get behind the trees.

He scoped out the security. There were a few guys scattered around Santiago's property. They seemed to be keeping a close eye on things, but they weren't stopping people from wandering about. If he timed it well, he should be able to walk in without a problem.

He'd discussed his entry with the team. They'd suggested he go in the front door like all the other guests. The problem was, he couldn't get on to the island without being on the guest list. It was Star Island after all, the most prestigious zip code in all of Miami. No one was getting inside unless they were invited, at least not by the front door.

He had been worried that if he showed up at the gate and they called Santiago, he might say no. He'd wanted to kill Santiago back then, and he'd made a scene after Mattie's funeral, accusing Santiago of setting Mattie up. Santiago wasn't the type of guy to forget that detail. Nor would he necessarily believe that all was forgiven, but if Santiago believed he had the upper hand, then it might work for Elias. This was Santiago's territory, his home turf. He'd be the most comfortable here. Hopefully, that meant he would drop his guard a bit.

Elias hoisted himself up on the wall and moved over to the tree line. He crouched behind some large bushes. He had no idea what they were, but they were thick and green and did a great job of hiding him from sight.

Elias unzipped the suit and started to pull it off. He managed to get out of it and then he opened the bag. He dried his face and the bit of hair that had gotten wet on the towel. He was pulling on his socks and shoes when he heard it. A crashing in the bushes. He peered through the bush to see a couple had pushed through the bushes on the other side of the planting and were now making out against the tree.

Fuck! Of all the shitty luck. He stayed still and waited.

"Oh, yes," the woman said.

"Lift your leg higher, baby," the man demanded.

Elias stifled a groan. They were having sex. He could only hope the guy was quick on the trigger. He needed to get over to the party. He tried to block out the sounds of the copulating couple, but it wasn't possible. The moaning and grunting were loud. Jesus, he hoped he didn't sound like this guy when he was having sex. *Pathetic.* The grunting sounded like the man was trying to lift a heavy object.

Finally, a minute later, there were some louder groans, and then it was over. "Baby, you were fantastic," the man said. The woman didn't say anything in response. That was not a good sign. *Take a hint, buddy.* Elias peered through the bushes again to get a better look at the couple. The man had a big belly and a fringe of hair around his head. He adjusted his suit pants and fixed his blazer. It was light-colored with a pink T-shirt underneath. He looked like a Miami Vice reject.

The woman fixed her hair and her dress. She was tall and rail thin and younger than the man by a large margin. She flashed the guy a big smile, but as soon as he turned his back to go back to the party, the smile disappeared, only to be replaced by a look of revulsion.

He watched them go and then went back to pulling on his shoes. Who the fuck knew why people did what they did? It wasn't his business. He gave himself a mental shake and focused on the task ahead.

He glanced down at his charcoal gray pants and white dress shirt. To try to fit in better to the relaxed atmosphere, he rolled up the sleeves. He then ran a hand through his hair. It was as good as it was going to get. He tucked his knife into his sock. Then he packed up the towel and put it in the bag. He tucked the dry bag deep inside one bush and the dry suit underneath the next bush over.

He then moved in a bit farther and hid the rebreather in the bushes surrounding the next palm tree. Spreading things out meant there was a chance they wouldn't find everything. He finally was ready to move. He quietly pushed into the center of the bushes. He stayed low and peered at the security guards through the plants.

There were two men in suits guarding the grounds in this area. Elias watched them for a bit. They weren't amateurs. They knew what they were doing. Not easily distracted. He was impressed. No doubt there were cameras everywhere as well. He looked around and spotted a couple up in the trees. There was nothing he could do about those. He just had to hope no one was paying close attention. The fact that he was going to walk out of the trees wasn't the problem; it was that he hadn't walked into the trees from the party. If anyone noticed that, it might be more difficult. Still not the end of the world. Santiago would know Elias was there soon enough.

He waited until both security guards were dealing with a fighting couple and then he emerged from the trees and walked across the yard. He grabbed a glass of champagne from a waiter as he walked past. Then he put it down on a table adjacent to the dance floor. He stood next to the table for a moment and took in his surroundings.

There on the patio. Andrea stood with her back to him, but he'd know her anywhere. Jesus, what was she wearing? The uber-short dress made her legs look amazing. He instantly recalled what it was like to have those legs wrapped around his waist. He picked up the champagne and downed it. "Here goes nothing," he murmured.

CHAPTER TWELVE

"**A**ndrea, you look"—Santiago's eyes drifted down over her body—"divine," he said with a smile. He got up from his chair and came to stand directly in front of her. "It's been too long." He leaned over and kissed her cheek.

She fought the urge to throat-punch him. She wanted to crush his windpipe and watch him die, flailing around like a fish out of water. "Santiago." She smiled back. "It's been a minute. It looks like life has treated you well."

He nodded. "I have been busy since you left."

"I can see that." He'd built an empire on the backs of addicts and gangbangers. She only hoped she could topple him. The mighty must fall at some point.

He went back and sat down in his chair. "So, I'm hearing stories about you. Ignacio tells me you were responsible for bringing back not only the merchandise but the money as well from last night's little adventure. How did that happen?"

She started to answer, but one of the servers, a tall blonde dressed in a tight white button-down and short black skirt came to the table to place a glass of red wine in front of Santiago, so Andy waited. She had to admit, he looked good for a total sleaze bag. His designer clothes fit him like a glove, and the shaved head suited him. His eyes were still reptilian, though, and she had no doubt he'd kill her as soon as look at her, no matter how charming he appeared.

The waitress moved off, and he indicated she could answer. Interesting how he made her stand in front of him instead of offering her a seat. He really did think of himself as a king.

She took a breath to calm the butterflies in her stomach. "Soto tried to rip off the sellers. They figured it out before we had a chance to leave. The shooting started, and they all ended up killing each other."

She had decided to keep it as brief as possible and not elaborate unless asked. Details were how mistakes were made.

"I see. What did you do with the bodies?"

"I dumped Soto and Tommy over the side, and I left the other boat to drift out there."

He nodded. "It's been found, the other boat. There were three bodies in it. The police are processing it now."

Her heartbeat ticked up. They hadn't thought about the autopsies of the three sellers. If Santiago had someone at the morgue, then he'd know it didn't go down like she said. She tried to keep her face neutral. No point in worrying about that just yet.

"Why weren't you shot? If all these bullets were flying around, how come you weren't hit?"

She met his gaze. "I hid in the galley once I realized Soto was trying to rip off the sellers. There was no way that was going to end well."

He narrowed his eyes, then gave her a slight smile. "Andrea, I would love to believe you, but there are a few… issues with your story."

Her heart rate accelerated as fear raced through her veins,

but she didn't blink. She held his gaze. "What issues?" she asked, keeping her voice as steady as her gaze.

"Soto and Tommy were lousy shots. The pair of them. They couldn't hit the broad side of a barn on a good day, let alone at night with men shooting back at them." She opened her mouth, but Santiago raised a hand. "Also, one of the sellers was killed by a bullet to the head with a high-powered rifle and not at close range. So, now do you see how your story doesn't really work? Who was there with you, Andrea? Who took the shot?"

"I did." The voice came from her right.

She turned, and the bottom fell out of her world once more. Elias stood there in a white button-down shirt with rolled-up sleeves and dark gray suit pants. His thick, dark hair curled slightly in the humidity, and the shirt stretched tightly across his well-muscled chest. There wasn't a woman at the party who didn't stop to check him out. Confidence oozed off him. He looked like he belonged—no, more, he looked like he owned the place.

"Elias Mason," Santiago grunted. "I should have guessed."

Elias walked over and cozied up next to Andy. "Santiago."

Santiago's eyes narrowed again. "You are looking well. I heard you were shot."

Elias shrugged. "I healed."

"So, you were there as well last night. Do tell."

"I went as backup. Andrea alone with Soto and Tommy on the boat wasn't a great idea. When things turned to shit, I took out the sellers. They'd already killed Soto and Tommy."

He said it with such casual confidence, even Andy was impressed. Of course, it was probably the truth. The Coast Guard guys had killed the buyers, so Elias *could* have been the one who'd actually pulled the trigger. She'd heard years ago that he was part of some elite unit, but she had no details. She could see it. It would suit him. He liked to be in control.

"I thought the Coast Guard was all about saving stranded sailors," Santiago said with a slight sneer.

"Part of it. I am part of a different type of unit. MSRT. Marine Security Response Team. We respond to domestic terrorism situations. Shooting people is part of my job."

Santiago smiled. "Andrea, why didn't you tell us about Elias in the first place?"

"Because he's been keeping a low profile since he's been back in Miami. He's sort of benched from work. He was just helping me out. I didn't want to involve him anymore than I had to." It was an easy sell since part of it was the truth.

"How did you two hook up again?" Santiago's eyes darted back and forth between the two before settling on Elias.

"I saw her at a bar at the beach. We started talking," Elias said. It was the simplest answer he could come up with that was plausible and hard to confirm or deny by anyone else.

Santiago cocked his head. "So now your story is that you two met up at the beach and got back together. Andrea decided to try and get ahead using Soto, and when the deal turned to shit, you came to the rescue."

"Pretty much." Andy debated giving Santiago a smirk, but settled for a simple nod of her head.

When Santiago eyed Elias, Andy's belly knotted. If he didn't believe this version, they were both in big trouble. He already thought she'd lied to him once, and switching up their story would just make him antsy. He didn't like to be nervous. He killed people if they made him nervous.

Santiago stood and took a step toward them. "Now, that story, I believe." He clasped Elias's hand and did a shoulder bump. "Good to see you, Elias." He stepped back. "Hell of an eye, taking out one of the buyers with a head shot at a distance on the water."

"It's what I'm trained to do." Elias didn't elaborate.

"I see. Are you back in town looking for work? Or are you still with the Coast Guard?"

Elias shrugged. "I'm benched, so they're leaving me alone at the moment. Why? You got something in mind?"

Santiago seemed to be assessing Elias more closely. "Maybe." He gestured to one of the waitresses walking by. "Bring us champagne." She nodded and moved swiftly away.

"How long are you here for?" Santiago asked as he sat back down.

"Don't know. They didn't give me a date range or anything." Elias put his hands in his pockets.

The waitress arrived with the champagne and some glasses. She opened it and poured a bit into a glass. Santiago tasted it and nodded. She filled two more glasses and then topped off Santiago's. With that done, she placed the bottle in an ice bucket she had brought over and left.

Santiago handed them each a glass of champagne. "To old friends," he said as he saluted them his own glass. They were hardly old *friends*, but Andy didn't argue, just clinked her stem with the other two men and took a sip from her glass.

Elias just held his glass. "If that's all, then we'll head out."

Santiago smiled a cold smile. "No, that's not all. I would very much like it if you would be my guests this evening. There are a few more details I would like to…verify." He then directed a flat stare at Andy, "Obviously, Elias being back changes things. If you told me the truth at the beginning…" He let his voice trail off.

"And if we'd said it was me, how would you have reacted? We didn't exactly part on good terms," Elias demanded bluntly.

Andy gripped the champagne glass tightly. Antagonizing Santiago was not the best plan. Elias had no idea of what Santiago had been up to these last few years. If he'd told her he was going to be here, she could have warned him. Actually, stopped him from coming altogether. Elias and Santiago had always been a volatile mix. Elias had always hated Santiago, even before Mateo's death. They were oil and water. Even though Elias had most likely saved her life with his explanation of events on the water, his presence also elevated her tension. She just didn't like feeling out of control and, at the moment, she had no real say in what was going to happen. It made her nervous as hell.

Santiago shrugged. "It's true. We weren't close. I guess I can understand why you were…hesitant to tell me, but now that you have, I like to think we can move beyond the past and possibly build a better relationship in the future. That is, if you're telling me the truth."

"It's the truth," Elias responded.

"About what's happened out there?" Santiago indicated at the water with his chin. "I have no doubts. But it's the truth about the rest of it I want to check. As you said, we weren't exactly friends before. I want to make sure you aren't trying to fuck with me."

"Fair enough." Elias put his arm around Andy's waist. "We'll stay until you've verified my story, but make it quick. I'm tired and I want to sleep in my own bed."

Andy tried hard to keep her face neutral, but it was almost impossible with their past. She had no interest in having Elias so close to her. He'd crushed her heart but that didn't mean she was immune to his charms. The traitorous organ had skipped several beats when he'd showed up.

"I'm afraid that won't be possible. It will take me several days to check out your story. You will both be my guests here in the meantime. I am sure you will find the house has everything you need." Santiago pointed at one of his men. "Peter here will show you to your room." Without another word to them, he turned, walked out from underneath the pergola, and greeted another of his guests.

Andy frowned. She'd wanted to argue with Santiago, but there was no point. He wasn't going to let them go until he checked out Elias's story. She prayed Elias had done his homework and had his Coast Guard buddies fix his record so it reflected what he'd said. If Santiago found one discrepancy in their story, he'd kill them both.

They followed Peter into the house and upstairs. He took them down the hallway away from the party to a quieter wing of the house. He opened a door and turned on the lights and then beckoned them inside. Elias allowed her to enter first and then followed. Peter then stepped out of the room and closed the door. They heard him lock the door from the outside.

"Fuck," Andy mumbled. "Now we're locked in here for as long as Santiago wants."

Elias just stared at her. Then he turned and checked out their surroundings.

Andy took a look around as well. It was large and carpeted with a thick gray rug over a white marble floor. There was a full bathroom on the left that was also done in marble. It had a claw foot soaking tub as well as a shower. Beyond the bathroom a king-size bed on the left wall was flanked by two beechwood nightstands. The duvet cover was white with lots of bright flowers scattered across it.

On the right was a sitting area. There was a light gray sofa and a couple of matching overstuffed chairs. There was a beechwood coffee table in front of the couch and a TV hanging on the wall opposite.

Windows directly across the room from the door over-looked some greenery and had a water view beyond. The room was warm and inviting. Andy thought it would be a lot like an upscale hotel room if it weren't for the door locked from the outside.

She glanced over at Elias. She had an overwhelming desire to pop him one. He'd saved her life this morning, or last night, whatever time it was, but he'd also made her life a living hell all those years ago. He'd left her high and dry after calling her some of the worst names possible. They'd been together for four years before that. He'd never even said goodbye, just disappeared and cut her out of his life completely.

She gritted her teeth. The whole situation was upsetting. She was pissed she'd been held captive for almost a day now and she was tired and hungry. Most of all, she was mad as hell Elias had showed up because, goddammit, whatever his strategy had been had worked. *Fuck!*

Andy returning to Miami was probably not her best decision ever. She found herself wanting to hit more and more people. When this was over and she got out of here, if she got out of here, she'd put in for a transfer. She was done with Miami. It hadn't ever brought her anything but sadness and heartbreak.

CHAPTER THIRTEEN

E lias was doing a walk-through of the room. He was searching for anything that might come in handy, like a weapon or something he might be able to use to unlock the fucking door. He was conscious of Andrea behind him, leaning against the wall not far from the bathroom door.

"What are you doing?" she asked.

"Looking around." He still had his knife in his sock and his burner phone, but he had no doubts that, at some point, Santiago would realize he hadn't been frisked and they would come looking for him. Andrea didn't seem to have a cell phone on her or a purse.

The dress was so short there was no way she was hiding anything. It was also damn hard to keep his eyes off her legs. If this was what she wore on all her undercover assignments, then no wonder men got caught. She was a serious distraction, as much as it galled him to admit it. He might hate her for what she did or actually *didn't* do, but there was no denying she was still hot as hell.

He moved around the room, but there was nothing really to see. Obviously, Santiago had held people here before, hence the lock on the outside of the door, so it stood to reason it was "child" proof. No weapons or anything that may come in handy.

Andrea moved toward the sofa. "Did you back—"

He whirled around and caught her in his arms, pulling her close so he could whisper in her ear. "Do not say anything you don't want overheard." There wasn't a doubt in his mind the room was bugged. There might even be cameras. Santiago seemed like the sort to do that.

Andrea froze. Understanding dawned briefly on her face before she nodded and moved out of his embrace.

"How's the family?" she asked in a loud voice. He cocked an eyebrow at her, but she continued. "Is your mom gonna worry if you don't reach out to her tonight? I know she's been keeping close tabs since you came back to town."

He frowned. *What the fuck was she talking about?* Then it dawned on him. She meant his team. "My mother always worries. It's her job, but it should be fine. As long as she knows I'm close by and not off in some far-flung or dangerous corner of the world." He swallowed a grin at the thought of Nick Taggert being called his mama. Hilarious. "What about you? Is your aunt gonna worry?"

"Yes. Like you said, mothers always worry."

Elias shrugged. "Not much we can do about it at the moment. They'll just have to get over it."

Andrea grunted her agreement and went over and sat down on the sofa. She leaned her head back on the cushions. "Why did you come tonight?" She turned and glared at him. "I thought we agreed that I would handle it."

Elias stared right back. "Santiago was never going to believe your version of events. It was better to get the truth out there. Safer for you."

She was mad as hell at him for showing up. Well, tough

shit. He wanted to take down Santiago, and he didn't trust her to do it on her own.

There was a sound at the door. Someone was unlocking it. Elias turned so he was facing the door. Ignacio walked in. "Elias, man. It's been a while. I heard you were here and had to check it out for myself."

"Ignacio." They bumped shoulders. "How's your family?" Elias asked. It was so fucking strange to treat everyone like he'd run into them at the grocery store rather than being held as a hostage.

Ignacio grinned. "They're all good. Wait 'til my sister hears you're back in town. She was crushed when you left." He glanced over Elias's shoulder. "No offense, Andrea, but my sister has had the hots for Elias since we were in grade school."

Andrea wore a serious scowl, which wouldn't help them at all, so Elias smiled. "Tell your sister I said hello."

"Listen, can I get you guys anything? Something to eat, drink?"

"How about you let us go?" Andrea asked.

He shook his head. "Sorry, Andrea, I would, but Santiago wants to be thorough."

She sighed loudly. "In that case, can you bring me something to eat? I'm starving."

Ignacio smiled. "I'll send something up. Don't worry. It will all be over soon." He turned and exited the room. The lock clicked and then his footsteps receded down the hall.

"What do you make of that?" Andrea asked.

"I have no fucking clue. It's just weird, but whatever. You wanted in, and this seems to be what you have to do to get there. I'm just along for the ride."

She shot him a glance but said nothing. She closed her eyes and leaned back against the cushions once more.

Elias crashed down onto one of the chairs. He let his

mind wander as he tried to relax. He was in a tough spot. His team was out there waiting on him, but he couldn't tell them what was going on. There was no way to make a call on his burner phone and know for sure he wasn't overheard. He thought about sending a text but if they found his phone then they would know what he was really up to. He was feeling antsy, which was never good. He needed a poker game. That always settled his mind down.

His mother hated that he played poker. It was the one thing—well, now that he discovered she hated Mattie, one of the two things—she disliked about Elias's life. His father had played, and the man was an addict. He lost all his money constantly. It was a relief for his mom when he left. It was easier to raise two kids on her own than have him around, which was a statement in itself.

When she found out Elias had taken up the game, she was furious. He didn't blame her. The thing was, he wasn't an addict. Not like his dad had been, at least, from what he could glean from the stories people told. Elias didn't have to play, nor did he feel the need to gamble with his money. He gambled with his life on a regular basis, which seemed to override any other need for risk-taking. He liked to hang on to his money and see it grow.

After he dealt with Mateo's death, Elias still played poker. It was his outlet for dealing with all kinds of shit, including getting shot. It allowed him to rein in his brain. The game gave him something to concentrate on so that his mind slowed down and focused. Work had the same effect. Except in a situation like now. He needed something to do to occupy his brain or he wouldn't be able to wind down at all.

He'd been letting his gaze wander around the room when it finally registered what he was seeing. In the corner of the room on a bookshelf behind a potted plant was a camera. It blended well, but he caught the reflection of the light off the camera lens. He'd been wondering about it in the back of his mind for a few minutes. The pieces of the puzzle clicked into place.

When he stood up, Andrea looked over at him. "I'm sorry, hon," he said.

He held her gaze, but she only frowned at him. He needed to get her to understand what was going on without giving anything away to whoever was watching, and he was sure someone was.

"I know you're upset because I came, and we'd discussed me staying out of it, but I thought you might be in trouble. Santiago is a smart guy. It was always a reach to tell him it was just you out there. It just seemed smarter to come clean."

Andrea was staring at him, her mouth open. He moved over to her, grabbed her hand, and pulled her to her feet. He wrapped his arms around her and hugged her in close. "I know you wanted to do this on your own, but it was too big a risk," he said in a normal voice. Then he whispered, "Camera behind the potted plant. They're watching us."

She'd held herself rigid in his arms until this point, but then suddenly relaxed and melted in his arms. He was unprepared for the wave of desire that rushed through him. Her hair smelled good, and her curves fit against him even better than they had when they were young. She'd filled out, and so had he. She was all softness against the hard planes of his body, and he instinctively reacted to it, crushing her against himself.

"Thanks for the apology, but you're right. It wasn't worth the risk," she said clearly. Then she wrapped her arms around his neck and whispered in his ear, "We have to pretend."

He pulled back slightly and met her gaze. In the heels, she was only a few inches shorter than he was. She tipped her head back to look up at him, and he swooped down and captured her lips. He kissed her like he was a dying man in the desert and she was a hidden spring. He drank from her deeply, crushing her to him, his tongue demanding in her mouth. She responded in kind and fisted her hands in his hair.

It felt so fucking amazing to kiss her. To crush her to his chest. His dick immediately rose to the occasion. All those years fell away, and they were kids again, only better. Less fumbling and more confidence. He cupped her ass through the dress and pulled her against his cock. Her tongue danced with his as she swept her hands down his back.

It wasn't until the door opened that he broke off the kiss. He would lie and say he'd heard the key in the lock if anyone asked, but the truth was, he hadn't heard a fucking thing because he'd been so caught up in Andrea. He mentally gave himself a dressing down for being so stupid. A move like that could have gotten him killed.

He stepped away from her slightly as Peter and some other guy entered the room and put food down on the coffee table. Peter had a smirk on his face. They were definitely being watched, and the audience was enjoying the show. "Brought you some dinner. Have a good night." The smirk was broader now as he walked out of the room with the other minion following behind. The key turned in the lock once more.

He shifted his weight and moved around Andrea to go over to the table. "Looks like sandwiches," he commented before unwrapping the plastic over the food. When Andrea came to stand beside him, he glanced over at her. Her eyes were shooting daggers at him. She cleared her throat, snatched up a plate and a bottled water, and then went to sit down on the couch. She picked up the sandwich and took a bite.

He had the distinct impression she was stuffing the food into her mouth to stop herself from saying something she didn't want Santiago's men to hear. He also picked up a sand-wich and took a bite. Roast beef. It occurred to him suddenly that the food could be drugged, but then what was the point of that? They were already hostages. There was no benefit to keeping them drugged. Neither had fought Santiago when he demanded they stay. With that thought put to bed, he finished the sandwich.

"How long do you think it will take before Santiago is satisfied?" Andrea asked as she unscrewed the cap on her bottle of water.

Elias shrugged. "Assuming he's waiting for the prelimi-nary lab results on the autopsies of the sellers, then probably tomorrow."

She sat back on the couch. "Well, I hope he gets his confirmation soon. I would love to get out of here. I want to sleep in my own bed."

"Yeah, it would be nice." He took a water bottle of his own and opened it. After taking a long drink, he stood up and headed to the bathroom. Once inside with the door closed, he stood in front of the mirror. He looked tired. Fatigue had etched deep lines in his face. His leg, which had been fine until now, was starting to throb. The adrenaline had kept the pain at bay, but now it was back in full force. He'd almost wished Santiago had drugged him; at least he'd get some sleep then. The pain in his leg and the proximity to Andrea were going to make sleeping damn near impossible.

He idly wondered if Santiago's guys had broken into his place yet and found the gun. He hadn't left it in plain sight, but he had made it pretty damn easy for them. He'd put it under the bed. Even the dumbest muscle should know to look there.

He used the facilities and then gave himself a pep talk about staying focused and not being a dick. He needed all his wits about him. This was about taking down Mattie's killer.

He'd do it for Mateo because he owed his best friend that much.

He came out of the bathroom and walked back over to the couch. Andrea had her head back on the cushions and her eyes closed. He wanted to leave her there, but if they were really dating, he wouldn't do that, so he had to make it look good. He moved over to stand next to her. "Come on, babe, let's go to bed."

Her eyes shot open, and he immediately realized his mistake. She wasn't resting; she was doing her best not to kill him. She was livid with him. Well, tough shit. He wasn't exactly pleased with her. He smiled at her and offered her a hand.

Her teeth came together with a click. She pasted a false smile on her face, and when she took his hand, he helped her to stand. Even when she dug her nails into the back of hand, Elias kept his face neutral. He wasn't going to give her the satisfaction of knowing she was causing him pain.

"Thanks," she said as she moved by him and went over to the bed. She sat down facing the door and pulled off her shoes. Those shoes and that dress were a deadly combination. All kinds of thoughts popped into his head. He shifted his weight to his injured leg on purpose to bring on the distracting pain. Nothing like a little agony to focus the mind.

"Turn on the light." He indicated the bedside lamp with his chin. She leaned over and flicked it on. Then he walked over and turned off the overhead lights. He went around to the other side of the bed and sat down. He debated taking off his shoes but decided to leave them on. He swung his feet up on the bed and laid back on the pillows. He was tired. His body was hurting, and it had been longer than he could remember since he'd had a full night's sleep. He'd settle for a couple of hours tonight to get him through.

Andrea leaned over and turned off the light, sending the room into complete darkness. It took a minute for Elias's eyes to adjust to just the ambient light. Andrea eventually stood up and pulled the covers back on the bed and climbed in. He knew they should be talking like they were a normal couple but, at the moment, he just couldn't get his brain to work. He closed his eyes. He felt Andrea get comfortable beside him and then he drifted off to sleep.

The sound of a key in the lock woke him.

The room was still dark. He glanced around. It wasn't dawn, but the sky outside was getting lighter. He'd had maybe two, two and a half hours of sleep. He glanced at his watch. Yeah, two and a half. He stood up as the door opened.

Peter was standing there. "Santiago wants to see you. Both of you."

He glanced over at Andrea. She pulled off the covers and threw her legs over the side of the bed and stood as well. Peter turned back and flicked on the overhead light. Elias's eyeballs seared from the sudden brightness.

Andrea was fumbling, trying to put her shoes on. He went to her side and steadied her by the elbow as she slid her foot into the first shoe. He held her close as she slid on the second one. He leaned in and whispered, "Keep your eyes open for trouble," before dropping a kiss in her hair. He kept his arm casually around her waist and walked with her to the door.

Peter stepped out of the way and let them go out into the hallway. There was another guard there. This guy was big, Elias's size. He turned and started down the hallway. They followed. Andrea stepped away slightly, so he had to drop his arm. It was fine by him. He liked to have his hands free.

The guy in front of them seemed to know what he was doing. Elias figured him for former military. He didn't look Hispanic, possibly not a local then. He was a hired guy for sure. They made their way through the enormous house. The floors were all done in marble, and the walls were all white and there was a wide variety of artwork that added color. There wasn't a speck of dust anywhere. It was very sleek and modern. Had to be Santiago's way of screaming to the world that he'd made it.

Elias tucked that thought away. He never knew what might come in handy when on an op. Understanding the way his enemy thought was always a plus. Santiago had an ego, and he wanted the world to bow down to him. That hadn't changed from when they were younger, but now he had the power to enforce it. That was also worth noting. If Santiago got mad at him, he may not have time to talk his way out of it before someone tried to take Elias out.

They finally entered a room at the opposite end of the house. It was done in creams and beiges. A modern man's office with a rectangular fireplace on the far wall. The desk off to the left was sleek, all chrome and glass. It was too cold for Elias's taste. He wasn't much of a chrome and glass man when it came to his office, but it was attractive to look at.

Santiago was seated behind the desk, with three men standing in front of it. They all turned to look as Elias and Andrea walked in. These men were also large. The guy on the far left was wearing a dark suit, but he had blond hair and bright blue eyes. He was definitely former military, the way he stood, his wary reaction to Elias and Andrea entering the room, the vibe he gave off. The other two, wearing similar suits, had darker hair. The shorter one had a mustache. They were more like wannabes. They were trying hard to emulate the blond guy, but they didn't have his skill level. Maybe they were just being trained.

On the table on the right side of the room were weapons. Guns. Lots of them. These must be the weapons from the meet. He couldn't get a good look at this distance, and he doubted Santiago was going to let him get any closer. But he was wrong.

"Andrea, Elias, thank you for joining us. Sorry for getting you up so early."

Elias said nothing. He and Andrea stood in the middle of the office.

"The information came through. It happened exactly as you said." He was telling them they were in the clear. Andrea's shoulders dropped slightly. *Don't relax yet,* he wanted to tell her. There was definitely something in the air. Something was going on. He took in the fact that Santiago didn't just come right out and say their story added up. He didn't seem to want his guests to know what was going on. *Interesting.*

Finally, Elias said, "Glad to hear it. If that's it then, I think we'll head out." But Santiago gave him a slight shake of his head, so Elias hedged, "Unless, of course, you need something else…" He wasn't sure what game Santiago was playing, but Elias would do his best to play along for the moment.

Santiago pointed at weapons on the table. "The guns are here for your inspection. Take a look and see if they are everything we were promised."

Elias turned and walked back to the guns. Peter and his bulky partner said nothing but shifted slightly so they had a better angle on Elias should he try anything. The other three security men hung back at Santiago's desk.

Elias was shocked Santiago was letting him near the guns. Whoever Santiago had lined up to do the inspection of the merchandise was not around. He didn't want to dwell on the reason why too much. Chances were good that person was never coming back. And this was the real reason for keeping him and Andrea at the house. He needed Elias to check out the guns.

A wave of unease spread through him. The guns were Russian. There were some Tokarev and MP443 Grach pistols, some Makarov submachine guns, Kalashnikov assault rifles and some AK-15 machine guns. Then it hit him. The RPG that had been lost at sea was also Russian. A Barkas.

He picked up the first gun and checked it over. It seemed to be in good working order. He looked closely and realized that the gun was new. All of them were. These weren't confiscated from a reject pile or stolen from some storage unit somewhere. These were brand-new, straight off the factory line. He checked over each one, but it was a no-brainer. These guns were all fully functioning. He finally turned around to Santiago. "They look good."

Santiago then turned to the blond man. "We have a deal then." He then pointed at Peter, who disappeared and came back a minute later with a briefcase. He gave it to the blond man, who immediately opened it on the chair behind him. It was full of cash. Payment for the guns.

"And again, my sincerest of apologies."

The blond man closed the briefcase and picked it up. "If a fuck up like this happens again, you will pay a hefty price." He nodded to the two men next to him and then walked out of the room.

Santiago dismissed the two other men. Andrea moved over to stand beside Elias, and while Santiago was preoccupied with instructing Peter to have the weapons boxed up, Elias whispered, "Are these the guns that were at the exchange?"

"Yes," she said in a quiet voice.

"The sellers, did they have Cuban accents?"

She cocked her head and then nodded.

Two pieces of the puzzle clicked into place and Elias tensed. He desperately needed to talk to Tag and the team ASAP. This was a much bigger deal than they had thought. He glanced out the windows that overlooked the pool. The sun was rising, and it reflected off the statuary around the far end of the pool. The gold dazzled in the sunlight.

Yeah, this was a fucking bigger deal than they'd been thinking.

Santiago was just the beginning.

CHAPTER FOURTEEN

Andy did her best not to move too much in her heels. Her feet were killing her. She tried not to shiver, but the dress didn't offer much coverage, and Santiago must have kept the house at sixty-five degrees. She really wanted to be done with this whole mess. Catching Santiago had seemed so important, but now, she just wanted this assignment to be over. It was bringing up too many bad memories. She wanted to look ahead, not behind. She missed her place back in L.A. but, really, she just missed having a home.

She glanced over at Elias. Even at the butt crack of dawn, the man looked sexy as hell. Rumpled suited him even more than neat, and she hated him for it. She knew she looked like hell, and he looked like a god. It wasn't fair. Nor was the fact that he'd kissed her, and she'd responded without a thought. It was like the last twelve years hadn't happened. Forget that he'd broken her heart and left her to deal with Santiago. Forget that she'd gotten over him and went on to have several long-term relationships. She was right there again, wanting him like she wanted air to breathe.

He'd always had that effect on her. When she'd seen him

on the boat dressed in his gear, holding that gun, God help her, she thought he was the sexiest thing she'd ever seen. It didn't matter that she hated him. She still wanted him. But now she just wanted to be out of here so she could keep her sanity.

She'd promised herself that one day she would get Santiago for her sister. Carmen was dead, though, and nothing Andy did would bring her sister back. She'd told herself all these years that it would matter, but standing here, looking out at a sunrise, she knew she needed to get out now before she was killed. Maybe even out of the ATF altogether. At the very least out of the Miami office. Maybe she'd try New York or North Carolina, somewhere she could start again and put all of this behind her for good this time.

She shivered, and Elias wrapped an arm around her. She shot him a look but realized he was totally distracted and had done it out of reflex. She couldn't step away without causing a scene, so she tried to relax and go with it. His body heat was very inviting, and she found herself leaning into him.

"So…" Santiago said, and they both turned to look at him. Peter stood inside the door, but his partner had disappeared. "You must have figured out by now that the man that was here came to collect the money for the guns that his people didn't get the other night. He was not pleased that he had to fly here to get it."

He studied Elias for a second. "I need someone to make sure these transfers happen in an efficient manner. The last man did not…do well. Soto was a disaster. I did warn Ignacio about him, but Ignacio didn't think Soto had the *cajones* to try and steal the money and the guns. It does not make me happy to be right." He smiled a cold smile. "Ignacio will not doubt me again."

A shiver crept across her skin that had nothing to do with the temperature in the room. Was Ignacio still alive? Probably. She couldn't imagine Santiago would kill his right-hand man. Still, who knew what Santiago would do to him?

Elias didn't say a word. Anyone else would have been trying to either get the job by saying how well they could do it, kissing Santiago's ass, or trying to get out of it by making up some excuse. Elias just stayed silent.

"Elias, I would like you to do this job for me. You will go out and meet the sellers and bring back the guns." A pause, then, "With no issues. I will contact you when the next delivery is scheduled."

Elias shifted his weight slightly. "I'm not interested."

Santiago's eyes narrowed as he looked up at him from his position behind the desk. "You seem to be under the impression that you have a choice." He gave a slight smile. "You will do this for me, and you will be paid well for it. If you don't, I will have to kill Andrea."

Andy's stomach knotted and her heartbeat took off at a gallop. The way he had said it so casually made her blood run cold.

Elias's expression didn't change, nor did he move in any way. "No. You won't kill Andrea. If you come anywhere near her, or any member of my family, you won't live long enough to regret it."

Santiago stared at him for a tense moment before he threw his head back and laughed. "You have not changed a bit, my friend. Always the tough guy, hmm?" He smiled at Elias.

Elias cocked his head. "You can get one of your flunkies to go out and get the guns. If I'm going to work for you, I want a real job. You're buying all these guns. Are you afraid of someone?"

Santiago snorted. "I'm not afraid of anyone. I'm buying guns because I like to be…prepared."

"Prepared for what?" Elias asked.

"What job is it that you think you can do for me?"

"I can train your men on how to use these guns properly."

The chair creaked as Santiago leaned back. "They are already being trained. The man in here earlier helps with that. He and his people. As you can see, I have already thought ahead. The only thing missing is someone to make the exchange. You will be that person. Or she"—he pointed to Andrea—"will die."

The room was so quiet that a pin could drop and they'd all hear it. They all held a collective breath.

Santiago waved his hand in the air dramatically. "Oh, and I have your gun. The one you used to kill the sellers. If you run or try to hide, I will make sure the police get it, and then you will be a wanted man." He stood up. "Now, I have business to attend to. You may leave." He smiled and walked out of the room.

Elias ushered Andy to the door with his arm around her. They went down the hallway to the front door. Peter opened the door for them, and they went down the steps. He closed the door, and they were alone on the driveway.

"Did you bring a car?" he asked as he dropped his arm and took her hand.

"No. Didn't you?"

He shook his head. They continued down the driveway to the gate. It opened for them, and they walked out onto the street. She tried to take her hand back, but he held it tight. "They're still watching."

She gnashed her teeth in frustration. "How are we going to get out of here?" She glanced at him. "How did you get in?"

He shook his head. "Another time."

They walked back to the guard house and asked the man inside to call an taxi for them. They stayed silent on the sidewalk, waiting for their ride. Once they were in the car, they said nothing.

Andy didn't want to speak. She was afraid she'd lose her shit with Elias if she did. He'd taken over her entire investigation. She'd been sidelined. Frustration and anger mounted as she thought of the work she'd put in to get on the inside of Santiago's outfit. In a matter of hours he'd swept in and had a job, taken over. She wanted to strangle him. Never mind that an hour ago she'd been all prepared to throw in the towel. He didn't deserve to be in that fast. She was not going to be dismissed no matter what he thought.

Finally, the taxi dropped them off in front of the club. Elias's truck was parked across the street. "You still have the truck," she murmured.

"Yeah, my sister's husband looked after it for me. You want a lift to your aunt's place?"

She wanted to kill him, and he was offering a lift to her aunt's place? What, so he could take over? No fucking way. She wasn't going to be pushed out of her own investigation. "I'm going wherever you're going," she snarled and strode across the street to stand beside his truck.

He walked over, unlocked her door, and she climbed in. A minute later, he pulled away from the curb. She waited until they were several blocks away from the club before she whirled on him. "What the fuck do you think you're doing?" she demanded.

He glanced at her. "Driving?"

"Don't be such a fucking smartass. You know what I'm talking about."

Elias sighed. "I'm doing my job. I saved your ass, and you know it. I can't help it if he wants me to take over instead of you."

"You fucking well can help it. This is my case. Santiago is

my collar, and you are not muscling in." She slammed the dash with her hand.

"Calm down."

"Don't tell me to calm down. You are fucking up my case. I want you gone!"

"We both know that's not going to happen. Santiago wants me. If I don't pony up, he'll kill you. I have to show up. Even if we weren't worried that he would actually kill you if I don't come through, it will set off warning bells for him and he won't let you in anyway. It's this or nothing."

She wanted to scream. It was so unfair. Goddammit! But it was true. Elias was right. Either they did this, or Santiago would become suspicious of them. She'd be locked out again, if not killed. She let out a yell of frustration and smashed the dash one more time.

Elias stated, "If it makes you feel any better, this wasn't going to be your case any longer anyway."

"What?" She whirled around and stared at him. They were stopped at a red light, and he pulled out his cell phone. He sent a text and then put it back in his pocket. The light changed, and they continued. "Where are we going?" she asked. It suddenly occurred to her she had no clue what was going on.

"We're going to my place. My team will meet us there. I am going to stop for some food, and that should give them enough time to show up. My assumption is that my truck now has a tracker on it, but on the off chance they are following us, and they are so good I'm not seeing them, I want the team to arrive at my home first so Santiago's men don't see them walking in. RECON will stand out in that neighborhood."

"RECON?" Andy asked. *What was he talking about?*

"The name of my team."

Andy was torn. She desperately wanted to go back to her

aunts and have a shower and get into her own clothes, but she did not want to miss whatever Elias and his team were going to discuss. "I want pizza. I've been eating Cuban food since I got here. I want some pizza."

Elias glanced over at her. "Okay, but it's barely seven a.m. Where are we going to get pizza at this hour?"

"I know a place."

She gave him directions to a food truck next to the water in Miami Beach. He pulled up and parked. There was already a line.

"It says breakfast."

She hopped out of the truck and stood in line.

Miguel waved from inside. "You're usual, Andy?"

"Yes, please. And an extra-large pepperoni as well. Can you add a couple sides of bacon?"

Miguel grinned. "You got it." He turned and spoke to someone inside and then went back to taking orders from the people in line.

Andy thought about going back to the truck and leaving Elias here to pay on his own, but it struck her that, if they were dating, she wouldn't leave him there on his own. Just in case they were watching. It could also be she felt safer next to him than in the truck by herself, but there was no way she was going to tell him that. She walked over and leaned on the back of the food truck. Elias followed.

"Do you have any money?" she asked. She had nothing with her. Not even her cell. Antonio had all of that. It didn't matter about the cell. It was a burner that she only used for this operation and her purse had nothing but some cash and her driver's license. Not even credit cards. She was going to have to track down Antonio, though, and get both back.

Elias stared at her for a second and then nodded. "I have a few bucks. As long as this doesn't cost the world, we're okay."

"Good." She leaned around the side of the truck. "Hey, Miguel, can you add some cafe Cubanos as well? Two please." She looked over at Elias. "You want some?"

He grinned. "Yeah, I'll have the same."

She hated that her stomach had that butterfly feeling when he stood that close and smiled. It was as if her body was betraying her. "Make that four, Miguel."

"No problem, Andy."

"Andy, huh?"

She went back to staring out at the water. "I went by Andy out in L.A. New town, new name. When I first got here, I discovered Miguel and his amazing pizza. I introduced myself as Andy without thinking about it."

"People at work call you Andy."

"Yep," she said, snapping the P at the end.

He studied her for a moment, then nodded.

A little flutter in her chest made her catch her breath. She hated that he did that to her, and she should hate him, the man. But she also still found him sexy as hell. The fact that he made something of himself was impressive. He was a smart, sexy beast of a man that had a killer smile. It was a wonder he wasn't already married.

Back when they were together, she'd thought they would settle down and get married. She had originally planned to go to law school, and Elias had wanted to work with his sister's husband at the garage. She'd secretly thought that he would get bored of the garage and would need something more, but she'd never said.

Turned out she was right. It never would have occurred to her to suggest to him he should join the Coast Guard, but she could definitely see how it suited him. He needed the discipline and the camaraderie. She was sure he got off on the ops he took part in. He was always a bit of an adrenaline junkie. *Takes one to know one.*

"Andy, your order is up." Miguel held two boxes out to her.

"Thanks Miguel. See ya later." She grabbed them and headed back to the truck. Elias paid for the food, grabbed the coffee and bacon, and followed her. He unlocked the doors, and they climbed in. The cab of the pickup filled with the smell of melted cheese and tomato sauce along with bacon. Her stomach growled.

"Where do you live?"

"Not far." He took them back off the island and turned north. A few minutes later, they were in a more industrial setting. There were buildings and warehouses and the occasional corner store, and that was about it. Elias made a final turn onto a street full of old buildings on one side and warehouses on the other. He parked and got out.

Andy followed him, carrying the pizzas. They approached an old warehouse-looking place that had been converted into apartments, an upgrade that had happened a long time ago and the landlords obviously hadn't kept the place up. Paint was peeling everywhere, and the door screeched when Elias opened it. They went in and up the stairs to the second floor.

He went to the middle of the hallway and an unlocked door marked *206*. He waved her through. She was surprised when she entered the place. It was one big open room with a kitchen area. Down a hallway on her right must have been the bedroom and bath, but most importantly was the fact that a group of large sexy men were already inside, lounging on the furniture. They all looked at her when she entered.

"Breakfast," she declared as she put the pizzas on the kitchen island and then sank down on a stool. She kicked off the shoes once more. Her feet were going to need a week to recover.

Elias set the bacon and coffee down on the counter and

did the whole shoulder bump greeting with his team members.

"We swept the place. No bugs. Andrea, your boss is looking for you," Nick said.

Andy looked up from her feet. "I'm sure he is."

"You might want to let him know you're okay."

She sighed. "Yeah, I guess. He's not going to be happy, so I'm in no rush."

"Good," Elias said, "because we're going to need to figure out a few things before you reach out to him."

She narrowed her eyes at him. "What things? This is still an ATF operation. My boss gets to call the shots, and in his absence, I do."

"No." Elias shook his head. "This is now a Homeland Security situation. Guns are only one small part of the shit going down with Santiago and the Street Aces."

CHAPTER FIFTEEN

"Grab breakfast and then I'll explain." Elias turned and headed down the hallway. "I'm going to have a quick shower and get changed. Save me some pizza. And bacon." He went into his room and grabbed some clothes, then he went into the bathroom and closed the door. He turned on the shower and stood in front of the mirror, gripping the sink. He hissed out a long breath.

It had been a long night with very little sleep and too much time next to Andrea. He was in over his head with her. It had never occurred to him that she would still have this effect on him. In that dress and those shoes, it had been a constant struggle not to kiss her. It didn't help that he'd just stolen her case. She was angry, and rightfully so, which pissed him off even more. He didn't want her to be right about anything. He wanted to hate her. He wanted her to suffer for betraying Mattie, but instead he found himself worrying about her.

He stripped off and then ducked under the spray. Maybe with the changes taking place in the op, she'd be out of the picture now. He could only hope. Continuing to work with her was going to be a distraction at best, hell on earth at worst.

He emerged from the shower, toweled off, and quickly dressed in faded jeans and a white T-shirt. He ran his fingers through his hair and left the bathroom.

In the living room, everyone was stuffing their faces with pizza.

"Where did you get this pizza?" Axe asked Andrea. "It's amazing."

"Yeah, it's really good," Finn agreed.

Andrea tugged on her dress, as if trying to stretch it farther down her legs, which only drew his entire team's attention instead. "Miguel runs a food truck in Miami Beach. The guy who owns it insists he does breakfast foods, that sort of thing, but Miguel makes the best pizza in the world. He's saving for his own shop. The food truck is Sunrise Eats. If you look it up online, you can see where he'll be each day. Tell him Andy sent you if you want some pizza."

"So," Nick said as he took a piece of bacon off his plate, "what happened with Santiago? By the way, you were right. Santiago had his guys break in early this morning. He has the gun."

Elias grabbed a plate and picked up a slice of the green pepper and mushroom pizza. "So he said. He threatened me with it." Elias added on a few slices of bacon and began to relate the events. "I learned some interesting things about the Santiago's operation," he said, then took a bite of his pizza.

"Like?" Cain asked as he sipped his coffee.

"First, I know where Waters died. Santiago has a swimming pool with a large S on the bottom in gold leaf. There's also some gold leaf on the statuary by the pool. Santiago holds court by the pool. I would imagine he got pissed off at Waters about something and smashed his head onto the statuary and then let him drown in the pool."

"So noted." Nick helped himself to another slice of pizza. "If we get the opportunity, we'll have to get the local cops to get their forensics unit down there to check it out. Any idea why Santiago killed him?"

Elias cocked his head. "Sort of? Santiago got us up at the crack of dawn so I could examine the gun shipment for him. He wanted to make sure they were in working order before he handed over the money to the seller. Turns out the seller came to his office to make the exchange since the one at sea didn't go well. Santiago now wants me to be his gun guy. He wants me to make the exchange. He told me not to be stupid because that's what happened to the last guy. He meant before Soto. My guess is the 'last guy' was Waters."

"Wait." Axe frowned. "The seller came to Santiago's house to get the money? Isn't that a bit odd?"

Andrea chimed in, "Yeah, super weird. That's not usually how things work at all. The seller and buyer meet on neutral territory to make the exchange."

"Unless they're doing more than one type of business together." Elias grabbed a second slice from the box. "The sellers who were on the boat were Cuban. The guy in Santiago's office was definitely former military and not ours. He had the slightest bit of an accent. Former Eastern Bloc or Russian." He let that statement sink in.

Less than a minute later, Cain swore. "You sure?"

"Yeah," Elias said. "And it's not just guns. The relationship is close because Santiago said the guy in the office was training Santiago's security."

"Shit," Finn frowned as he set his plate on the coffee table.

"That changes things." Nick started digging out his cell.

"Yeah, it does," Elias agreed.

"Would someone like to fill me in on what you're talking about?" Andrea demanded as she glared at Elias.

"The men that were selling the guns were from Cuba. The guns were all brand-new, Russian made—"

"Shit, the RPG was Russian made," Nick said. Then, "Wait. New?"

Elias nodded. "As in straight from the factory. Anyway, what it looks like is the guns came from Cuba, which is why they agreed to make the exchange so far out. Cuba is only ninety miles from here. They came most of the way, and Santiago's people met them. The Russians have been making noises about having a larger presence in Cuba in recent months. These are Russian guns."

"So, you're saying the sellers are Russians from Cuba?" Andrea asked as she pushed her plate away.

"Yes. Not only that, but the Russians are also training Santiago's men. I noticed that the security at the party was very professional. I thought they might be former military. Now I think they've just been trained as such."

"By the Russians," Andrea stated. "But what does that mean?"

"That's a good question," Nick agreed.

"Not sure. It makes me nervous, though, that the Russians are supplying guns and RPGs via the Cubans to a drug kingpin in Miami *and* training his men. You have to ask yourself, what do they gain from it? The Russians won't do anything unless they get something in return."

"But maybe it's just some Russian guy who lives in Cuba who had access to a bunch of guns. You don't know for sure it's the Russian government," Andrea argued.

"No, you're right," Elias agreed. "I don't know for sure, but these guns are brand-new, never been used, straight from the factory, and this isn't the first time Santiago bought guns from them. Just the way he and the guy were talking, it's obviously an ongoing thing. So, how could an average guy have the kind of connections that would allow him to take all those guns from the Russian factory to the buyer without someone catching him?"

"Maybe there's a gun factory in Cuba?" she suggested.

"If there is, that's a major problem for us, but the fact that the seller is also doing training says there's more going on here."

"Agreed." Nick stood. "A major drug dealer in Miami, having his men trained by the Russians and buying RPGs, is setting off all kinds of bells. I've gotta go make a call. Andrea, if you wouldn't mind sticking around a while longer, it would be helpful."

She shrugged. "Fine." She turned to Elias. "I am going to take a shower, though. Find me something to wear." With that command, she rose from her chair and strode into the bathroom, slamming the door behind her. Nick walked down the hallway and went into Elias's bedroom, closing the door more quietly than Andrea had.

Cain got up off the couch and came over to the kitchen island. He dropped another slice onto his plate. "You think the Russians are planning something?"

Elias shrugged. "The Russians don't do anything without a plan. There's a long game here, but we're not seeing it. At least, not yet. I have to stay in there with Santiago. I'm guessing the longer I'm around, the better chance I have at spotting whatever is really going on."

Axe and Finn came over to the island and sat on stools. "At least we know where Waters died," Finn said.

"Yes, but not why," Axe pointed out.

"Do we need to know why?" Cain asked. "He's dead. Doesn't really matter why."

"It might." Elias drank some coffee. "Maybe he was like Soto and tried to rip off Santiago, in which case, it doesn't matter. On the other hand, maybe he saw something and decided to do something about it. He used to be one of us.

Maybe he made the Russian connection and decided to stop Santiago somehow. Maybe there's more we don't know. The why could be important."

"You're going back in with Santiago? You ready for that?" Axe asked, his face full of concern.

Elias started to say something glib then stopped. He shrugged. "I don't really know. It's kind of surreal. This is the life I probably would have had if Mattie was still alive. I probably would have been drawn into the gang life and whatever came after. He wanted to be exactly where Santiago is, and if I'd survived that long, odds are I would have been his right-hand guy."

"But that's not what happened," Finn pointed out. "Are you still good with being undercover?"

"Yeah. This started with me wanting to take Santiago down, and I still want to do that, but when I saw those guns, it all changed. All the personal shit just fell away, you know. Now it's about what those guns mean. This isn't just some small-time gun hustle. It's bigger than that. Much bigger."

"Bertrand agrees with you," Nick spoke as he rejoined the rest of the team. "He's making some calls. Turns out Homeland and the rest of Washington has been aware of a slow migration of Russians to Cuba recently. They've been watching and waiting to see what's going on but have no intel on it as yet. This is the first anyone has heard about Russian guns arriving on U.S. soil. Needless to say, Bertrand agrees you should go back undercover and find out as much as you can."

Elias nodded. "Santiago will call me when he wants me to go make the exchange for him. He'll probably call me before to feel me out a bit. I would if I were him."

"Just be ready and stay in touch with us." Nick frowned. "I'm not sure Andrea has realized the full implications of this yet."

"She knows that she's lost control and this is no longer her operation, but she has to stay involved." Elias grimaced. He wasn't happy that she had to remain a part of the operation. "Santiago thinks we're back together as a couple. He threatened her life to make me do what he wants me to do. If I suddenly say she's not important anymore, he's the kind of guy to go out and have her killed just to see my reaction. He'll see it as me trying to protect her by lying to him, and he'll punish me for it by killing her and possibly my family."

"Shit." Axe scrubbed a hand through his hair. "I didn't even think about them. We need to keep an eye on them."

"It's under control," Cain stated.

Elias gave him a grateful nod.

"Care to explain?" Nick asked.

Cain met his gaze. "Sometimes it's better if you don't ask questions."

Nick gave him a long look, but let it go.

Elias was thankful. He and Cain were cut from the same cloth. He knew that Cain would go outside the lines to protect his family, and Elias was very appreciative. He would do the same for Cain. There was no question. Cain most likely had some people he knew keeping an eye on Elias's family, but these people may not be law enforcement types. It didn't matter to Elias as long as his family was safe. It might not be a good thing, though, if Bertrand found out.

"Andrea is in then. What are we going to do about her boss?" Finn asked.

"We're going to tell him that we're taking over, and if he has a problem to call his own boss and complain." Nick stole a piece of bacon from the to-go container. "I already asked Bertrand to make the call and let the ATF know they'll be taking a backseat. They should be happy their agent is still involved at all."

"So, what do we do now?" Axe asked.

"We wait and we watch. Once Santiago calls, then we can start poking around. Until then, it should be business as usual or what he thinks is business as usual for Andrea and me."

Elias moved away from the island and headed toward his bedroom. Andrea would be getting out of the shower soon, and he needed to get her some clothing. He dug around and came up with a navy T-shirt and a pair of sweats with a drawstring waist. He walked back to the bathroom and knocked on the door. The fan was on so he couldn't hear if the water was running. He waited a beat and then opened it.

Andrea was standing there toweling off. He caught a glimpse of her breasts before she wrapped the towel around herself. She glared at him as she tucked the corner of the towel into her cleavage. "You could have waited for me to say something."

"I didn't think, sorry. Here's the clothes. It's the best I can do." He handed her the clothing and quickly stepped out of the bathroom.

The last thing he needed was to be involved with the woman who'd gotten his best friend killed. But seeing her nearly naked was enough to make him waiver. She was as stunning as he remembered. More so. The sooner this whole thing was over, the better, not just for his mental health, but for his balls, too.

CHAPTER SIXTEEN

ndy stood with the towel wrapped around her, her heart thudding against her ribs. She wanted to be furious at Elias for walking in on her, and she was, but it was her second reaction that alarmed her more. She wanted him to stay. That wasn't good. Not one bit. She really needed to get her head on straight. She could blame it on the lack of sleep or the stress of the situation, but the reality was the past still haunted her. She'd always thought they would end up together. Life without Elias had never entered her mind until the day her sister and Mattie died. The day her betrayal and his happened.

She'd thought it was all behind her. She'd put it in its place and moved on, but the longer she was around him, the more it became evident that it simply wasn't. She still had feelings for him.

Maybe it was better that she acknowledged them instead of burying them. That's what her shrink had said out in L.A.: *Acknowledging your feelings doesn't mean you have to act on them.* But that had been about her crush on her boss. She'd ignored her therapist's advice, and it had promptly blown up in her face.

Robins had her moved out here to Miami with him, and she had agreed, not because they were lovers, but because he'd dangled Santiago in front of her. Of course, by the time she'd gotten here she'd realized sleeping with her boss was a massive mistake.

This time, though, she did not want to make a mistake. She still wanted to take down Santiago, and if she had to be sidelined a bit to stay in the game, she'd just have to live with that. She needed to heed her ex-shrink's advice. Admit to herself that she still had unresolved feelings for Elias and being involved in this mess was bringing up the past in ways she hadn't anticipated.

She still had unresolved feelings for her former boyfriend Elias Mason.

There, she'd said it to herself. She let out a breath. Not so bad. She was still standing. Of course, the fact that she wanted to fuck his brains out probably wasn't helpful either, but one admission at a time.

Andy finished drying off and got dressed. The T-shirt and sweats were huge, but at least they were clean, and so was she. She used her fingers to comb out her hair the best she could and let it hang down her back. If she couldn't find a brush, the chances of locating a hair dryer were astronomical.

She opened the bathroom door and walked back into the living area. The room was empty, but a voice came from the kitchen. "Elias went to pick up a few things. The guys all went to grab some sleep." Nick walked out from behind the island.

"Oh, okay." Andy stood there, uncertain what she should do.

"Have a seat." Nick pointed toward the living area.

The view of the water beyond was amazing with all the

container ships loading and unloading. "Leave it to Elias to find a place with the best view," Andy commented as she sat down on the sofa.

Nick came over and sat on a chair to her right. "We have to talk about how this is going to proceed. You were there when Elias broke it down. This isn't just about guns. There are much broader implications, and until we know the full scope, we're not comfortable with ATF running things."

Andy clenched her jaw. Where did he get off telling her what he was comfortable with? Why did his opinion matter so fucking much?

"And by 'we,' I mean my boss and the higher ups at Homeland Security. Look, I know you put a lot of time and effort into this, and it must suck to have us come in and take it over, but at this point, it's our job. A Russian buildup in Cuba is the job of many collaborating departments, but not one of them is ATF."

She didn't say a word, but some of the anger ebbed away. He was right. It wasn't her job to keep the border safe, and that was what this was boiling down to.

She cleared her throat. "There's an argument to be made that since this is about guns, we should be involved. Besides who are you exactly? Your team, I mean. Are you all," what had Elias called it, "MSRT?"

Nick frowned. "No. We're... sort of a mixed bag of top operators from the Coast Guard's elite units. Elias and Cain are MSRT. Finn and I are MSST and Axe is TACLET. I can explain those to you," he said but she waved him off.

"I can look them up if I want to know them."

He nodded. "We call ourselves Team RECON if that helps. We were all benched from our regular duties and put on this team. Now we...solve problems for the Coast Guard."

She cocked her head. "I see. That still doesn't explain why

the ATF shouldn't be involved. We're supposed to stop the selling of guns."

"Agreed, and you *will* be involved. You will continue with Elias, posing as a couple for the operation, but I will be running it. Your people will not be told the truth. Robins, your boss, will be the only ATF agent read in on the situation and, even then, it will be the barest of details. He will not be told the full story. Hell, we don't even know what that is just yet. He will not be allowed to discuss it with any other member of the team, including you. You cannot discuss what you know with him or anyone else. These are the ground rules for you continuing."

She curled her hands into fists in her lap. *It wasn't fair.* Jay and Peña had worked just as hard as she had. "That's not fair to the others."

"Life isn't fair."

She bit her lip. She wanted to argue with him. She wanted to tell him to go shove the op up his ass and storm out, but the reality was, this was too close to home. She knew when she'd started this that she had to finish it no matter what. Other than her doubts this morning, which she was blaming on lack of sleep and being too close to Elias, she was solid in her desire to see this through.

The only family she had left was her aunt, and as horrible as it was, she was willing to risk that woman's life, as well as her own, to bring down Santiago. Sacrificing her team members' hard work was a no-brainer. She knew that didn't make her a very nice person, but she hadn't joined the ATF to be nice. She had joined to take assholes like Santiago off the street, to stop the violence that happened every day.

"Fine. Agreed."

"My boss is talking to Robins as we speak. You will go talk to him after this. You are going to tell him everything that happened last night with the exception of us, the rest of the RECON team. Elias was working on his own. He does not have our support. He's pissed off and pulling a lone-wolf situation."

She frowned. "Why?"

"The top brass feels the fewer people who know the real situation, the better."

"Sounds like a hell of a lot of CYA, cover your ass, shit to me."

Nick smiled briefly. "Yeah, well, that's probably not wrong, but as far as you are concerned, Elias showed up on his own with his own story and you went with it. Today, you saw me ream his ass for it and things did not look good, but you have to roll with it because it's the only way you guys get to stay in the game."

She frowned.

"Don't worry. We've got his back no matter what happens, and yours, too. As long as you're in this with us, we'll take care of you."

"I wasn't worried about that. I was just thinking it could be a hard sell. Elias is there. Why would Robins believe that he's not sanctioned?"

"Tell Robins that Elias is doing this because of Mateo's death, but we want to pull him out. The brass is working on a new plan, and they are sending some new people in, but it's going to take a few days to get organized."

"But why, though? Why go through all this?"

Nick gave her a hard stare. "Because now we're into terrorism and foreign actors on our soil. It's a whole different level of game play. The fewer people who know the reality, the safer it is for everyone concerned. If the Russians really are making some kind of play, you can bet your ass they're prepared. Some asshole making a stupid offhand comment could get us all killed. We need to limit involvement and knowledge as much as possible."

Andy nodded but let it all sink in. Were they overreacting? Robins, Peña, Jay, they were all trustworthy—but it hit her. Nick was right. How many times did they say some small thing while getting coffee? Nothing major, nothing that would give away any details, but if someone heard it and reported back, it could be enough to change things. If they made one comment about Elias, just one, and someone was listening, it could get her and Elias killed.

Nick wasn't overreacting. His bosses weren't hitting the panic button. They were making the smart play. Leaving Elias out there as a lone wolf. Santiago already knew he was with the Coast Guard, so he wasn't going to trust him much anyway. If there was even the slightest hint that he was doing this with his team, Santiago will have him killed. But that also gave Santiago an overinflated sense of confidence since he held that rifle. He thought he had Elias by the *cojones*.

"It makes sense. Okay, I'm on board and won't say anything, but I want to be kept in the loop. No secrets from me. I want to be read in on everything."

"I'll do my best." She opened her mouth to protest, but he cut her off. "I can't promise anything. It's not really my call."

She nodded.

Elias opened the door and entered the apartment. He had bags of groceries in each hand. "Hey." He put them on the counter.

"Hey." Nick stood up. "I'm going to go. Get some sleep. We'll connect later. Call if Santiago reaches out."

"Okay, Tag," They bumped shoulders and Nick left.

Andy stood up. "I have to go, too. I need to change and go see Robins."

"Do you want a ride?"

She shook her head. "No. I've got to go face the music with my aunt and then do the same with Robins. Having you around for either is not helpful. My aunt will have heard by now. She's not your biggest fan."

"I am not surprised. Call me when you're done. I'll pick you up. We have to keep the cover going for Santiago."

"Okay." She borrowed Elias's phone and called an Uber. Then she grabbed the stilettos and carried them to the door. No need to torture her feet any more than necessary. She stopped, put them on, and then opened the door. She glanced back at Elias, but he was busy putting away groceries. At some point, they were going to have to talk about the past and the truth about what happened.

Andy went down the stairs and smiled as she passed an elderly gentleman in the hallway. "At least he's got great taste in women," the old man said to a short, round Hispanic woman wearing some sort of muumuu. Andy laughed to herself and kept going out the door.

Twenty minutes later, she pulled up in front of her aunt's house. It suddenly hit her she had no money for a tip, but thankfully, as a stroke of fabulous timing, Antonio was just leaving her aunt's house. He looked dapper in a pair of white linen pants and a blue button-down. "Antonio, do you have my purse? I wanted to tip the driver in cash."

Antonio smiled as he walked toward her. "Nice outfit."

She rolled her eyes. "Yeah. Thanks." He pulled out his wallet, but she put her hand out to stop him. "You don't have to do that. I'll pay for it. Is my purse in the house?"

"It is, but I got this." He pulled out some bills and tipped the driver generously. "So, you made it through last night. I'm very glad."

"Me, too," she said and laughed. "It didn't look so good there for a while."

"Why didn't you tell me Elias was back in town and back in your life?"

She shrugged. "I don't know, Antonio. He isn't big on

dealing with the old crowd. He's having a hard time since he got shot. He's…rethinking things."

Antonio's eyes bore into hers. "You brought him along to the exchange."

"Wouldn't you? Jesus. You saw how Soto was acting. Crazy. I think he was on steroids. He was just *loco*. I didn't think I would get out of there alive if I didn't have some kind of help. I tried to get out of going, but he held me at gunpoint once we got to the marina. Scariest few hours of my life." None of it was a lie. She had no problem looking him in the eye when she spoke.

"What about you and him?" Antonio squinted at her.

"That's…a bit more complicated. We're sort of hanging out. Santiago thinks we're right back the way we were, but I —I'm not sure, Antonio. It's different now. We're different. I thought I could get ahead a bit through Soto, make some money, but now, I don't know. Maybe I'll throw in the towel and move again." Also, all true.

Antonio surprised her and gave her a hug. "It's tough, *chica*." He kept his arm around her. "You two have been through a lot together and apart. Maybe it's better you take some time and think about things. Either way, you have to keep up appearances for Santiago. He's on edge these days. No matter how relaxed he looked last night, he's like a dog on the Fourth of July with all the fireworks. Don't do anything to upset him."

She nodded. "I'll do my best. Trust me."

"Good."

"Oh, Lola's dress. I forgot it at Elias's. I'll get it dry-cleaned and get it to you later?"

He laughed. "No rush."

She held his shoulder as she pulled off the shoes. "Here, you can take these death traps now. Oh, my god, my feet are killing me. How does she wear these for hours on end?"

"You know Lola. It's all about appearances. She had Botox injected into the balls of her feet so she can wear stilettos all the time and not be in pain."

"Jesus, is that a thing?"

"It is in Las Vegas."

She's a better woman than I am, for sure."

Antonio leaned over and kissed her on the cheek. "You looked beautiful last night. Don't forget it. You even look… cute today."

She laughed. "I don't, but I appreciate the compliment all the same. I'll drop off the dress once it's clean." When he started walking toward his car, she called after him, "Are you working today?"

He shook his head. "No. I'm off for the next couple of days. Going offshore with a friend for some rest and relaxation."

"You have fun." She waved, then turned back and went up the walk to her aunt's house. Andy let herself in and walked straight through the living room into the kitchen, where she knew her aunt would be.

Her aunt was making some sort of pastry and didn't bother to look up. "You're alive. Nice to know that. If Antonio hadn't come by, I would still be wondering."

"I'm sorry. I didn't have my phone so I couldn't call." She didn't want to mention that she'd been with Elias and used his to call the Uber. She just couldn't deal with the fallout right now.

"You didn't have your phone because you went out with Soto. Now he's dead, and Santiago is watching you. *Chica*, what are you doing with your life?" her aunt yelled. "Hanging out with these lowlifes. It's stupid. You're not stupid. Why are you doing this?"

Andy stood there silently. She wanted to tell her aunt the

truth, but she couldn't, and there was nothing she could say that would make it any better.

"And now you are back with Elias? He left you on the floor, sobbing your eyes out. He was supposed to love you, and he just left you heartbroken. Why would you take him back? Your sister died, and he just left. Why? Why would you even look at him again?" Her aunt slammed the rolling pin down on the table.

Andy remained silent. She should have known her aunt would know about Elias. She couldn't come up with anything to say that would appease her aunt.

"No." Aunt Esther shook her head. "No, *chica*. I won't have you under my roof if you are going to live this way. You want to be with Elias? Fine, you go live with him. You want to hang out with these losers? You go. Do it, but don't come crying to me when he breaks your heart again. Don't come back here looking for sympathy when it all blows up in your face, and do not call me for bail money. *Dios mio.* You will be lucky if you need bail money. I will end up burying you like your mother and your sister before you. I thought you were the smart one, but no. You come back and you make more bad choices. Go. Get out. I'm done with you."

Her aunt's words stung. Andy tried to swallow the tears that were building in her throat. Even though she knew what she was doing was important and necessary, having her aunt kick her out made her feel hollow and sad inside. She walked down the hall to her room. She kept telling herself that it wasn't real. As soon as she could tell her aunt the truth, all would be well, but it didn't make it hurt any less now. She valued her aunt's opinion. It was killing her that her aunt thought she was a lost cause. She sniffed and tried not to let it get to her.

She threw all her stuff into her luggage and even dug out the cell phone from the heating vent. She sent a text to

Robins and told him she'd meet him out in the alley in twenty minutes. Then she put it in her purse. God forbid Santiago or his men came looking for Andy here and found the phone. He'd kill her aunt without blinking an eye.

She finished packing her stuff and then pulled on a pair of jeans and a blue tank top that had an A-line shape, along with a pair of socks and her sneakers, sighing as her feet hit the cushy insole. If she never wore sky-high heels again, it would be fine by her.

Then after she took one last look around the room, she stuffed Elias's dirty clothes into the front of the suitcase and zipped up the bag. She wheeled it out of the room and down the hallway. Her aunt looked up.

"I—"

"I don't want to hear it." Her aunt held up her hands and turned her face away. "There's no excuse, *chica*. None."

Andy grimaced. "*Te amo, Tía* Esther," she said in a loud, clear voice and then wheeled her bag out the back door and across the grass to the fence. She let herself out into the alley. Robins pulled up in their undercover op van. She opened the door to the back and got in with her luggage and then closed the door behind her.

When Robins took off quickly, she fell back and whacked her head on the side of the van. "Ouch."

"She kicked you out, or did you decide to move in with your ex-boyfriend all on your own?"

The acid in his voice grated on her nerves. She did not need this right now. "She kicked me out, but it's probably for the best anyway."

Robins muttered something, but she couldn't hear from the back of the van with the road noise. She really just didn't give a shit at the moment anyway. Twenty minutes later, they were in Miami Beach at the park near Ocean Drive. Robins started to get out of the van but changed his mind and slammed the door closed again.

He whirled around in his seat. "What the fuck is going on? I get a call from my boss telling me we're off the case. Well, you're not off the case, but Homeland and the Coast Guard is taking it over, and now you're working for them? What the fuck, Andy? Why didn't you call me? What's going on?"

She took a deep breath. "I couldn't call you. We agreed on that. I couldn't leave once I dropped off the guns. Ignacio wouldn't let me, and he made Antonio stay with me the entire time. Then when I was taken to Santiago's, I couldn't call you either. I called as soon as I could."

He shook his head, glaring at her. "What the fuck happened in there? Why was your former boyfriend there?"

She regretted sharing about Elias, not that she'd had a choice. He'd had such a violent reaction to her, she'd had to tell Robins something. But she should have lied. "He came to Santiago's. I had no idea he was going to be there until he appeared beside me. He said he was there at the exchange, and he was the one who shot the weapons dealers."

Robins snorted.

"It was a damn good thing he did because Santiago wasn't buying my story. But he bought Elias's hook, line, and sinker. We're in. He wants Elias to take the next meet with the sellers."

"What about us? Why is Homeland involved?"

She shook her head. "I don't know. All I know is Elias showed up. I don't think he's working with his people, or he's not telling them the whole truth. It's hard to know what's going on. It's not like they're sharing details with me."

His eyes narrowed. "So, you're just what, going along with it?"

"Do I have a choice? I mean, I can walk away, but if I do,

we lose the small part we have left of this investigation. We'll have no chance at taking down Santiago and no claim to the bust. At least if I'm there, I can try and point out it was our op in the first place. Besides, if I pull out now, Santiago will just kill me. He's using me to keep Elias in line. He thinks we're lovers again."

"Are you? Are you sleeping with him again?" His eyes bore into hers.

"Are you for fucking real? When were we going to screw? At Santiago's? This is the job. Elias is doing it because of Mateo. I'm doing it because of my sister. I don't give a fuck why you're doing it, but we've all got our reasons, and I want to be there to see that motherfucker Santiago go down."

Robins glared at her some more and then shook his head. "Is there anything you can tell me?"

"I don't know anything. My job is to literally stand around and be arm candy. They aren't sharing anything with me. What did they tell you? Surely, you must know more than I do. Did they tell you why they're taking it over? What did Landon say? He's the boss, for Christ's sake. He has to know something."

She hoped by changing tactics, he'd stop quizzing her. If she made it seem like he knew more than she did, he'd feel better. Robins's ego was fucking enormous. It hadn't taken her long to figure that out. He really thought he was the smartest man in the room. He wasn't. Not even close. How she'd ever found him attractive, she'd never know.

"Landon didn't say much. Just something about the guns coming from an unexpected source, and it rang alarm bells in Washington, so everyone is all bent out of shape about it."

"So, they figured out who the sellers were?"

"Yes." He hesitated. "It's delicate."

"Do you know who they were? Can you guess where they came from?" She put on her wide-eye look that he'd always fallen for when they were together. Back then, she did it to boost his ego and make him feel good. That was before she realized he was an asshole and his ego was so large it didn't need boosting.

"I can't say anything."

She sighed. "I understand, but if you know, then you must know what the hell is going on? Why does Homeland have the case?"

He'd backed himself into a corner. Either he'd have to admit he didn't know, or he'd have to stop demanding answers from her.

Robins looked uncomfortable for a minute. "I'm sorry, Andy. I really can't talk about this. You're just going to have to muddle through with these guys. Of course, I'll support you any way I can. Peña and Jay cannot be read in, so it will be difficult, but reach out if there's anything you need."

Such a bastard. *What a fucking idiot.* She swallowed her scorn and pasted a false smile on her face. "I feel better just knowing that."

CHAPTER SEVENTEEN

E lias tried to get his mind to shut down so he could sleep, but he wasn't having much luck. He needed a poker game or a good workout, anything to stop his brain running in a loop. He was bouncing between being pissed at Santiago and wanting Andrea.

Andy. At first, he hadn't liked the name, but it was growing on him. *Shit.* That was a problem. He needed to stop thinking about her, but easier said than done.

He glanced at his watch. She'd been gone a couple of hours. She should be back by now. Was she colluding with Santiago? Or someone else? Or was she in some kind of trouble? What was taking her so long?

He gave himself a mental shake and switched to thinking about Santiago. What was he getting ready for with all the guns and training? Surely, he could hire people here to train his guys, so why go with the Russians? It was puzzling.

The phone that connected the door to the building buzzed. Andrea must be back. He got up and went down the hall to answer it. He glanced at the screen, but there was no one there. He immediately went back into his room and got his gun. He padded quietly back down the hall and stood to the left of the loft door.

There was a knock.

He glanced at the screen and hit a couple of buttons. The camera above the door showed Andrea standing there talking with Mrs. Jimenez. *Great.* Just what he needed. He tucked his gun in his waist band and unlocked the door. He pulled it open.

"Hey." Andrea looked up at him and gave him a smile. "Mrs. Jimenez was just telling me about Mr. Tanez and the parking situation. I promised her we'd be more careful in the future." She waltzed passed him into the apartment, pulling her luggage behind her. He smiled at Mrs. Jimenez and then quickly closed the door in her face. She was too nosy for her own good.

"How did it go at your aunt's?"

Andrea sighed. "Not great. She kicked me out." She sat down on one of the stools. "I can't wait until this is all over so I can tell her what's really going on. I hate that she's disappointed in me."

Elias didn't know what to say to that. He had never been a favorite of her aunt's, so there was no love lost. "Do you want something?"

"No. I'm just tired. Is it okay if I crash?"

"Sure."

She kicked off her shoes and trudged into the bedroom, dragging her bag behind her, and closed the door.

Good thing he wasn't tired. He went over and turned on the TV to the sports channel and sat down. He put his gun on the coffee table and laid down on the couch. He was asleep in seconds.

A few hours later, his ringing phone woke him. He sat up and glanced at the screen. *Unknown number.*

He picked it up, swiped the screen, and said, "Hello."

"Be ready at ten. Someone will come pick you up."

"Santiago? You just did a deal. You're doing another one already?"

"Be ready." He hung up.

Elias sat there trying to piece it together, but he couldn't get it to make sense. He tapped the screen a couple of times and then raised it to his ear. "Tag, it's me. Santiago just called. He says I have to be ready at ten. Someone is coming to get me."

"Already? He's doing another deal?"

"I asked, but he ignored me and then hung up."

"Okay, we'll be there. We'll keep a safe distance, but we'll make sure we're with you."

Elias paused for a second. "Maybe someone should stay here with Andrea. I don't trust Santiago. He could be taking me out somewhere so he can kill her."

"Why would he do that?"

"No fucking clue, but I don't want her on her own here. She's too vulnerable."

Nick grunted. "Okay. I'll have Finn stay with her."

"Thanks." He clicked off the call.

"What's going on?" Andrea asked. She was standing beside the island. He hadn't heard her come up the hallway.

"Santiago called. He wants me to be ready at ten. Someone is coming to get me."

"Another deal so soon?"

He shrugged. "The guys will follow me, but Finn is going to come stay with you."

She frowned. "I can take care of myself."

Elias sighed. "I'm sure you can, but I live in a building full of old people. I don't want any of them to get hurt if Santiago's guys come back for another visit. You can take care of you, but you can't take care of a bunch of elderly people at the same time."

"And Finn can?"

Elias met her gaze. "He's a hell of a lot better equipped to take out multiple targets than you are. It's what he's trained to do."

She opened her mouth to argue presumably, but his phone went off again. He glanced at the screen. Wild Bill. He picked it up and answered. "Hey, what's up?"

"Big game tonight. Lots of heavy hitters. You can make some good coin. You want in?"

"Can't tonight."

"You sure? It's going to be easy pickings. Lots of out-of-towners with money to burn."

"Sounds good, but I can't. Keep me in the loop for next time."

"Okay, man, will do." Wild Bill disconnected.

Elias leaned back on the couch. He'd love to go to a game like that. The last time Wild Bill had called him for a game with a group of out-of-towners, he'd made six figures.

"I'm hungry," Andrea declared. "What time is it?"

"Just past five. You want me to make you something?"

She stared at him in astonishment. "You cook?"

"How do you think I survived on my own? If I didn't cook, I would starve." He got up from the couch and went to the kitchen area. He opened the fridge. "I can make a salad."

"Salad? Seriously? I'm hungry. A salad is fine to start, but I want real food."

Elias glanced over at her and had to grin. She'd always had a healthy appetite. Nice to see not everything had changed. "How about I make a salad to go with a steak? I can barbeque it."

"Sounds great. Wait. Where's your barbeque?"

"On the roof." He started pulling salad fixings out of the fridge.

"You have a rooftop deck?"

He nodded as he started rinsing the lettuce. "It's the reason I rented the place, or one of them at least."

"How do you get up there?"

He pointed toward the hallway. "There's a door opposite the bathroom."

"I guessed that was a linen closet." She looked down the hallway.

"Yeah, it kind of looks like that." He started chopping vegetables.

Andrea sighed. "Do you have any wine?"

He looked up and nodded. "White or red?"

"Surprise me?"

He moved back a step and opened the wine fridge that was on his side of the island. It had two sections. One at fifty-eight degrees for the reds one at thirty-five for the whites and champagnes. He pulled out a bottle of red that would go nicely with the steak. He'd become a bit of a wine snob after dating a woman who was a sommelier. She'd dumped him because he was away too much. He'd been sorry that it ended but the upside was he was now interested in wines.

"Here, try this one." He opened the bottle and then retrieved a red wine glass from a cabinet. He poured a small bit for her to taste.

She smelled it and then took a small sip. "This is really good." He smiled. She put her glass back down, and he filled it. Then he put a stopper in the wine and went back to chopping vegetables.

"You aren't going to have any?" she asked him.

He shook his head. "I've gotta be on my game with Santiago tonight. Best I don't have a glass just yet."

He finished with the last of the vegetables and mixed them with the lettuce. The steak was nicely marbled when he unwrapped it and put it on a plate. He stacked a couple other plates under the steak. "If you can grab the cutlery, I've got everything else."

"Sure," she said and got off her stool. After grabbing the cutlery, she reached across the island and grabbed the wine. He tried not to smile. He didn't blame her one bit. Wine would be good right now.

He strode down the hallway and stopped in front of the door. She opened it for him, and he waited for her to go first.

When they exited onto the rooftop, she exclaimed, "Oh, my god. This is amazing! You have a hundred-and-eighty-degree view of the bay."

The barbeque was in the left corner, and he set the steak down on the metal area beside the grill. He placed the salad on the round table that was in the middle of the roof deck. There were four chairs around the table, and the whole set was white metal. There were two lounge chairs closer to the wall by the right corner with a small round table between them. He'd hung some plants off the back fence that separated his section from his neighbor's.

Andrea leaned against the wall. "This is just beautiful. I can't get over it."

Elias didn't respond. He was having a hard time reminding himself that this wasn't real. Andrea wasn't his girlfriend. This wasn't their life. It all just seemed so easy, so much so that he could almost forget the past. Pretend it didn't happen. Life would be good.

But it had happened.

Andrea turned toward him and caught his eye. He took a deep breath and braced himself for whatever was about to come.

"We never talked about the past. You never gave me a chance to explain. You left without a word." Her eyes were accusing.

He started scraping the grill. "I..." He found himself at a

loss for words. He cleared his throat. *God, I don't want to get into this now.* It would play with his head, and he needed a clear mind when he met with Santiago. "Now isn't really the time."

"When is the time? You wouldn't hear me out then, and you won't hear my side now. So, when am I allowed to speak?"

Her anger smacked him like a rogue wave. He didn't blame her. She was right; he hadn't let her explain anything. What could she possibly say that would make a difference? Mattie would still be dead. She'd known beforehand and could have warned Mattie, but she chose not to.

"Andrea, I can't do this now." He decided to be honest with her. "I need a clear head to deal with Santiago. If we start talking now, I'll be…all worked up. Unable to focus. People die when they're distracted. I know I owe you a chance to explain, and you can have it once this mess is over." He was doing his level best to be logical and calm, but anger he'd held onto for years started to bubble in his blood. He didn't want to hear her excuses. There was no excuse. Mattie died. She could have stopped it.

It was his turn to take a deep breath. The moment had shattered, and the ease and comfort he'd found in her company was gone. Now, he just wanted to eat the steak and be done. He finished cleaning the grill and turned on the flames. He gave it a couple of minutes to heat up and then put the steaks on. He watched out of the corner of his eye as she refilled her wine glass. Maybe the wine wasn't such a good idea.

"How's your mom?" she asked.

"Fine." One more thing he didn't want to unpack with her was his family. All roads led to Mattie. She looked over at him with a hurt expression on her face. She was trying to be civil, and he was being an asshole.

The thing was, he didn't feel like being civil. He glanced out at the bay and tried to let the view soothe him. "Why the ATF?"

The metal legs of a chair screeched on the roof deck as she pulled it out and then sat down at the round table. "When you left, I decided I needed a change, too. I had a distant cousin out in L.A., so I made my way out there. It was immediately apparent that I needed a job, but more than that, a career. I had most of my criminology degree finished already, so I took a couple more classes while I worked as a waitress. Once I graduated, I applied to all the law enforcement agencies. The ATF were the first to respond."

"What happened to being a lawyer?" he asked as he flipped the steaks.

"Mattie and Carmen died. That changed everything. I wanted to get Santiago even back then. It just took a while."

He turned to face her. He was surprised. Shocked would have been a better word. Was she spinning some line to lull him into a false sense of camaraderie?

"You want to avenge Mattie's death?" He couldn't make that scenario work. She was the one who could have stopped it in the first place.

"Carmen's." She hesitated. "Santiago was supplying her with drugs."

That made more sense. He flipped the steaks one more time and then plated them and brought them over to the table. He handed one to her. "Here you go."

She took the plate and smiled. "Smells good." She put it down and then took up some salad. She also refilled her wine glass.

He was tempted to say something, but what was the point? It was none of his business. He got some salad and started eating. They ate in silence until Andrea finally popped the last bite in her mouth and put down her knife and fork.

"That was delicious. I hadn't realized how much I missed a good barbequed steak."

He nodded as he chewed his last bite. He glanced over the wall to the west. The sun was setting. The sky had turned pink and purple. In a few minutes, it would be dark up here. He liked to sit here at night by himself and decompress. He glanced across the table at Andrea. Their gazes locked.

"Elias," she said, barely above a whisper.

He felt a familiar tug in his groin. The last rays of sunlight glinted off her dark hair, making it glow. Her green eyes seemed to be lit from within. Damn, she was gorgeous. He had a strong urge to kiss her. Being with her up here was just like those nights at the beach. He wanted her now just as much as he had then.

"Andrea," he growled.

She bit her lip. Then she stood up, never breaking eye contact with him. She moved around the table until she was standing beside him.

He turned in his seat to face her. "This is a bad idea."

"Yes, it is. A very bad idea."

"Please walk away." He was having a hard time concentrating. She flicked her hair over her shoulders, and he caught a glimpse of her neck. He remembered what it felt like to kiss the hollow at the base of her throat. She used to make this sound…a soft groan that drove him wild. He gritted his teeth. "Andrea, you need to go downstairs. Now."

"Hmmm," she said, "you're probably right. I will probably regret this, but at this moment, I don't care. I want you, Elias. I want to feel you inside me. Just like at the beach."

"Jesus. Andrea, this is just—"

"Stupid? Yeah, it is, but it doesn't change the fact that I want you and I know you want me." She glanced down at his crotch where he was obviously hard.

"Andrea, we can't go back. This is—" He stopped speaking. Why the hell was he trying to talk her out of the thing he wanted so badly it hurt?

She moved forward and captured his mouth with hers, their tongues dancing the way they had all those years ago. It felt so fucking good. She started to climb into his lap, but he stopped her and broke off the kiss. "Are you sure you want to do this?" His voice came out as a croak.

"Oh, fuck yeah."

He bent down and picked her up. She wrapped her legs around his waist, and he cupped her ass. He carried her over to one of the loungers and set her down. He pulled off his T-shirt while she started rubbing his cock through his jeans. He reached down and pulled her tank top over her head. He groaned out loud when he saw her black lace bra. She needed to stop rubbing him, or this wouldn't take long.

And she did. She stopped and laid back on the lounger. "Fuck me, Elias," she whispered. "I'm ready for you."

In an instant, Elias bent down and grabbed the ends of her jeans. He pulled them off her and dropped them onto the deck. She was wearing a black lace thong. He was so hard he was in pain. He pulled off his jeans and dropped them beside her shirt. Then he lowered himself down on top of her and captured her mouth. His kiss was punishing, and she responded in kind.

She reached for his cock again, but he grabbed her wrist and brought her arm above her head. He brought the other one up and held them with one hand while he captured her lips in a scorching kiss. She tasted like fine wine and sweetness. God, he'd missed her. She felt so damn good.

He kissed her neck and then kissed his way down to her nipple. He was hard as rock with her pressed against him again. Touching and tasting her was better than he remembered. He undid her bra and pushed it out of the way. He sucked her nipple and she arched under him.

"Elias," she breathed, "I want to touch you."

"Not yet." He moved to nip her other nipple. Then he swirled his tongue over it. Her hips rocked under him. He let go of her wrists as he kissed and licked his way down her belly to the apex between her legs. As he pulled her thong down, she lifted her hips to help him. He dropped it with the other clothing.

"Fuck, you're beautiful," he ground out before dropping his mouth to her hot center.

She fisted his hair, and he wasted no time. He licked and sucked her. She moaned. He dipped his fingers inside her. First one, then two. He glanced up to see her. She was bucking beneath him, her head thrown back in abandon. He smiled. He could always make her come. He moved his fingers at an increasing rate while he continued to drive her crazy with his tongue.

Andrea bit her lip. "More," she whimpered as she thrust her hips to his rhythm. He added a finger and increased his speed. Within seconds, she bucked her hips hard once and let out a strangled sound. She called out his name as she came.

CHAPTER EIGHTEEN

Andy opened her eyes as he stood up. She reached for him and pulled his cock free of his underwear. She ran her tongue down the length of it. A low, guttural groan erupted from him when she closed her mouth around his girth and swirled her tongue again and again.

"You need to stop." His voice was ragged.

She stood up. "Your turn."

He turned and sat down on the lounger. He cupped her ass and brought her to his mouth again. She sunk her fingers into his hair. He'd always been good. The sex between them was the best she'd ever had, even back then, but this, this was fucking amazing.

She moaned and then pulled back from him. "No, I want to taste you."

She pushed him, and he laid back on the lounger. She kissed his chest and sucked his nipple. Then she moved lower and took him in her mouth again. She moved in and out slowly. He grabbed her head and groaned, and his hips started to jerk upward.

She stopped sucking and sat up. Then she lowered herself

on top of him. Just taking the tip of his cock in first, but then bringing all of him inside her. It felt so fucking good. Elias always filled her up in exactly the right way. She threw her head back and looked up at the stars as she moved her hips against his. Pure fucking heaven.

Elias sat up and captured her mouth. He moved in long strokes, building the tension inside of her. God, this felt so right.

"Faster," she breathed.

He wrapped his arms around her and turned her, so she was on the bottom now and he was above her. He entered her slowly again, but she reached back and cupped his ass, pulling him in deeper. "Fuck me harder, Elias."

He let out a soft curse and then pulled out and entered her again. Faster and faster. Within seconds, he was slamming into her, and she reveled in it. She needed this. The fear and the anger of the last few months was always hanging over her. She needed a release. Elias bit her neck and sunk one hand into her hair as he thrust deep inside her. She couldn't breathe, couldn't think. It was pure animal lust, and it was fucking amazing.

"Elias," she growled as she came a second time. He buried himself to the hilt and pulled her head back as he came inside her.

Her bones had turned to liquid. "That was...incredible. Even better than it used to be," she said as she lay naked on the lounger.

Elias had already risen and was now pulling on his clothes. He wasn't making eye contact. Always a bad sign with him. He was having regrets. Well, too bad for him. She wasn't. She hadn't had great sex like that in a long time. Sure, it was stupid to screw her ex. But the fuck had been amazing, and after all she'd been through, she just needed a release. A few minutes of pleasure that gave her respite from the stress and fear.

Elias walked over and started cleaning up the plates, because of course he did. Why bother talking to her? She sighed and stood up. The hell with being embarrassed. She'd just fucked his brains out, and she was fine with that. She gathered her clothing and went downstairs, still naked. He could do all the dishes he wanted. She was taking a shower.

She dropped the clothes on top of her suitcase and went to the bathroom. She grabbed a towel from the real linen closet, which was in the bathroom, and got under the hot spray. Too bad he was such a spoilsport. She could have gone for round two. Possibly three.

She washed and conditioned her hair and then lathered the soap so she could wash her body. She thought briefly about what would happen tonight with Santiago, but she couldn't guess what was going on.

She caught herself fantasizing about a future with Elias, and her heart immediately sank. An hour ago, she'd been all like "fuck him." She wanted her say, and then one too many glasses of wine and she literally did fuck him. Now she was all confused. She was supposed to hate him for deserting her, but instead she was wondering how she was going to get him into bed again. Shit. She needed to arrest Santiago and get the hell out of Miami.

This place was bad for her. She seemed to be washing her bravado off along with all the dirt. It was going down the drain. She closed her eyes and let the water rain over her. She'd been under a lot of stress for the past few months. That's why she overdid it and screwed Elias. Well, that was the story she was going with if it ever came up between them. The truth was so much more complicated and down-right scary to even contemplate.

She got out of the shower and toweled herself off. She

then opened the bathroom door and went down to the bedroom. As she was closing the door, she heard voices. Elias's team was here again. She glanced at the clock. He had hours yet. Why were they here now?

A small ball of worry started in the pit of her stomach. She quickly grabbed a pair of jeans and a navy tank top out of her suitcase and pulled them on. She towel-dried her hair and brushed it out, then tied it in a bun at the back of her neck.

She braced herself and opened the door. All the conversation in the other room stopped as she walked down the hallway. Nick, Finn, and Elias stared at her. The small knot of worry grew into a large fist-sized rock of fear.

"What?" she asked. "What is it?" She stopped at the island and put on hand on it to steady herself. "What's wrong?"

Nick glanced at Elias and then back at her. "Why don't you come sit down?" He indicated the chair to the left of the sofa. He was in the opposite chair, and the other two were on the sofa.

"Just tell me." She sent up a silent prayer that nothing had happened to her aunt. She talked a good game about willing to risk everything to get Santiago, but when push came to shove, she really didn't want to lose the only family she had.

"I just got word from our Admiral Bertrand, who was contacted by the ATF. Your boss, Derek Robins, was found dead this afternoon in Miami Beach." Nick's voice was soft, almost painfully gentle.

Andrea blinked and frowned. "What? No. I just spoke to him a couple of hours ago. He was fine."

"Someone grabbed him and tortured him. Then they shot him in the back of the head."

"Why? Why would they do that?" She shook her head

and then sat down on a stool by the island. "I don't get it. Why would Santiago kill Robins? Wouldn't he come kill me first?"

Her head was spinning. Robins dead. Derek, her former lover, was dead. She was numb. She didn't feel anything.

"Andrea."

She looked up, and Elias was standing in front of her, a mug of tea in his hand. He gave it to her, and she took a sip. Hot and sweet with a touch of milk. Just how she liked it. How could he remember things like that and not care about her?

Jesus. She needed to get a grip on herself before she completely unraveled. She slid onto one of the stools at the island. "Sorry." She shook her head again. "It's just such a shock. I can't seem to get my brain around it."

"We know," Nick agreed. "It doesn't make sense. There's no way Robins should have been in danger. At least not from this op."

"It had to be Santiago, though, doesn't it?"

"Does it?" Elias asked. "Like Nick said, there's no reason why Robins should have been in danger from Santiago. Santiago shouldn't even know he exists. So, unless he has a mole in the ATF, Robins was killed by someone else."

She stared at Elias. Was he accusing her of being a mole for Santiago? He was out of his fucking mind. Clearly. "Are you asking me if I did this?" She fisted her hands as her heart thudded against her ribcage.

"Did you?" Elias asked.

It was a sucker punch to the stomach. She was tempted to throw the tea mug at his head. How could he believe that of her? They'd just had sex. How could he think she'd stoop that low? Obviously, he did not have a very good opinion of her. He still thought she'd had a choice not to tell him that Santiago was going after Mateo. If he'd have listened to her side of the story earlier, things would be different now.

"No, I most certainly am not a fucking spy for Santiago," she said through clenched teeth.

Fuck Elias. He was going to listen now because she was going to tell everyone what happened. To hell with him needing a clear head.

She turned and looked at Nick and Finn. "My sister, Carmen, had the misfortune of being beautiful. Santiago liked beautiful things. Still does. He chased my sister for months. She turned him down again and again until one day at a party he introduced her to cocaine.

"My mother was an addict, so it was almost as if Carmen didn't have a chance. She was hooked immediately. She dated Santiago because he was always there to get her high. He kept her supplied with anything she wanted, and she went everywhere with him and did whatever he told her."

She took a sip of tea. "After a while, though, Santiago grew tired of her. The drugs were taking their toll. She was no longer this bright, pretty young thing. He dumped her. She cried and wailed and begged him to take her back for weeks. I tried to get her to go to rehab, but she wasn't interested. You can't force an addict into rehab. It won't work, or so the doctors told me."

She swallowed. This was the hard bit. Her stomach knotted. "We—Elias, Mattie, and I—were all hanging out all the time at that point. Carmen was running all over Miami, trying to score and doing God knows what to make it happen. Santiago knew it. He knew he could get her to do whatever he wanted as long as he gave her the next fix.

"One day, I showed up at Carmen's place, and she was a mess. She was stoned out of her mind. She told me that Santiago was skimming from the Street Aces. He was banking the money so he could take over the gang. He kept the money at her place in a safe. He was no fool. He knew she wouldn't be able to break into the safe, but he also knew the money being kept there would keep her in line. After all, that's where her next fix would come from."

She licked her lips and took another sip of tea to try to get dissolve the lump that was building in her throat. "I didn't realize Mattie knew about the skimming until he mentioned it a day or so before he died. He said he thought Santiago was stealing, and he was going to go to the head of the gang and tell him. Unfortunately, Carmen was there with us that night. She went back and told Santiago, even though I begged her not to. She even told Santiago that I knew, too."

She swung her gaze to Elias. She needed him to hear this. The truth of what happened. "I went over to Carmen's later that night to plead with her to leave and go to rehab, but Santiago was there. Carmen was already stoned, completely out of it. She was shooting up by this point. Santiago had one of his minions hold me down while he prepared a shot of heroin. He went over to my sister and stuck the needle in her arm. He told me if I said one word to you or Mattie about what he was doing, he would kill Carmen. Then he came over and stuck the same needle in my arm and said that I would be next."

In the blink of an eye, it was like she was back there again, staring in horror at the hypodermic plunged into her arm, the terror she'd lived through that night as real now as it had been then. Heart thudding, she gulped more tea and tried to calm her breathing. Elias's expression had gone flat. No reaction whatsoever. She'd always thought if he knew the truth, he'd forgive her and understand why she did what she did. Maybe she was wrong.

She met his gaze again. "I couldn't tell you or he'd kill me and my sister. In the end, you hounded me until I broke, but it was too late. Mattie was dead. Santiago made good on his promise. My sister died that night, too. An overdose. Santiago came to me a couple of days after Mattie's funeral, after you were gone, and said the only reason I was alive was because he'd killed Mattie and you'd left. There was no longer any threat. If you'd gone after him, he would have killed me, too."

Elias's face looked like it was chiseled out of granite. Well, she'd had to live with the truth for years. Now it was his turn. She looked back at Nick and Finn. "So, you see, there is no way in hell I would ever do anything to help Santiago. I would die first."

Nick stood up and came over to her. He touched her arm. "I'm sorry you had to go through that, but I'm glad you're okay."

His definition of okay was probably very different from hers, but she appreciated the gesture. She glanced at Elias, but he remained where he was, and his expression hadn't changed. What did she think would happen? That he would fall on his knees and beg forgiveness? No. But some reaction would have been nice.

Finn also came over and squeezed Andy's arm on the way by. He went to lean on the counter next to Nick. "The thing is, whoever killed Robins is still out there. If it was Santiago or one of his minions, then chances are good he's going to kill you two tonight."

"I guess," Andy mumbled, "but it still doesn't make sense to me. Santiago finds out I'm ATF and assumes Elias is with me and goes and kills my boss but then decides to wait until tonight to kill me and Elias. He's not exactly a patient man. Why the wait? Why the subterfuge? Why not just drive over here and kill us now?"

Nick opened the fridge and pulled out a bottle of water. He held it up, but everyone else shook their head. "From what you've said, Santiago is the type of guy that likes to inflict pain and play games. Maybe this is just another one of his games."

She cocked her head. It was a possibility, she supposed, but it just didn't sit right with her. She glanced over at Elias, but he was still a blank slate. "So, what does this mean for tonight?"

"It means," Finn said, "that Axe and I will stay with you here and Nick and Cain will follow Elias. Axe is on his way over now."

Andy shifted on her seat, trying to get more comfortable. "No offense, but do you think the three of us will be able to handle Santiago's hit squad? He's not the type to send just one guy when putting on a show of force."

"I think we'll be fine." Finn glanced at Nick, who gave a slight nod. "We discussed moving you, but as we're still not sure it was Santiago who killed Robins, it seemed premature. We don't want to blow the op. That said if you'd be more comfortable somewhere else, we can move you."

She shook her head. "No, I agree. If there's a chance to keep this in play let's do it. I do think that Robins' death has something to do with this case, though. He wasn't working on anything else."

Nick shook his head. "But he didn't know anything."

"Maybe that's what got him killed." Elias finally spoke, but his voice was like gravel.

"What do you mean?" Andy asked.

Elias shifted his weight so he was leaning on the counter in front of the sink, facing everyone else. "Maybe someone thought he knew more about the op than he did. You said he was tortured, right, Nick? So, what if he was tortured to find out details, and he had none to give, so they killed him."

"But who, though? Who besides Santiago would be interested in what's going on?" Andy asked.

"The sellers," Elias said. "If they've gotten wind of the investigation, they'd want to know what's going on."

Nick nodded. "Fair point. They would. You think the Russians have some men on the ground here and they somehow found out about the investigation?"

"I think it's a possibility. We have to look at this from every angle. Either way, it certainly seems like it puts a big target on our heads."

"That's what I'm afraid of." Nick sighed. "I would prefer it if there was a way we could wire you up tonight so we knew exactly what was going on at all times, and can jump in if you need help. As it is, we're flying blind."

Andy shook her head. "Santiago will check him for bugs so unless you have the top-level shit—you know, the stuff the CIA has—it won't work because he's got top-of-the-line detection equipment. The best you can do is be close by with a line of sight and have a signal."

"It'll be fine. I'll scratch my nose if I get into trouble. You can track me so you should be able to get close enough to see what's going on." Elias glanced at his watch. "I've got to get ready." He walked out of the kitchen area and down the hallway. He entered the bedroom and closed the door. Finn and Nick exchanged a look.

What did that mean?

Nick focused on her. "How's his leg?"

"Um, his leg?"

Nick's eyes narrowed. "Yes, his leg. Was he limping earlier? Did he mention his leg was hurting? He always tries to hide it."

"Um, I didn't notice." She willed the heat to stay out of her face. She hadn't thought at all about Elias's leg when they were having sex on the rooftop. It must have been hurting him, but she'd had no clue. And it had gotten darker once the sun had set. She didn't see any sign of an injury.

"Okay." Finn straightened. "We need to set up for tonight. I want to get a look at the camera feeds for the front and back of the building."

"He's got them going to the TV as well as his laptop," Nick supplied. Finn nodded and headed for the sofa. Nick got on his cell phone and started talking to the other members of the team.

Andy stayed on her stool. So many thoughts whirled around in her head. Robins was dead. It was so surreal. Derek was a self-important asshole, but she didn't want him dead, and certainly not tortured. A wave of guilt washed over her. Derek was her former lover, and yet she just couldn't seem to well up any real emotion about his death. It was sad and senseless, but it was like he was a stranger. She wanted to chalk up her lack of feeling toward him to the fact that she was in a very stressful set of circumstances, but she knew that wasn't the truth. No, the truth was she just didn't like him all that much.

CHAPTER NINETEEN

E lias sat on his bed staring at the wall. He couldn't get his brain to slow down and focus on one thing. Robins was dead. Did that mean Santiago was coming to kill him?

Maybe.

Maybe not.

He tried to focus on that because the truth was, what Andrea had said out there had turned his world upside down.

He'd stopped breathing when she'd told him Santiago had threatened to kill her. He did not take another breath for minutes on end. His lungs just froze. He was surprised he wasn't passing out. He figured it was because of all his training. He could hold his breath for a long time.

Then when she said that Santiago had killed her sister and the only thing that saved her life was Mattie's death, he'd just shut down. His brain went into overload and all his senses collided. He had no idea what was said for quite a while after that. As if he was a robot, he shut off like someone had hit the kill-switch. That's what had happened when Mattie died, too. He shut down, and then he filled with rage.

He thought he'd put it all behind him, but hearing her story, he now remembered in technicolored detail the horrible things he'd screamed at Andrea. Blaming her for the death of his best friend. Calling her a traitorous whore. He'd gone over the edge. Even now, he could feel the echo of that rage, the all-consuming nature of it.

The truth, the one he'd never admitted to anyone or even contemplated saying out loud, was that he was scared of himself. He knew he was beyond control, and if he didn't get out of Miami immediately, he was going to kill someone, or himself. He couldn't breathe any longer. It was as if someone put something heavy on his chest and he just couldn't get his lungs to inflate anymore. That was always his body's reaction when anything traumatic happened. He stopped being able to breathe.

He'd only signed up with the Coast Guard because the recruiter promised him that he could get him in immediately. They had a few slots in the class that was starting the next week because of some car accident. He'd left right after Mattie's funeral, making his way up to Connecticut where he spent the next weeks working as hard as he could, both physically and mentally, to put everything behind him. He spent a handful of years that way. It was how he had made it on to the Maritime Security Response Team. And that team had saved his life in more ways than one.

It was the first time he could get his brain to focus on something other than Mattie. He would go weeks, and finally months, without thinking about his friend and how he'd failed to save him. His career was the thing that had pulled him through.

Now, he was in danger of jeopardizing that because he couldn't get his shit together. He could not go out that door tonight if he couldn't focus and calm down. Before, he wanted to take Santiago down. Now he actually wanted to kill the other man in cold blood. He killed Mattie and Carmen. Worst still, he threatened to kill Andrea and made Elias believe she'd betrayed him. He lost not only his best friend, but also the love of his life.

Andrea. God, he owed her an apology.

He owed her so much more than that. He should have known she wouldn't just turn her back on him. He should have stopped and listened to her. Shoulda, coulda, woulda, what if—it was all in the past, and there was no going back. He'd been an asshole. No, he'd been the worst kind of asshole to her.

And yet she'd had sex with him earlier. Why? Was she crazy? Did she want to hurt him back somehow? Maybe it was just lust 'cause, God knew, he'd felt that and then some. Andrea was as beautiful now as she was then. More so. It had felt so good to have her back in his arms. To bury himself deep inside her. It had been like finding heaven and coming home all wrapped into one.

He'd had to get up and move away from her or he would have spent the rest of the night having his way with her. She had always been his drug of choice, and no amount of time would change that.

Now, though, now he needed to make amends to her somehow. Fix the horrible mistake he made all those years ago. He had no idea how to do that, but at the very least, he could take Santiago out of the picture. It was no longer just about Mattie anymore; it was about justice for Carmen, and for Andrea.

Elias rubbed his face with both hands and then stood up. He winced as he leaned on his leg the wrong way. The sex earlier had been outstanding, but it had taken a toll on his leg. Now he was going to have to put up with the pain and not let it stop him. He grabbed the ibuprofen bottle off his nightstand and popped a couple. That would take the edge off at least. He'd refused pain killers when he was shot and at every doctor's visit since. He'd grown up seeing what drugs had done to people. He had no interest in becoming a statistic.

He went out of his bedroom and down the hall to the bathroom. He closed the door and turned on the shower. He'd stand under the hot spray and see if he could loosen up his leg a bit. He needed to be in top form tonight. If Santiago wanted to kill him, then he welcomed the challenge. He wasn't backing down.

Twenty minutes later, he was back in his room, pulling on a pair of jeans and a lightweight black sweater. He put a gun in his ankle holster and tucked another one in the small of his back. He went back out into the main room. "Are we good?" he asked.

Finn looked at him and gave him a thumbs up. "You did a nice job on the security system here. The cameras are good quality. Nice sharp video."

"Yeah, front, back, and the side alley. Part of my rental agreement." He grinned.

"Yeah, I saw that. Excellent. We'll be ready when Santiago's guys show up."

Elias turned to Nick. "Is Axe here?"

Nick nodded. "He's lurking on the street, keeping an eye out."

"Cain?"

"He's already set up in his truck to follow you. We're all set. What about you?"

"I'm good." And he was shocked to realize he actually was okay. He knew what he had to do, and he was going to do it. He was always better with a goal, and tonight that goal was to kill Santiago before Elias got killed. He was ready.

He glanced at Andrea where she sat in the chair by the TV. She had her back to him. He wanted to say something to her, but now wasn't the time. He'd do it later. He'd grovel if he had to so she would listen to him.

Elias's phone buzzed. "Looks like it's show time. Santiago just texted. He says he's pulling up down front."

"You good?" Nick asked.

Elias nodded. "I'm good."

"Okay then. You have your tracker?"

"Yeah. Finn hooked me up earlier. Put a tracker on my keychain. It looks like an apple and says I heart NYC so I'm good to go."

"Good luck." Nick said.

"Thanks."

"Yeah, good luck, Elias, man. Watch your six," Finn called from the couch.

Andrea turned around and met his gaze. "Good luck, Elias." She turned back around without waiting for a response.

He walked out of the loft, and a minute later he was on the sidewalk. Santiago lowered the window of his black Escalade as Elias approached the car. The passenger side door opened, and Peter got out.

"Santiago. Peter."

"Elias. Peter here is going to go upstairs and stay with Andrea until we get back." He gave a cold smile. "My insurance policy."

"No." It was out of his mouth before he knew it.

Santiago's face darkened. "I think you're forgetting. I own you. You do as I say. You don't question me."

"No. If you want Andrea as an insurance policy, then she needs to come with us. I'm not leaving her here with Peter." Elias kept his face neutral, literally using his poker face. It wasn't that Finn and Nick couldn't get out of the apartment fast, but if Peter stayed and he ended up taking down Santiago tonight, Peter could kill Andrea before anyone was close enough to stop him. He couldn't have that. Andrea was safer if she was with him. At least then he could protect her. His team would help protect them both. She had better odds if she were with him than alone in the apartment with Peter.

"Fine. That works, too. Peter, go get her."

Elias shook his head. "Don't bother. I'll text her." He shot off a text, and two minutes later, Andrea was standing next to him on the sidewalk.

"Where are we going?" she asked as she grabbed his hand.

He squeezed her hand and smiled slightly. "We'll soon find out." Peter patted them both down, confiscating Elias's two guns. It amazed him that Peter and Santiago didn't care about anyone watching but he guessed that was what it was like if you were the drug and gun kingpin of Miami. Who was going to argue? Certainly not the old folks that lived in his building. He was sure Mrs. Jimenez would have something to say to him later.

Santiago moved over, and Andrea and Elias got into the back of the SUV.

"Where are we headed?" Elias asked. He wasn't thrilled that Andrea was between him and Santiago but being in the middle had its disadvantages as well.

"Patience, Elias." Santiago took out his phone and started sending emails. He seemed somewhat preoccupied.

Elias glanced at Andrea, and she frowned at him. She'd caught it to. It wasn't so much what Santiago was saying, but what he wasn't. That is, he wasn't saying anything at all. Santiago was not a guy to sit in silence. He liked to talk, and he wanted people to listen. Even more, he liked to lord his importance over people. By rights, he should have been needling both Elias and Andrea, but he was sitting in stony silence, sending out emails and texts.

It was weird. The whole situation felt off.

Elias glanced at the driver and determined that he was one of the guards that had been watching over the garden area when Elias had emerged from the bushes. Peter was sitting directly in front of him so he couldn't see the man's face. Neither guy was going to give anything away. The driver kept running a hand over his hair. He wasn't straightening it. It was a nervous tick.

That was the issue. There was a nervous energy in the SUV, and nervousness was not something he'd ever equated with Santiago. So, what was he nervous about?

An hour later, they were well into the Everglades. They'd taken Alligator Alley, and then about five minutes ago, they pulled off onto a small side road. Elias did not like how things were looking. This was a great place to dump a body or two. He took Andrea's hand and squeezed it. She squeezed back. She had to be thinking the same thing.

"Santiago, you want to tell me what's going on? I thought you said you wanted me to do the exchanges. The ocean is in the opposite direction."

Santiago finished typing a text and hit send. "I said you needed to take care of exchanges. I didn't say they would all be on the water. That was the buy. This is the sell. Only these people are not going to be happy that there are no RPGs. I need you here to explain what happened and to take care of anyone who gets…too excited."

Elias locked gazes with Andrea. The picture snapped into sharp focus now. Santiago was the middleman, and he was nervous about his buyers. This just got a whole lot more interesting.

The SUV rolled to a stop in a small clearing. There were two vehicles already there, a white Transit van and a black Ford pickup. The van had Colorado plates and the pickup had Oregon plates. Two groups, or more likely, two chapters of the same group.

The doors of the vehicles opened, and four men got out. Each one had on jeans and a camouflage bulletproof vest. There was one guy with a black hat on backward. They were all carrying handguns. Definitely some sort of fringe group. Elias heard his mother's voice in his head. *It takes all kinds.*

Santiago nodded at Peter who'd been watching him. Peter and the nervous driver got out of the truck. Peter was empty-handed, but the driver had a semi-automatic. He wasn't playing around.

"Which one of you is Santiago?" the guy with the hat yelled.

Peter ignored the question. "Gentleman," he said, "I'm going to need you to put down your weapons."

"No fuckin' way," the biggest guy snarled and spit toward Peter as if to emphasize his point.

Santiago must have rehearsed the scenario with Peter beforehand because Peter didn't seem like he was super bright, but his next words were smart. "I understand your hesitation, but you all have guns, and we have guns. If somebody sneezes the wrong way, we're all dead. How about if one of you keeps your rifle so you all are still protected but there's less chance of things going badly. We'll do the same. Sound good?"

The men glanced at the guy in the hat, and he nodded. "Rupert, keep yours." The big guy who snarled earlier nodded and spit again. "So, are you Santiago?" asked the guy in the hat.

Santiago handed Elias his Glock back. "If you so much as think about pointing that at me, she will die an agonizing death. Get out," Santiago said as he opened his door.

Elias tucked the gun in his waistband and opened his door but whispered to Andrea, "Stay in here and keep low just in case."

"Yes," she said in a soft voice as he climbed out. Everyone left their doors open for a quick escape.

"I am Santiago," he said as he walked around to the front of the SUV. Elias hadn't noticed in the truck, but Santiago was wearing a loose black Henley and jeans. Not remotely his usual attire. He was trying to blend in more. Very interesting. Elias went and stood next to him.

"Where are my weapons?" the man in the hat asked.

"I have them. Where is the money?"

"I want to see the weapons first."

Santiago nodded at Peter, who then went to the back of the SUV and started pulling out the bags with the guns in them.

Elias tensed. The setup was all wrong. He was going to have to change all the rules if he had to be part of another exchange with Santiago. He needed to minimize the risk. They were sitting ducks out here as far as he could tell. He was damn glad the team were out there watching, otherwise he might actually be worried.

Peter put two of the bags on the ground in between the two groups of men, then went back to the SUV and returned with two more. The headlights of each vehicle lit them up. Hat man nodded at the shorter man on Rupert's left, and he went to the pickup and pulled out a backpack. He came around and put it on the ground next to the guns. Peter reached over, opened the backpack, and then nodded once at Santiago. The short guy opened the bags. "Looks good. Wait. Where's the RPG? You promised us you could get us an RPG?"

Santiago looked at Elias. *Great.* He was the sacrificial lamb. He cleared his throat. "At the bottom of the ocean. There was a mishap during the transfer, and it was lost over the side."

"No RPGs...no deal," snarled Hat Man.

Rupert raised his gun.

Elias raised his hands as if to calm the situation. "Obviously, we will deduct the price of the RPG and five percent more for your troubles."

Santiago glared at Elias before he said to Hat Man. "You will have your RPG. It will come in the next shipment. It's already been set up."

"You told us it would be here this time. Why should we believe you?" Rupert waved the barrel of the gun around.

Elias defended their story, "And we did have it for about two minutes until a major wave hit and knocked our guy and the RPG overboard. We managed to get our man back, but the hardware was gone. Do you know how hard it is to transfer stuff when the waves are high? We were all lucky to get back in one piece."

Santiago cut in. "We'll have a new one for you in the next shipment."

Hat Man asked, "When's that going to be?" He smacked his neck, killing a mosquito. "It's too damn hot and muggy down here. We don't want to hang around long."

"There's a shipment coming in a few days. You'll have the RPG by mid-next week at the latest," Santiago promised.

"What about the training? Is that still happening at the end of the month? Our boys need to be trained. We want to be prepared. We definitely need to be back for that."

Santiago grimaced. Elias was sure Santiago hadn't wanted Elias to know about that part of things.

"Yes," Santiago agreed, "the training is still on at the end of the month. As I said before, our man will contact you once he lands and is on his way. He will teach your people all you want to know about the equipment."

"The equipment?" Rupert said in an indignant voice. "We know how to use the equipment. We need to learn the warfare techniques. The special ops stuff."

"Rupert," Hat Man said, "shut up."

"He'll teach you that, too," Santiago agreed.

Hat Man narrowed his eyes but finally agreed. "Okay then. We'll wait, but no later than the middle of next week. You're damn lucky Gerald Finch and his boys say you're a good guy, otherwise…" He left the sentence unfinished. Elias assumed that was supposed to be some kind of threat.

"I appreciate that." Santiago nodded to Peter, who reached for the bag.

"Wait," Rupert barked. "We need some of the money back."

Peter reached in and grabbed one wad of bills and glanced back at Santiago. Santiago then held up two fingers. Peter dug in and pulled out a second wad.

"Make it three," Hat Man said, "for our troubles."

Santiago's nostrils flared, and his jaw was clenched so tight Elias could see the man's pulse in his temple, but he finally nodded. Peter pulled out the third bundle and handed it all to the stocky guy across from him. The guy took the money and handed it to Hat Man. Then he picked up two of the bags and headed for the van.

Peter grabbed the backpack and stood up. He walked back to the front passenger side of the SUV and got in.

"We'll be in touch," Santiago said.

"You'd better," Rupert responded.

Everyone got back in their respective vehicles, and five minutes later, they were on the way back to Miami.

Santiago was fuming. When he finally addressed Elias, there was acid in his voice, "You speak when I tell you and say what I tell you. You do not ever speak for me,"

Elias tried to remain calm, but it was hard after what he just witnessed. "You needed the deal to go through. They were getting cold feet. I made it happen. Five percent isn't much. I know your markup on the guns is steep. Plus, the whole training thing. You can't tell me you aren't getting paid something for that. You might not be doing the training, but I am sure you are making a profit off of it, otherwise, what's the point?"

Santiago started to speak, but his phone went off, and he answered it. From the side of the conversation Elias could hear, Santiago was trying to placate someone. Girlfriend maybe. Elias tuned the conversation out. It was far more important to figure out who those men were and where the hell they were going to use an RPG.

CHAPTER TWENTY

Santiago sat clicking on his phone beside her, and Andy did her best to keep distance between them. It was taking everything she had not to reach over and push him out of the car. They were almost back in the city now, which meant that Santiago wasn't likely to kill her and Elias.

That also meant he was not the one who killed Robins.

As they made a sharp turn, she held on to the inside of Elias's thigh to keep herself from brushing against Santiago. Elias glanced over at her but said nothing. He put his arm between her legs, moved her slightly closer to him, and held her in place. She swallowed.

Having his arm there reminded her of earlier on the rooftop. It had been wonderful, but now she wondered if it would ever happen again. Did she want it to? Yes and no. Actually, make that hell yes! And oh boy. If she were smart, she'd get as far away from him as possible once this was over. It was too easy to lose her heart to him. Honestly, she was never sure if she'd gotten it back. He'd been horrible to her, but that didn't mean she'd just stopped loving him. Maybe she never had.

She gave herself a mental shake. It was ridiculous to begin thinking that way here and now. Santiago swore beside her. She turned to see what had caused the outburst.

"Fuckin' asshole." He almost slammed his phone on the seat ahead of him but stopped himself in time.

Peter tossed a worried glance back at his boss, and the driver promptly looked in the rear-view mirror, but no one said a word.

She started to ask, "What the—?" but Elias squeezed her thigh, so she stayed quiet.

"We will go out to meet another shipment Saturday night. Be ready."

"We?" Elias asked. "You don't trust me now?"

"Shut the fuck up," Santiago snarled.

It was quiet for the next few minutes while they wound their way through the streets of Miami. She had so many questions but no answers. This was like one of those puzzles where she needed to find a certain piece to make all the other pieces fit and make sense. She just didn't have that piece yet.

They pulled up in front of Elias's building. "Saturday night. Be ready," Santiago instructed.

Peter turned in his seat. "Um, boss, there's a storm coming in Saturday night. It's looking like it might be ugly."

Santiago's face paled, and he almost smashed his phone again. "Fuck the weather. Saturday fucking night!" he yelled. "Drive!"

Elias opened the door and climbed out of the SUV, pulling her with him. As soon as her feet hit the sidewalk, the SUV took off. They didn't even have time to shut the door. It swung closed as they drove.

"Jesus Christ. What the hell is wrong with him?" Andy asked.

"Stress." Elias grabbed her hand and went over to the door. He let them in, and they went up the stairs to his apartment. He unlocked the door and ushered her in. Then he closed the door behind him.

Andy startled when she turned and saw his whole team was already in the apartment, staring at them. Wait. Not the whole team. Cain was missing. There was a knock at the door. Elias hauled it open again, and Cain walked in.

"Now that we're all here," Nick said as he opened the fridge, "you can tell us what the fuck happened out there?" Nick pulled out a bottle of water. "Anyone want one?"

"I want a beer," Elias said. He glanced at Andy, but she shook her head. She had a bit of a headache from the wine earlier. Plus, she decided alcohol and Elias were a dangerous mix. She crossed the room and took a seat on the chair to the left of the sofa and stared out at the view for a minute. She took several deep breaths to calm the nerves rioting in her gut.

Nick sat down in the middle of the sofa. Axe sat down on his left and Finn on his right. Cain started to take the chair opposite of Andy but changed his mind when Elias limped over. His leg was obviously bothering him.

"Thanks," Elias said as he sat down in the chair.

Cain sat down on the floor on the other side of the coffee table. He took a sip of his beer. "So, what happened at the exchange? We couldn't hear anything. The parabolic mic failed. We need a new one. We also need a better place to store our equipment."

Nick sighed but remained silent. Andy glanced at Elias, and their gazes locked for a second before he took a sip of his beer and then started. "So, it looks like Santiago is selling the guns to some sort of militia group. I'm assuming you got pictures."

"Yup." Finn nodded. "Already sent them along so they can run facial recognition on them at Homeland."

"They are anxious to get their hands on the RPG.

Santiago had to give them some cash back to cover the loss of it." He grinned. "I made him give up another five percent as a show of good faith."

Andy chuckled. "I thought Santiago was going to go apeshit when he realized he had to turn over the other wad of cash. Did my heart good to see him so pissed off."

Elias grinned at her, then sobered again. "Anyway, these guys got Santiago's name from another guy that goes by the name of Gerald Finch. The way the guy in the ball cap spoke about him, he must be someone important in that world."

"Gerald Finch is the leader of a militia group known as the Sons of Freedom," Axe said. "Heard about him when I was assigned to oversee part of the security for the Super Bowl a few years ago. He'd made some threats against the halftime show performers. His group is on every watch list there is. They are alt-right and extremely dangerous."

Brooding silence held a moment as Axe's info sank in.

"So, this guy Finch recommended Santiago to the men there tonight…" Nick contemplated. "That's not good."

"It gets worse," Elias continued. "Santiago isn't selling just guns and equipment. He's working as a go-between for the Russians to train these militia operators. Rupert, the one with the gun, said they knew how to use the equipment, but they wanted the special forces training that Santiago promised them."

Cain swore.

"Jesus," Nick said as he leaned back on the sofa. "Russians training far right militias on American soil. I can't get my brain around it."

Andy sat there silently. She'd had a bit more than an hour to get use to the idea, and she still couldn't fathom it. "It's a hard one to believe. How could we not know about this?" She cocked her head. "Or maybe someone does know about it. Do you think the CIA or the FBI know, and they're running some sort of operation?"

"If that's the case," Finn said, "then we'll hear about it pretty damn quick. The pictures I sent will send up every red flag there is, and the phone lines will be burning up. If Bertrand calls within the next couple of hours, we'll know what happened."

"You are not wrong," Axe agreed.

"On the other hand, what if they don't know?" Nick posited. "What if these unassuming Russians fly in under a false identity, or whatever, and then go train these men for a month or so and then fly out again?"

"Well, they can't fly in from Cuba," Andy reasoned.

"No, that's true," Nick agreed. "But they could easily fly into Paris or London on one passport and then wait a couple of days and fly out from another big city on a new passport. Claim they are Ukrainian or Polish or whatever. Considering what's going on in Ukraine, this could be state-sponsored."

Axe raised an eyebrow. "You think Putin put them up to it? Seriously?"

Nick shrugged. "I think there's a chance that this is a foreign government planned operation. Think about it. It's not like these militia groups can't buy guns and get ex-special forces guys to train them. Hell, most of these groups have ex spec-ops guys in them. So why go with the Russians? They wouldn't unless somebody somewhere, like this Finch guy who everyone looks up to, says it's a good idea."

"You think they paid Finch? Or worked their way into his good graces?" Andy asked.

Nick frowned. "I don't think it really matters. The long game is to have someone on the ground, influencing the group. Someone to whip them up into a frenzy until mob mentality takes over. Then they stop listening. And if it's happening on the right, then chances are good it's happening on the left. The Russians don't have to sell guns or train people; they just have to have an excuse to be here to sow the seeds of discontent. They did it online until we smartened up, and now they want to do it in person."

"Then everyone gets mad and stops listening to one another. We all take sides and—boom!—an event like January Sixth happens," Andy said.

"Yes," Nick agreed. "The truth has always been, and will always be: United we stand. Divided we fall. Who wants us to fall the most?"

"Russia and China," Finn murmurs.

"Jesus, that's just…frightening." Elias shook his head. "You're suggesting we're being seriously influenced by outside actors whose sole purpose is to bring down the United States."

Nick sighed. "I don't know about sole purpose, but it's certainly a goal. We have always been the nation that stands up for the little guy and keeps the power balanced in the world. If the US falls apart, it becomes a free-for-all for Russia and China."

"We are not equipped to deal with this type of thing," Finn stated. "I'm all for doing my bit, but that shit is just too far above my pay grade."

"Agreed." Nick emptied his beer bottle. "I'll call Bertrand and tell him what we've found and what we think is going on. He'll pass the rest of it on to whoever deals with this shit."

Elias took a slug of his beer. "So, what's our next step then?"

"We take down Santiago and stop the flow of the Russian guns into Miami, at least temporarily." Nick sighed.

Andy cleared her throat. "To that end, Elias has to go out with Santiago on Saturday night again for the next buy."

"What?" Nick looked over at Elias for confirmation.

"Yeah. Santiago got a text, and he went apeshit in the car. Almost destroyed his cell phone twice. He told me to be ready on Saturday night. He also said 'we' have to go out."

Cain cocked his head. "He's going? That's unusual, isn't it? Why the change?"

"It certainly wasn't his idea," Andy stated. "He was livid about it. If I had to guess, I would say the sellers are making him go."

"I agree." Elias shifted and rested his leg on the coffee table. "I'm guessing because of the fuck-ups of the last two drops and the loss of the RPG, they want him out there as a show of good faith or as a way to determine who is boss."

"How do you know the last two drops went wrong?" Nick asked.

"We know what happened during the last one." Elias nodded at Andy. "Santiago had said something about losing the person who was supposed to look after the exchange, and he wasn't talking about Soto. Soto was a stand-in for Waters is my guess, and Waters must have been a stand-in for the guy before that because this shit has been going on for a while."

Andy stifled a yawn. "So, you think they're holding his feet to the fire? They want to get everything back on track, so he needs to be there in person to make sure it goes off without a hitch."

"What's today? Thursday?" Finn asked.

Elias glanced at his watch. "Friday, actually."

"Well, we have less than forty-eight hours to figure out how to be at the exchange to provide backup without being seen."

"It's supposed to storm that night, too, according to Peter, one of Santiago's henchmen," Andy supplied.

"Well, that sucks." Axe sighed.

Nick leaned forward and put his beer bottle on the table.

"Don't sweat it yet, Axe. We'll figure it out." He yawned. "Maybe we should call it a night. We're all tired. God knows we could all use some serious sleep."

"Wait," Andy said. "Aren't you forgetting something?" The chatter stopped, and everyone looked over at her. She continued, "Santiago didn't kill us. And let me tell you, I was thinking it was over for us when we turned off Alligator Alley into the Everglades. But he didn't."

"I'm not understanding," Nick said.

"If we're not dead, then Santiago is not the one that killed Robins."

"Shit," Finn mumbled. "Where does that leave us?"

Nick shrugged. "Maybe his death is just a—"

"Coincidence?" Andy finished for him. "Do you really believe that?"

"No, I guess I don't, but at this point, we don't have anything else to go on. Let's table it and get some sleep. We'll start again in the morning."

Andy wanted to argue, but she was bushed. She couldn't hold back the yawn this time.

"I'll take that as a yes." Nick smiled as he stood up. All the guys followed suit. They headed toward the exit. Nick opened the door. "Make sure you keep your security system on. Call if you need anything."

"Will do," Elias said, and they all filed out.

Andy stood, too. "Do you think we'll be okay tonight? Should we sleep in shifts?"

He shook his head. "We're both exhausted. Santiago doesn't need anything from us tonight. I don't think he'll bother doing anything." He went over to the keypad and turned on the system. "I let Santiago's goons break-in to steal the gun on purpose. I didn't want them to hurt any of the other tenants, so I made it easy for them. But in reality, I have this place wired pretty intensely. We'll be fine."

She wanted to argue, but she was too damn tired.

"You take the bedroom, and I'll sleep out here."

This time she did argue. "Your leg is killing you. You need to be in a bed."

He shook his head. "I need to sleep on the couch. It means I can keep an eye on the security cameras." He pointed to the TV.

"But you need sleep, too."

"I'll sleep. Please, Andrea, go to bed."

She gave in mostly because her mind and her body were both pushed well beyond their limits. "Okay, Elias. See you in the morning." As she walked back toward the bedroom, she sent up a silent prayer that nothing would happen until morning. She honestly didn't think she'd be able to handle anything else.

CHAPTER TWENTY-ONE

Elias opened his eyes and yawned. He glanced at his watch, and then promptly raised his eyebrows. *Holy shit!* He'd managed a solid eight hours of sleep. It had been a while since that had happened. He glanced at the TV screen. The security feed was still on. Mr. Tanez was walking out of the building with Mrs. Jimenez nattering away beside him.

He rose from the couch and prioritized his first task as the coffee maker. He got it ready and then turned it on. He was in desperate need of some caffeine. He walked down the hall to the bathroom just as Andrea opened the door. She let out a small scream.

"Sorry. Sorry. I didn't realize you were in there." Elias backed up to let her out. She was wearing a towel, and her hair hung loose over her shoulders, dripping water down her back.

She had her hand pressed to the center of her chest, as if to calm her suddenly racing her heart. "No. It's my fault. Just a bit on edge." She gave him a quick smile as she brushed by him and went into his bedroom.

He watched her go. Her legs were amazing, and so was

the rest of her. He let out a sigh as he went into the bathroom and then closed the door. He turned on the spray and ended up having a quick, cold shower. He got out and toweled off. He wrapped the towel around his waist and ran his fingers through his hair to flatten it out.

He opened the bathroom door just as Andrea was walking by, and she let out another small scream. He grinned. "We have to stop meeting like this." He leaned on the door frame.

She laughed. "I don't know why I'm so jumpy."

"I can think of a few reasons. People threatening to kill you probably tops the list."

"Well, there's that." She chuckled. "I cannot wait for this to be over."

She stretched. Her red tank top pulled tight across her chest, and he just couldn't help but admire her breasts, remembering what it was like to have her. He straightened. More thoughts like that, and he'd be in trouble. The towel wasn't going to hide much.

"Excuse me," he said, "I need to go get dressed. There's coffee if you want some."

"Thanks." When she bustled off to the kitchen area, he went into the bedroom and pulled on jeans and a black T-shirt.

It was nice to hear Andrea laugh. Once this was over and they both could relax, maybe they could hit the beach one day. Rent Jet Skis or something. He stopped in the middle of pulling on his socks. What the hell was he thinking? She was being nice, but he'd been so awful to her that the moment this was over, she'd be gone. Why would she want to spend time with him? He'd abandoned her and never once gave her a chance to explain.

He let out a deep sigh and finished pulling on his socks. Then he stood up. It was time to face the music. He left the bedroom and entered the kitchen area. He poured himself a cup of coffee and then went over and sat down on the sofa. On his left, Andrea had sat in what he already thought of as her chair.

"The view here is really incredible. I can see why you like the place. The neighbors are quiet, too."

He smiled. "Yes, they aren't the partying sort, although Mrs. Jimenez does crank her TV up during Jeopardy. She says she can't hear the new host very well."

He looked over at Andrea and met her gaze. His heart hammered against his ribs. Sweat broke out on his palms. "Andrea," he started, "I owe you an apology. No. I owe you more than that. I owe you…" He didn't know what he owed her. It all seemed inadequate. "A lot," he finished lamely. "I should have taken the time to listen to you back then and trusted you more. We'd been together for four years at that point. I don't know why it never occurred to me that you must have had a reason for keeping Santiago's secret."

He frowned. He wasn't vocalizing what he really wanted to. He tried again. "I'm truly sorry I left you alone and hurting. I know how hard that must have been. I was alone and hurting, too, but it was easier for me because I buried myself in my new career right away. It was so damn exhausting there was no time to think. Anyway, I just should have been… more for you."

Andrea studied him. The weight of her stare felt like stones tied to his chest. Her face was impassive. Finally, she cleared her throat. "You are right. You do owe me an apology and more. A lot more. You were the only person I really felt I could trust at that point besides my aunt, and you turned on me so quickly it gave me whiplash. I had to mourn my sister on my own. It wasn't like the neighborhood cared. They all dismissed Carmen as another junkie with no hope. Even my Aunt Esther was like that.

"All my life I heard, 'Don't turn out like your mama and your sister.' Nobody even knew who my father was, so they didn't even bother to say anything about him. I was deemed a failure before I even got a start. You remember what people were like. But you, you were different. You never compared me to my sister or my mother. You only ever encouraged my dreams. I thought…" Her voice died out. Then she took a sip of coffee. "I thought we were invincible as a team, and we'd be together forever. And then one day it all turned to dust. You just flipped on me like everyone else in my life had. You said mean, cruel things, things that gave me nightmares for months, even years, afterwards."

Elias's gut rolled. He actually felt queasy. He closed his eyes. He remembered every word he'd uttered. It was like he was outside his body looking in when it happened. It was all still there. "I was just so…lost. I wanted to hurt you, punish you, for what happened because I couldn't punish myself enough. I was drowning in guilt. I thought what happened was my fault. I should have been able to stop Santiago. If I could take it back, I would. Every single word."

Her eyes were bright with unshed tears, and his heart cracked. He'd caused her so much pain. He needed to make her understand. "I… When I got there after you told me what was going on, I found Mattie on the ground, bleeding from his belly. I called nine-one-one, but even then, I knew he wasn't going to survive. I remember hauling him into my lap and hugging him." He swallowed hard. He'd never told anyone this next part.

"Mattie opened his eyes. He looked up at me and smiled. I told him the ambulance was on the way, but he kind of half-laughed. He said, 'It's too late for me bro.' I kept telling him to hold on, but he shook his head. He said, 'Elias, we almost made it, brother. Almost made it…to…the top.

You…can make it. You…go…and make…me proud. I'll…
be watching.' Then he died in my arms.

"I never heard the ambulance arrive; I don't remember
them taking me to the hospital. I was almost catatonic. I just
couldn't believe Mattie was dead. It was as if something
inside me shattered. I…couldn't get myself together at all. I
would try, but my thoughts just went everywhere or nowhere
at all. Mattie had been my rock for so long and, suddenly, I
was lost without him."

"You had me," Andrea said, her eyes sad.

He shook his head. "No. You see, it was knowing Mattie
was there that made me feel like I could support you. It was
Mattie's strength that I leaned on when I needed help. My
mama had too many other things going on, and so did you. I
never wanted to lean on you. You had so much to deal with I
never wanted to burden you. Mattie always had my back,
and suddenly that strength was gone."

He blinked and had to gulp some coffee to swallow the
golf-ball size lump in his throat. "Looking back now and
knowing a few things, I can tell you I had a breakdown of
sorts, an inability to pull myself together. The only thing that
helped me get my focus back was anger. I realized that anger
let me fix on something and, for a few seconds, I didn't hurt.
It was pure rage that got me through without totally losing
my mind."

He met her gaze once more. "And I took that rage out on
you. It was unfair and horrible, and if I could take back every
word I would but, Andrea, it was the only thing that kept me
going. I would have ended up in an asylum somewhere, or
dead." He paused for a breath. "There is no excuse for what I
put you through.

"When I left and went up to Connecticut, I used my
anger to drive myself. It propelled me forward every day and
in every way. I eventually learned how to harness that anger,

and it gave me a career, but it didn't give me Mattie back. It ended up costing me the one other thing in the world that I truly loved. You. I am so very sorry."

She looked down at her hands in her lap. "Elias. I appreciate your explanation and your apology but, honestly, it doesn't really change anything. You crushed my soul and I had to start again on the opposite side of the country to get over you. It took a long time, but I have finally made peace with what happened. You were right. I could have saved Mateo's life, but I chose to try and save my sister instead. I didn't succeed, and I've had to live with that guilt every day.

"But the truth is, coming back here has been both a nightmare and catharsis. I have faced my demons, including you. I can look you in the eye and know that I did the best I could in the circumstances, and that's all I can ask of myself. I can finally hold my head up high in the neighborhood— well, at least once this is all over—and tell people that I made it without help from anyone." She shook her head, as if in wonder. "I made it. I didn't end up like my mother and my sister.

"As soon as this assignment is over, I'm leaving Miami. As a matter of fact, I think I will probably even leave the ATF. There's a big world out there, and maybe it's time for me to explore it. So, thank you for helping me exorcise my demons. I think I am finally ready to move on."

Elias swallowed hard. It was like someone had gutted him with a knife. He finally knew the truth. His faith in the woman he'd loved so fiercely had not been wrong. He was just the asshole who had doubted her, and now it was costing him all over again years later because he knew deep down no matter what he'd said or done, he never really stopped loving her. He had known it the moment he sat in his truck and all thoughts turned to her. She wasn't interested in being with him, and who could blame her? There wasn't anything he could say or do to fix things. Andrea was ready to move on, and he would just have to learn to let go.

"I'm happy for you. I wish you much success." He held up his coffee cup, and she clinked hers with his. Elias then gulped his coffee to stop himself from saying something he might regret. Like…

Stay.

Elias's cell phone rang. He glanced at the screen and then answered the call. "Wild Bill," he said by way of greeting.

"Elias, my man. Another game tonight. It's a big one. Local boys. Lots of money. You want in?"

He glanced over at Andrea. The thought of spending another night locked in the apartment with her, without being able to touch her, seemed like hell. "I'm in."

"That's what I like to hear. Usual place, usual time. See you then."

Elias dropped his phone on the coffee table again and got up to get more coffee. "Do you want some more?" he asked as he raised the carafe.

She shook her head. "Who's Wild Bill?"

He let out a little chuckle. "He's just a guy who sets up poker games over in Miami Beach. I'm not even sure if Bill is his real name."

"Nothing at all shady about that," she snickered.

He poured his coffee and stayed over in the kitchen area, leaning on the island. "Not a thing." He grinned.

"So, you're going to play tonight?" she asked casually, but he could see concern on her face. Was she really concerned about him? *No. Stupid.* She was concerned about her own safety.

"I am. It helps me to concentrate and get myself together. My form of meditation. But don't worry. I will have one of the guys looking after you at all times."

"Oh, I'll be fine," she said, but a quick look of relief passed over her face.

"So, what would you like to do today?" He thought the best approach was to keep it light.

"Well, it's cloudy, and it doesn't look like it's going to burn off any time soon. Maybe we can stay in and hang out? Watch some TV. Play some games. That type of thing."

He gave her a brief smile. "Sounds good to me." It actually sounded like a living hell to him since he would be cooped up with her all day, but he wasn't going to tell her that. She did not need to know that he found it very difficult to be around her without touching her.

For the next several hours, they sat on the couch and played all the old classic board games. He'd borrowed them from Mr. Tanez who kept them for when his grandkids visited. Andrea won Monopoly. She was better at banking and real estate than he was. He won Risk because world domination was his thing. They each won a game of Yahtzee, and they finally packed it in when it became obvious that neither one of them were particularly good at Trivial Pursuit.

"I still think you should have given me that one," Andrea said and then fake-pouted.

Elias shook his head. "Alfred Nobel did not invent an electric drill."

"I thought you said power tool, not power*ful* tool. I made a guess. I was close."

He snorted. "You weren't even in the right century and an electric drill is not close to dynamite."

"Fine." She rolled her eyes. "If you're going to be picky about it." Then the two of them cracked up.

It felt so good to laugh. It had been a while since he'd had a good, proper, lighthearted laugh. "Are you hungry?"

"Always," she said emphatically.

That made him smile. "Pizza? Where's your friend with

the truck at this time of day?" He glanced at his watch. Just after six p.m.

"Miguel? Don't know. Let me text him." She got her phone off the coffee table, and her fingers flew across the screen. "The truck is parked, but he'll drop off a couple of pizzas if we want. We have to pay extra, though."

"Deal," Elias said. "His pizza is much better than the local place."

An hour later, they were sitting on the couch, eating pepperoni pizza, watching the first *Die Hard* movie. "It is *not* a Christmas movie," he said. "Christmas movies are ones like *White Christmas* and *Home Alone*."

"This is totally a Christmas movie. It takes place at Christmastime."

"Well, yeah, but it's an action movie. It's not a feel-good movie," he argued.

She shrugged. "I don't know about you, but I feel pretty freakin' good when Alan Rickman goes flying off the top of the Nakatomi Tower."

He snorted with laughter. "You got me there."

She grinned and winked at him then went back to eating her pizza.

A couple of hours later, after the movie had finished, he stood up and took the remaining slices of pizza over to the kitchen and wrapped them up. He put them in the fridge. "Do you want anything else?"

She shook her head and yawned. "I'm beat." She got up from the couch and came to stand next to him. "Do you mind if I turn in? It's been a long time since I had a chance to sleep somewhere that I felt safe. I guess it's catching up to me."

"By all means, go and get some sleep. I'm heading out anyway."

"Right, your poker game." A frown appeared on her forehead.

"Don't worry. I texted Cain earlier. He's got it covered. You will be watched."

She cocked an eyebrow. "I'm not sure I like the sound of that."

"I meant you will be safe. You don't have to worry."

She smiled. "I know. I'm just giving you a hard time. Thanks for making sure I'm safe." She rose on her tiptoes and kissed his cheek. "Night, Elias. Good luck at the game."

"Night," he said, but his voice came out as a croak. He cleared his throat. He could still feel her lips on his skin and the way her breast had brushed against his bicep. Yup, it was a good thing he was getting out. He needed some space and something to occupy his brain that wasn't tall, gorgeous, and great in bed.

CHAPTER TWENTY-TWO

Elias arrived at the condo on South Beach right on time. Wild Bill greeted him wearing a western shirt and a Stetson, his blue eyes twinkling. "We got a lively crowd tonight."

"Locals?" Elias asked as Wild Bill's security patted him down. He couldn't bring a gun to the games. In the past, it had never bothered him, but tonight was a bit different. He would have liked to have the comforting weight of his Glock in his waistband.

"Uh huh. Some trust-fund kids and some serious players." He smiled and winked. "I think this is going to be a good night for you."

Elias always tipped Wild Bill well. He couldn't throw the game for Elias, nor would Elias want him to, but he could tell him when the right players were assembled to provide an enjoyable night of poker. Elias didn't want beginners at the table, or fools. He liked real competition. If Bill said it was going to be a good night, then it usually was.

The condo overlooked South Beach, and like so many other condos these days, it was done in shades of white and gray. Elias must have seen at least a dozen condos in the exact same color scheme when he'd been looking for an apartment.

The wood floor was done in a pale beige. The main living area had two story floor-to-ceiling windows that would have an amazing view when the sun was up. There was a white couch and matching chairs over on the left and a bar set up all the way at the end of the room. On the right was a large table with five chairs. There was also a set of stairs that presumably lead to the bedrooms on the second floor.

Elias went over and claimed the remaining chair at the table. He didn't like it because it meant he had his back to the staircase. He smiled at the dealer and exchanged his ten grand for chips. It was a steep buy-in, but Wild Bill's games were always good. Elias made a lot of money at poker. He could go pro, or so he'd been told by a lot of people, but he liked his job at the Coast Guard too much, especially his new position with the RECON team. It didn't make sense to him to quit.

He realized that, in general, he was happy, or as happy as he'd ever been since Mattie died. He'd be happier if Andrea stayed in Miami. He'd found the transition back to his hometown excruciating at times, but now he was adjusting. She'd been right. Facing down old ghosts made him feel better. If only she'd stick around so maybe they could put the past behind them and build a future.

"Mr. Mason?" the dealer asked.

It was obvious the woman had been trying to get his attention for some time. *Shit.* He needed to focus. No more thoughts of Andrea, or he'd lose his shirt.

"Sorry, lost in thought." He put his chips in the center of the table, and the woman dealt the cards. Wild Bill always used one of the same two women. Tonight, it was Bonnie. She was average height with bright blond hair and a nice smile. She wore a black short-sleeved blouse and black pants, but her nails were painted fire engine red. It always kind of creeped Elias out a bit. Her nails looked like blood on the cards when she was dealing.

Elias was sitting at the end of the table closest to the stairwell leading to the second level. On his right was a young guy—someone had said his name was Tan. He was tall and lanky. He couldn't be more than in his early twenties. Elias was pretty sure he still had acne, but he must have money or Wild Bill wouldn't let him play. Probably a trust-fund baby.

Next to Tan was Betty. She and Elias had played together a few times. She'd won a hand or two off him, but she usually dropped out when the numbers got big. She also had blond hair, although he was pretty sure hers was a wig. She was also older, likely in her sixties. She was friendly enough, and he didn't mind playing with her.

To Betty's right was some guy named Skip, of all things, and he looked like what Elias always thought a Skip would look like. Light brown hair that probably used to be blond hung over his ears but looked like he blew it dry. The red pants and a white button-down he wore screamed Martha's Vineyard or a Hamptons' summer season, or so the latest Vogue magazine had said when Skip had read it at his dentist's office. The expensive Rolex on his wrist, and his handmade Italian shoes made Skip appear to ooze money.

At the opposite end of the table was some guy named Jasper. Elias had noticed him the moment he walked in. Jasper had a hard face. People around him treated him with deference, and he expected it. It appeared that he was not the type to suffer fools. His thick dark hair, was slicked back from his forehead. He had on a pale blue button-down and a pair of gray dress pants. He also wore a diamond pinky ring. Elias hated men who wore pinky rings. He just didn't trust them.

A bulky looking man, an inch or two taller than Elias leaned in and spoke quietly into Jasper's ear. He wore a light gray suit and looked like he was about to burst out of it like the Incredible Hulk. Jasper shook his head once and the man stepped back away from the table.

The first hand went quickly, as did the second and the third. They played steadily for the first hour. Elias won a few, folded on most, and lost one. He liked to take his time so he could figure out the strengths and weaknesses of his opponents.

They moved through hour two and were in hour three when things started to get serious. Tan had misjudged Skip's hand and lost all his chips. He got another ten thousand, but he started to play much more conservatively after that.

Skip got too excited over his win and proceeded to lose most of it again over the next few hands. Betty had picked up a few of those chips, but it was mostly down to Elias and Jasper. Soon it became the theme of the night. The others would start in the game but drop out very quickly. Then Jasper and Elias would duke it out until one of them called.

"Elias, can I get you anything?" Wild Bill asked.

He shook his head.

"Jasper?"

Jasper glanced up at Wild Bill. "Bourbon."

Wild Bill nodded. "Anyone else?" There were no takers, and he went over to the bar.

Elias glanced at his watch. It was nearly time for him to head out. He wanted to get some sleep. Going out on the water with Santiago was not a situation that he wanted to go into being tired.

"Past your bedtime?" Jasper jeered.

Elias just glanced up but didn't bother to respond. He took three cards and bet accordingly. Jasper took two and raised the bet. Elias raised the bet again and Jasper called it.

There was about seventy grand in the pot. It wasn't the biggest hand of the night, but it was close. Elias knew before Jasper even turned his cards over that he had a flush. Diamonds. Elias was sitting on a full house, nines over threes. He waited for Jasper to turn his cards, and then when Jasper started to move a hand toward the pot, Elias turned over his cards to reveal the full house.

Jasper stopped moving. The whole room froze. Something had shifted. They'd gone from a friendly game of poker to something else entirely. Jasper was angry. Everyone started moving at once.

"I think I'll call it a night," Betty said. Tan quickly agreed, and the two stood up. Skip said he had to go use the facilities.

"Sit down," Jasper growled, and they all reluctantly took their seats again. "We play one more hand, winner takes all."

Elias wasn't big on the idea, but the way Jasper ordered the other players around pissed him off. This guy seemed like he was one step up from an animal. Everyone was afraid of him. Even Wild Bill had made himself more scarce than usual.

Elias cocked his head. Could he win one more hand? Possibly, but the reality was, even if he lost, it wasn't a big deal. It would be for Betty, though. Elias knew she gambled to pay her husband's medical bills. He had a rare type of blood cancer. Elias didn't know a thing about Tan or Skip, but they didn't deserve to lose their money because Jasper needed to be the big man at the table.

Elias said, "Fine, but just you and me. The others can watch."

"No."

"Then I walk." Elias started to get up from the table.

Jasper's bodyguard came toward Elias. Although he had Elias in size, he was stiff. Elias knew by the way he moved.

The guy didn't stand a chance against him. He'd have the bodyguard out cold on the floor in seconds.

"You do not want to touch me," he said.

Wild Bill stood next to the table. "Gentleman, it's a friendly game. If these players are finished, they can leave. We all play by the rules here."

Jasper glanced at Bill but then went back to glaring at Elias. "Fine."

Betty got up and hightailed it out of the condo in seconds. Tan and Skip wanted to watch so they stayed seated, but they refused to play.

They'd been playing Texas Hold'em all night. Bonnie dealt the two men their two cards face down. Elias had the three of clubs and the three of diamonds. He glanced at Jasper. The man had a pretty good poker face, but over the course of the evening, Elias had noticed a small tell. If his cards were good, he only looked at them once. If he wasn't as sure about them, he looked at them multiple times.

Bonnie played the next three cards in the middle of the table face up. An Ace of diamonds, the seven of hearts, and the three of spades. Three of a kind. Still not much of a hand. He watched Jasper. The man hadn't picked up his cards again. That didn't bode well.

Bonnie turned up the next card. A ten of clubs. Nothing good there. He watched Jasper. The man looked at Elias and then back at the cards that were face up on the table. He still didn't make a move toward his cards. Bonnie put her hand on the deck to deal the next card when Jasper glanced at his cards again.

Yes! Jasper did not have a rock-solid hand. Elias was still in the game.

Bonnie turned over the last card. The three of hearts. Four of a kind for Elias. The pot was his. He knew it in his bones.

Jasper smiled and turned over his cards. "Full house," he said. "Aces over threes." Jasper had two aces in his hand, and the one face up on the table made his full house along with the two threes from the dealer. Jasper started to stand up.

Elias remained silent and turned over his cards. A small gasp broke the tense silence. He wasn't sure if it was Tan or Skip, but once again the room froze.

Jasper's face hardened.

Wild Bill walked over with his security guy in tow. "Gentleman, it was a great evening. It's time to go. Thank you so much for coming."

Tan and Skip were gone in a flash. Elias stood up. His leg hurt, but it had been worth it. There had to be about a hundred and thirty-five thousand in chips on the table. It was a good night. Jasper moved away from the table and came to stand directly in front of Elias. Their eyes locked.

"You got lucky. It won't happen again," Jasper sneered.

Elias remained silent, and he didn't move. He just returned Jasper's glare until, finally, the other man moved away and headed out the apartment door with his hired muscle in tow.

Once the door closed, there were footsteps on the stairs. Elias whirled around to find Santiago standing there. "That was magnificent. You fleeced that motherfucker!" He had a huge grin on his face.

Elias blinked. What the hell was going on?

"See?" Santiago pointed at Wild Bill. "Didn't I tell you it would be a good game between them?"

"You did indeed." Wild Bill agreed. "Well done, Elias."

"What are you doing here? What's going on?" Elias demanded. His heart was double-timing in his chest.

Santiago finished descending the stairs and came over to stand beside the table. He pulled a cigar out of his pocket. "I arranged the game tonight. I wanted to see you play Jasper. I knew you could beat him." He got out a lighter and lit his cigar. "I've been asking around about you. You're good. Everyone agrees. Maybe even the best on the beach. I knew Jasper wouldn't be able to resist if he heard that."

"You wanted me to play Jasper? Why?"

Santiago puffed on his cigar. "Because I wanted you to beat that asshole. I wanted you to take every single dime, and you did."

Then it dawned on Elias. "Jasper is your competition."

Santiago stopped puffing and removed the cigar from his mouth. "That piece of shit is not my competition. No one is as big as I am here. *No one.*" He turned to face Bill. "Get me a drink," he barked. Bill hustled over to the bar at the end of the room.

"If he's not your competition, then why did you want him to lose so badly?"

"Because Jasper is like one of those nasty little dogs always nipping at my heels. He's always looking for a way in. I always have to be on my guard or else he'll nip nip nip at my business."

Wild Bill came back and handed Santiago a high ball glass filled better than halfway to the rim with a clear liquid. Vodka, by the looks of it. "I'll just go get your money, Elias," Bill said and then disappeared up the stairs.

Santiago stood there puffing on his cigar, the smoke a cloud around his ugly face. "You need to be ready for the exchange. I don't need any more hassles. It has to run like a well-oiled machine." He took a healthy swig of his drink. Not his first one of the evening Elias realized as Santiago swayed in front of him.

"Goddamned Russians are so fucking demanding. Making me come. Stupid. Who the hell do they think they are?" He opened his mouth, inhaled on his cigar and then released a series of hazy blue smoke rings. "Making me work for my money." His lip curled. "It's Jasper's fault I have to deal with the motherfucking Russians." Then his face cleared. "You fleeced Jasper. Yaasss!"

Wild Bill came down the stairs and handed Elias a backpack filled with his winnings. He opened it up and took out a bunch of cash. He handed it to Santiago. "The five percent. Courtesy of Jasper."

Santiago stared at the money and then threw his head back and roared with laughter. "This is priceless." He laughed some more and then walked down the hallway towards the bathroom.

Elias turned to Wild Bill, who put his hands up in a defensive position. "I didn't have a choice. Santiago wanted a game. It's not worth my life to argue with him."

"A heads up might have been nice."

"I wasn't sure you'd come if you knew that Santiago had set it up. I am sorry, Elias," Wild Bill said. "You did well though." He smiled.

Elias wasn't ready to give him a pass. "What's the real story between Santiago and Jasper?"

Wild Bill glanced down the hallway and then lowered his voice. "Jasper and Santiago were in direct competition. Jasper was seriously cutting into Santiago's business. He was taking over Santiago's territory with drugs and guns. He was even moving in on Santiago's prostitution angle when suddenly, out of nowhere, things went bad for Jasper. His shipments were hijacked and then the replacement shipments were stolen as well. His clients were not happy.

"Santiago moved in with a flood of cash and new muscle, taking his territories back, inflicting serious losses on Jasper on every front. It was ugly and bloody." He leaned closer and continued, "No one knows where the money or muscle came from, but it worked, and Santiago came out on top. He's relegated Jasper to picking up the crumbs ever since. He still hates Jasper though and he's always keeping an eye on him just in case things turn again."

The sound of a door opening stopped their conversation. Elias zipped up the bag and headed toward the exit. He had opened the door when Santiago called out, "Elias, you better be on your best game later, or you won't be coming back."

Elias nodded once and closed the door behind him.

CHAPTER TWENTY-THREE

Andy luxuriated in the huge bed. She did not want to get up. It had been a long time since she'd been able to sleep without one eye open. Even though Santiago was still out there, she didn't feel in immediate danger. She'd like to think it was because she knew what she was doing and could handle herself, but the reality was she was relaxed because Elias was there, and she knew he and the rest of his team wouldn't let anything happen to her.

If only her own team was like that. Jay and Peña had her back, but Robins… Well, you weren't supposed to speak ill of the dead. Did thinking ill count? When she thought back over the months and years she'd been working with him, she realized that he had always done something to make her feel just a bit uncomfortable. Like showing up late to collect her after a meet with a CI, leave her hanging for a bit when she asked for help, subtle but there. He wanted her to be a bit scared because he thought she would be more dependent on him that way, but that's not what happened.

Instead, she had withdrawn her trust in him. She relied on Jay and Peña. The whole thing with him not showing up at the marina and being late to come rescue her when the shooting started were just two more examples of his passive-aggressiveness toward her. Only, in that case, it was suddenly very obvious. If he'd lived, he would've been in trouble with the bosses at the ATF, and she was pretty sure he knew it.

She rolled over and glanced at the clock. It was later than she thought. With a sigh, she swung her feet over the side of the bed and got up, stretching out her limbs. After gathering her shower things, she headed down the hall to the bathroom.

A sound coming from the living room stopped her cold, but then she realized it was Elias, snoring softly. He had to be exhausted. He'd gotten in around three a.m. She'd heard the apartment door open and close and then him moving around in the kitchen. She had recognized the sound of his footsteps, so she hadn't panicked when the bedroom door opened. He had checked on her, then closed the door again softly and went back out to the sofa.

Andy entered the bathroom and closed the door quietly. Let him sleep. He was going to need to be well rested for tonight. She turned on the shower, pulled off the boxers and tank top that she'd slept in, and stepped into the warm spray.

As water sluiced down her body, she picked up the shampoo and poured it into her hand. The smell wafted around her. It smelled like Elias. Her breasts tingled. She washed her hair and tried not to fantasize about him being in the shower with her.

What the hell was she supposed to do about him? His apology yesterday had felt sincere. He'd meant it from the heart. She'd had no idea how far down the rabbit hole he'd gone when Mattie died. She'd known he was full of rage, but she'd had no idea now that the rage was the only thing keeping him putting one foot in front of the other.

It made sense. His mom was a lovely woman who'd

always been wonderful to Andy. She was the one person who did not prejudge Andy on her mother and sister's mistakes. But she hadn't been there for Elias, however that wasn't entirely her fault. Andy had always had the sense that Elias's father had broken some part of his mother, a part she couldn't get back. She worked hard and provided for her kids, gave them a solid upbringing with good morals and values. There was no doubt she loved her children, but there was always a bit of something being held back.

Mattie had been everything to Elias. The two of them really were brothers. It wasn't surprising then that Elias had fallen apart at his death. If only he hadn't turned on her afterward.

She sighed as she rinsed her hair. It was fine to say she was over it and she'd moved on with her life, but the reality was, it still hurt. He'd pushed her out when she'd needed him the most. That was hard to let go of.

Her shrink told her she needed to accept the pain and then release it, but how was she supposed to do that? He'd broken her heart and shattered her dreams in one fell swoop. Of course, she'd gone on to create new dreams and she'd put her heart back together. At least she thought she had until she'd seen him again. She couldn't hide from the truth. There was an Elias-shaped hole in her heart, and it would probably always be there unless they got back together.

Back together. No. That was just stupid. He'd hurt her too much for that, hadn't he? Or had he really? Should she let it go? Could she? The sex was certainly outstanding. Just the thought of it had her nether regions tingling. But playing board games yesterday had been fun, too, and watching the movie. They'd always had fun together. He was easy to be around. She enjoyed his company.

She grabbed the conditioner. She was waffling more than the IHOP down the street. Miami had been traumatic for her then, and now. It was definitely time to move on. Get out. Start fresh. There was no real future for her and Elias. Too much water under the bridge.

After finishing her shower and toweling herself off, Andy pulled on a pair of faded jeans and a button-down white shirt. She brushed out her wet hair, pulling it up into a bun which she secured with a couple of bobby pins. After wiping the mirror with her towel, she applied a bit of makeup.

She was going to have to talk to the guys at the ATF soon and possibly go see them. It didn't matter it was Saturday. They'd be chomping at the bit to hear what the hell was going on. Not that she could share anything, but she wanted to hear more details about Robins. She still wasn't convinced his death had nothing to do with Santiago.

Andy opened the bathroom door and heard voices. She stuck her head around the corner to see the whole team standing by the island. "Hey, guys."

"Hey, Andrea," Axe said.

"It's Andy, Axe."

"Sure thing." He smiled. The rest of the guys waved. She went down the hall to dump her things in the bedroom and came back out to the kitchen area. The guys were all sitting around the table, so she took the last open seat at the head.

Andy asked. "So, what's going on? How come you all are out so early? I mean, I know we have to plan for tonight, but it's only ten-thirty in the morning."

"I called them," Elias said as he started handing out plates and cutlery.

"Oh, why?" She suddenly spied the bags on the counter. "Ooh, what's for breakfast? I am famished."

Elias grinned. "You are always famished."

"Is there a problem with that?"

"Not at all." He went and opened the bags. "Here." He

handed Finn a couple of breakfast burritos, who promptly gave them to Andy.

She laughed. "I'm starving, but these are huge. One is enough."

Finn frowned. "Are you sure? There's plenty."

"I'm sure."

"Suit yourself." He handed the other one to Axe.

For the next several minutes everyone was too preoccupied stuffing their mouths with the delicious breakfast burritos to speak. Andy glanced around and saw the Cuban coffee on the counter. "Are you saving these for a rainy day?" she asked as she retrieved them from the kitchen. She brought over the coffees and set them in the middle of the table, then took one before reclaiming her seat.

She studied Elias as he ate. He looked a bit tired, and she was willing to bet his leg was hurting him. She was starting to recognize the signs. There was a tightness around his eyes and a slight downward pull at the corners of his mouth. Nothing obvious but, still, the signs were there. Playing poker last night had not been good for his leg. Sitting here probably wasn't helping much either.

"So," she started, but then her cell phone started vibrating. She'd turned the ringer off last night and hadn't bothered to turn it on yet. She glanced at the screen. Peña. She got up from the table. "Sorry, guys, I have to take this."

"Peña," she said as she walked across the apartment and back down the hallway.

"Andy, where have you been? I've been calling all morning."

She pulled the phone away from her ear and swiped down to view her notifications. Seven missed calls. She grimaced. "Sorry. I had my ringer off. I slept late. What's going on?"

"What do you mean what's going on? Didn't you hear about Robins?"

She sighed. "Yes, I heard." She'd been about to say that Nick had told her, but then she remembered that Peña and Jay weren't in on the current situation with Elias and the rest of the team. "It's been on the news," she finished lamely.

"Why aren't you coming in? What are you doing? Where are you?" he demanded. "Sorry," he then immediately apologized. "It's just Jay and I are really worried about you. We don't want you to be killed, too?"

"Yeah, I know." She didn't want to wind up dead either. "Do you know anything more than what was on the news?" She was so grateful that she'd read an article about it this morning. "All the article said was he was found dead by the beach. Do they know who did it or why?"

Peña's sigh was heavy. "Not much more. He told someone he had a meeting to go to and then just never came back. A dog walker found him. Andy, he'd been tortured. Someone burnt him with cigarillos. It was awful."

"Oh, my god." She closed her eyes for a second and sent up a silent prayer. He was an asshole, but no one deserved that. "Do they have any suspects? Any leads?"

"Not that I know of. I was hoping you had an idea. Could it have anything to do with Santiago?"

She drew in a breath. She needed to be very careful here. She wasn't allowed to say anything to Peña about the op. "To be honest? I've been thinking the same thing. Could it have been Santiago? I don't think so. I think if it was Santiago, then he would know about me, too, and he'd kill me. He's not one to tread lightly."

"That's true," Peña agreed. "So, you think it has to do with another case?"

"It seems farfetched, but possible. Maybe an old enemy

saw him and decided to take him out." As she said it, she realized how lame that sounded.

"I'm not sure about that. I think the coincidence is too much."

"You know what? So do I, but for the life of me, I have no idea how Robins' death ties back into Santiago."

"Is there anyone else involved in the op that you can think of that would know about Robins or want him dead?" Peña's voice sounded hopeful.

"No. That's the frustrating part. None of it makes any sense."

"Do you think Elias Mason could have anything to do with it?"

That question set her back. How was she supposed to answer that without tipping her hand? "I don't think so. What would he have to gain by it?"

"Don't know, but he's the only outlier in this."

She found herself gritting her teeth and made an effort to unclench her jaw. "I guess. I can poke around a bit and see." It just seemed better to say that than continue to defend Elias.

"Just be careful. If this guy killed Robins, you could be next. Where are you, by the way?"

"Who's taking over the case?" She wanted to avoid that question at all costs.

"Don't know exactly. It's all-hands-on-deck over here. Ridley wants it, but I think Christine is probably going to get it. You should come in ASAP. The op is done for us anyway. They're going to want to talk to you about any connection you think there could be."

"Yeah, I know, but I'm still in the game over here, and I don't want to give it up just yet. I'm close. I think."

"Close to what, though? Robins just said we were booted off the investigation because it went into areas outside our purview, but he wouldn't elaborate. He said that you were going to stay with the investigation in a tangential manner. What the fuck does all that mean?"

If Robins was good at anything, he was good at doublespeak and making himself sound more important than he was. She did not want to get into it now. If no one was in charge just yet, then she was in the clear to stay away from the office. She knew if she walked in the door, they weren't going to let her out again and all bets would be off.

"I've gotta run. I'll check in later. Keep me posted with what's going on. Tell Jay I said hey. We'll go for drinks when all this is over."

"But—"

She clicked off the call and promptly turned off her phone. She went back out to the table where the guys were still drinking coffee. "So, what did I miss?"

"Nothing," Elias said. "I was waiting for you. What's going on?"

She bit her lip as she sat down. "That was one of the guys on my team. Because of Robins' murder, everyone has been called for active duty. Peña doesn't know who is taking over for Robins, but everyone wants to talk to me. They're going to check out everything, but the prevailing theory is that Robins' death has something to do with Santiago. I said I didn't think it was him because I'm still alive, but Peña didn't buy that. He said"—she paused—"he thinks Elias might have killed Robins."

Nick frowned. "Did he say why?"

"Not really, but he mentioned that Elias is sort of the only piece on the chess board that's known and unknown at the same time, if you know what I mean." She couldn't help but smile after that convoluted sentence. "What I mean is, he's the only one that ATF knows is involved with the investigation but they don't know much about. He's the X." She glanced at him, and he smiled.

"I kind of like being the unknown. I'm a man of mystery." He chuckled.

"Actually," Nick said, "this could be a big problem. We can't have them digging around in this. It could tip Santiago off. I'll call Bertrand and make sure he crushes that before it gets out of hand."

Andy frowned. "I can tell you the pushback is going to be intense. One of their own is dead. If they think Elias is involved, they aren't going to listen to some admiral in Washington. I mean, would you?"

"She's got a point," Finn said.

"Yeah," Nick agreed. "I'll still make the call. Maybe Bertrand can talk to a higher-up over at the ATF and work something out."

Andy leaned back in her chair. What she'd just said earlier finally hit her. She had said, 'one of *their* own' was dead. She subconsciously had separated herself from the ATF. What the hell did that mean? And did it bode well for her future?

CHAPTER TWENTY-FOUR

Elias looked at Andrea where she sat at the end of the table. She was thinking something over. Ever since he could remember, she'd get a furrow right between her brows when she was deep in thought. Whatever it was she was mulling over, she wasn't too happy about it.

"Elias," Cain said, "why did you drag us over here?"

"Right." He absently rubbed his leg. "I got a call last night about a poker game, so I went." He glanced at Nick. "I needed to clear my head."

Nick frowned but said nothing.

"Turns out it was all a setup." Elias shook his head. "I guess the guy who tells me about the games is not as loyal as I thought."

"What do you mean by a setup?" Cain asked.

"Well, it was a game, but I was meant to be there. One of the regulars was there, and a couple of local boys that seemed like trust-fund babies or Silicon Valley types. But the main attraction was this guy named Jasper."

Andrea's head shot up. "Jasper?"

"Do you know him?" Nick asked.

"No. I've never met him, but I've heard some stuff. He's Antonio's partner. You remember Antonio from the neighborhood, right, Elias?"

Elias nodded. "They're partners?"

"It's on the down low according to Antonio," Andrea said, "but it's the reason Antonio works at the Blue Iguana. Jasper owns it, and Antonio keeps an eye on things for him. Antonio said Jasper had some business dealings that rub up against Santiago, and he wants to know what's going on so they don't conflict."

Elias cocked his head. "Interesting. That's not what Santiago said."

"Santiago?" Axe's voice rose above his normal tenor. "Was he there?"

"Yeah. Santiago got Wild Bill to call me and get me to come to the game. I guess he wanted to see if I could beat Jasper."

"And did you?" Cain asked before he downed the last of his coffee.

"Yeah, and it didn't go down well. Not well at all. Jasper is more than a businessman. He's Santiago's main competition."

"He told you that?" Finn frowned. "Since when did you two become best buds?"

"No, he didn't tell me, but how Santiago described him tells me all I need to know. He said that Jasper is like a little dog nipping at his ankles. Translation: Jasper is a pain in his ass and he's chipping away at Santiago's business. Also, if Jasper was just a nobody, Santiago would have killed him the first time he became a real annoyance. But he didn't. He has to live with Jasper nipping away at him. He said that it was Jasper's fault he was dealing with the Russians."

"Do you think Jasper somehow tied him up with the

Russians?" Nick asked. "Like Jasper made some sort of deal that roped Santiago in with the Russians?"

"Not likely. My contact told me that Jasper was actually poised to take over the whole drug trade, etc., from Santiago when all of a sudden, Santiago had a big influx of muscle and cash. He used it to steal Jasper's shipments and take his territory back. I think Jasper was growing too strong and threatening Santiago's existence, so Santiago made a deal with whoever he could in order to keep Jasper at bay. The Russians probably offered him a lot of cash and maybe even contacts. They helped him reestablish dominance. Jasper, in general, seems like a very pissed-off individual. He is also not my biggest fan."

Nick tapped the table. "I'll make some calls about Jasper. I think we need more information about him and his relationship with Santiago."

"So, what else did Santiago tell you?" Finn grabbed the last Cuban coffee from the middle of the table and downed it in one gulp.

Elias grinned. "I guess I should have left some paper out for you so you could make your animals. Now you'll be all hopped up on coffee."

"Funny." Finn put the cup back down on the table.

"Anyway, we were correct. The Russians are forcing Santiago to go tonight. I think it's a power play to remind him who's boss, which ties into the whole Jasper situation. Santiago sold his soul to keep Jasper off his heels, but he is none too pleased about the price he's paying. I think he hates the Russians and all of this shit. He was very uncomfortable the other night with the buyers. I would not be surprised to see him try and find a new partner to dance with in the not-too-distant future."

"So you're saying if we want to get him, we need to do it tonight," Cain said.

"I think that would be wise," Elias agreed.

Elias glanced at his watch. "He's late. It's gonna be close with this storm moving in." He looked around the empty parking lot. They were at a marina, waiting for Santiago. The lights weren't cutting the darkness much and the storm clouds blocked the moon. The air was thick with moisture.

Andrea nodded. "Yeah, it takes a solid hour to get out there in good weather. The storm's held off so far, but the water looks rough."

Elias gazed out at the boats bobbing up and down in their slips. It wasn't too bad here, but he knew it would get worse the farther out they went. He leaned against the railing that ran along the edge of the walkway. There were four different piers jutting out into the bay. Each one had many slips, but they were all full tonight. No one wanted to go out there in this weather, and he didn't blame them one bit. "Are you okay in rough seas?"

She held up her hand and wiggled it back and forth. "So so. It depends. I admit I got a little queasy last time, and the waves weren't all that big."

He grinned. "It's not so much fun."

"You don't get queasy, do you?"

He shook his head. "Nah, I've spent too much time at sea to feel it now. But when I first started, I was sick as a dog. It took a while to get my sea legs. Then after being out at sea on a cutter for a couple of weeks, I had to get my land legs back when we hit port. I was sick for a few days on land. Eventually, my body sorted itself out."

Andrea glanced at the parking lot. "Any tips you can give me?"

"Believe it or not, eat something substantial. An apple, or

pasta, something like that. When your stomach is busy working on the food, you tend to feel less nauseous. Never go out on an empty stomach. It's the worst."

"Well, I could have used a heads up a few hours ago. It's not like I can go grab an apple or pasta now."

He couldn't help it. He laughed. "No, I guess not. You know you can still stay here. Santiago isn't here yet. I could say you were sick and went to your aunt's or back to my place."

She shook her head. "As much as that appeals, I would rather be out there with you than back at your place with a gun to my head. This way I feel like I have options. Back at the apartment, I would just be trapped, and God forbid if things did go wrong, there's not much maneuvering room. Besides, it would split up the team. You guys wouldn't leave me unprotected, and everyone is definitely needed tonight."

He nodded. He didn't want to say it, but he felt better about having her nearby as well. At least, he could protect her then. If she was at the apartment, his focus would be split. He'd be trying to deal with Santiago at the same time as worrying about her.

"Interesting about Jasper," she said.

"What? That his drug shipments went missing? Yeah, makes you think doesn't it."

"Do you really believe the Russians are helping out Santiago?"

"I do. I'm willing to bet it's part of the deal. Santiago was losing out, so he's made a crazy call to hold on to his territory."

"Makes sense, I guess," she mused. "But why are they doing the exchange at sea when the Russians flew in last time? They were in Santiago's office."

"It's harder to get a shipment of guns across the border for a start. I think though the real reason is probably that they don't want to be seen as traveling in and out of the US too much. Every time they come it's a risk. I would guess they aren't traveling on their real passports. Why increase that risk exponentially by bringing guns with you when you can just drive a boat for an hour and do the exchange at sea?"

Andrea agreed. "You're right. Much less risk involved for the Russians."

A Cadillac with blacked-out windows entered the parking lot. Santiago. It parked a few spaces from Elias's pickup, and Santiago got out. Peter stepped from the passenger side, and the driver from the other day got out as well.

"You're late," Elias said.

"Fuck off," Santiago snarled back. He was wearing a pair of light gray dress pants and a black button-down. He had dress shoes on his feet. Peter was more sensibly dressed in jeans and a collared shirt. The bodyguard was wearing a suit.

Elias mentally shrugged. Obviously, Santiago had never spent any time out on the ocean. Elias was wearing a blue polar fleece with a navy T-shirt underneath and a pair of jeans. He also had on a pair of light rubber-soled boots.

Andrea was wearing another of his polar fleeces, this one in maroon, with jeans and sneakers. He found it warm standing there, but once they got out to sea, it was going to get cold fast.

Santiago stormed by them and continued down the walkway to the stairs. At the bottom, he turned left onto the first pier. Peter followed after Santiago, but the driver stopped next to them and, with a tilt of his head, indicated they should get going after the other two.

"What's your name?" Elias asked.

"Jacobo."

"Okay Jacobo. Let's go." Andrea said, "Nice to meet you," then turned and went down the walkway.

A couple minutes later, they all came to a stop at a slip about three quarters of the way down. Tied up was a powerboat with two massive engines.

Elias did his best not to appear nervous. Even though the powerboat was large, it was not a vessel designed to handle rough seas. He was glad his team would be out there along with Captain Myers and his cutter from the original bust and another cutter they brought down the coast. There were also two RHIBs with two teams, his and one other. Tag and the guys would take the lead, but it was damn nice to have serious backup.

They all boarded the boat, and Jacobo settled behind the controls in the captain's chair. Peter untied the mooring lines, and they were off in a matter of minutes. Elias and Andrea sat on the side bench. Santiago sat on the back seat behind Jacobo. He looked miserable.

"You want to go over a plan of some kind?" Elias yelled above the wind. He almost felt badly for the guy. Almost.

"What plan? It's your job to make this happen smoothly. Any trouble, and you take care of it. Or she dies." He gestured toward Andrea with his chin, then pulled up his collar and crossed his arms over his chest. He had to be freezing. The wind was colder out here, and they kept getting hit with spray.

There were stairs down to a cabin between Jacobo and the passenger seat where Peter sat. Elias was about to suggest that Santiago go sit down there, but he stopped himself. Let the asshole suffer. Instead, he wrapped his arm around Andrea and brought her in close.

It was rough going, and they bounced on the waves a fair amount. Elias glanced at his watch. They were running behind by his calculations. "You might want to try and pick it up a bit. You're late."

Santiago swore long and loud but still yelled at Jacobo to

go faster. The boat lurched and picked up speed. It also caught a bit more air, so the landing was hard sometimes. Santiago was miserable, and Elias couldn't help but grin. He hid it by turning to kiss Andrea's hair. "How are you doing?" he asked.

She nodded, but he could see she was a bit green.

Elias had been watching Jacobo the whole ride out and came to the conclusion the man was competent as a boat driver. He was steering into the waves as much as possible and making course corrections as necessary. It did ease the knots in Elias's stomach slightly.

Ten minutes later, Jacobo cut the speed. The roar of the engines and the wind dropped to a slight whine. Elias stood up. Peter roused himself, but Elias signaled him to stay put as he went over to Jacobo. He glanced up at the sky once again. It was pitch black out here. The cloud cover blocked out any moonlight and a light mist had started to fall.

The boat they were meeting was, nearby, bobbing vigorously in the waves. It was significantly bigger than this one, a yacht, in fact, at least fifty feet. "Bring us alongside the best you can. It's going to be tough with the waves."

Jacobo tipped his chin up in confirmation, and Elias went back to Andrea, who started to stand. He rested a hand on her shoulder. "Just wait a minute."

He looked out into the night. He couldn't see the RHIBs or the cutters, but he knew they were there, and it was a damn good thing. Chances were good someone was going to be in the water before this was over.

Jacobo did his best to bring them alongside, but it was damn near impossible. The waves were large, swells of over five feet, and it was hard to keep the boat steady. Peter stood up, as did Santiago.

A man appeared on the aft deck of the yacht. It was the

same blond man from Santiago's office when Elias had first inspected the guns. "You're late," he yelled.

Santiago mumbled, "Fuck you," but the guy obviously couldn't hear him. To them, he yelled, "Let's get this done."

The man nodded. He turned behind him and said something to somebody and then two other men appeared on deck. One was short and stocky with dark hair and the other was taller with his hair in a ponytail. Both picked up a large duffel bag and stood at the side.

"Okay, wait," Elias yelled. "This isn't going to work." He pointed to the back of the yacht. There was a swim platform. The two men looked back and then nodded at him.

"Jacobo, go along the back of the yacht. You're going to have to be very careful because we're going to be at a bigger angle to the waves. You've been keeping it at about forty-five degrees which is where it's supposed to be. Now you're going to be closer to sixty. No sudden moves, okay?"

Jacobo reached for the steering and throttle at the same time. He maneuvered the boat behind the yacht and turned it slightly. He was going to have to work the throttles the entire time since it was impossible to drop anchor.

The name of the yacht came into view. *Seas the Day*. Elias snorted. Whatever. He turned to Peter. "Come on." He went to stand next to Santiago. "You're gonna need to move."

Santiago turned toward Elias. There was terror in the man's eyes. He was scared beyond belief. What the hell? A wave hit a bit hard, and Santiago bumped into Elias. He could smell the booze. Santiago was drunk. Jesus Christ, this was rapidly becoming a shit show.

"Go sit over there," Elias directed at Andrea and pointed to the opposite side of the boat. Andrea got up and moved to the passenger seat opposite of Jacobo.

He turned to Peter. "You ready?"

"Yeah," Peter grunted.

Elias waved over the two men on the yacht. They started coming down onto the swim platform. They were in jeans and sneakers, and they were immediately immersed in water up to their knees. They also had tied ropes around their waists so if they fell, someone could haul them in.

The shorter guy grabbed the end of the first bag which was hanging off the back of the boat in the opening to the swimming platform. Then he moved back on the platform so the taller guy could reach over and grab the other end. Once they had it between them, they swung it towards Elias and Peter who caught it and pulled it into the boat.

One down. Elias turned and watched the men wrestle with the second bag. It seemed like it was heavier. They finally managed to hold it between them, and they started to swing it back and forth to gain momentum. Elias saw a huge wave coming and yelled at them to hold on, but it was too late. They launched the bag, and Elias and Peter scrambled to grab the merchandise, but a large wave hit, driving the powerboat away from the yacht.

The bag landed on the edge of the boat and started to slip into the water. Peter launched himself over the side and grabbed it. Elias pulled hard on Peter's waist, and they managed to get the bag back into the boat. Out of breath, Elias looked at Peter and shook his head. "Let it go next time. It's not worth losing your life over."

"Don't listen to him," Santiago roared as he stood up. "Do not drop a bag! Do you understand me?"

Elias turned and glared at Santiago. "You stupid—"

Santiago whipped out a gun and pointed it at Elias. "Just get the fucking bags."

Elias growled under his breath but turned back to Peter. In a low voice, he said, "Don't go in after a bag, or you won't be coming back out. You'll get trapped between the boats and get crushed."

Peter glanced over his shoulder. "If I don't, he's going to shoot me. Not much of a choice."

Elias wanted to tell him that help was close by, and even if he got shot, there was hope, but he remained silent. The wind picked up, and Elias looked out at the sea. It was hard to see more than twenty feet in any direction. That was as far as the lights of the yacht penetrated the darkness. The storm was coming. The mist in the air was heavier now. Another ten minutes tops before the skies opened up. He sure as hell wanted to be a good distance away from the yacht before that happened.

"Let's do this," he called to the other two men. They nodded. The short guy pulled another bag out, and the taller guy reached for it. He managed to grab the end and had started to pick it up when lightning lit up the sky. The boom of the thunder made everyone jump, and the tall guy dropped his end of the bag. Hauled off balance by the sudden weight shift, his partner pitched off the back of the platform, hitting his head on their boat as he fell.

Elias reached over the side to drag him out of the water, but it was too late. The guy was already under the platform.

"Pull the rope!" he commanded.

The tall guy had to climb over the bag to get back on the yacht to start pulling the rope. Unfortunately, the bag of weapons was on the rope, so the tall guy pushed the weapons into the water and then pulled on the rope again.

His partner came to the surface, but it was evident that he was already dead. He was face down with a huge gash across the back of his head. The blond man reached passed the tall guy and cut the rope with a knife. The shorter man disappeared under the waves.

His partner hopped up and screamed something in Spanish. Elias didn't catch it because the lightning flashed again, and thunder rolled. The blond man took out his gun, aimed at the tall guy remaining on the platform and fired. He fell back in the water and drifted out of sight.

He turned to Santiago. "Give me the money."

"Where's the last bag?"

The blond man looked down at his feet. "Give me the money, and I'll give it to you next time."

Santiago shook his head. "No way. I need those guns. No guns, no money."

The other man raised his weapon. "Give me the fucking money now!"

Santiago wavered a moment but then picked up the backpack and unzipped it. He pulled out some of the stacks of cash, went over to the side of the boat, and started throwing them at the guy. He threw ten stacks and then stopped. "You get the rest when I get the rest of the guns."

The blond man hadn't moved. He just stood there and stared at Santiago. As if in slow motion, he raised his gun.

Elias yelled, "Get down!" to Andrea, who threw herself down the stairs.

Santiago dove for the driver's seat and pushed Jacobo out of the way. A shot rang out, and the windshield of the power-boat shattered.

Santiago jammed the throttle of the powerboat all the way down just as Elias yelled, "No!" But it was too late. The boat shot forward, knocking Elias and Peter off their feet. Jacobo fell, too.

The boat launched in the air over the top of a wave and then came down hard. Elias looked up just in time to see a huge wave coming. He knew they weren't going to make it. He tried to get to Andrea, but the boat started up the wave. They were at the wrong angle, and the wave started to break. It crashed over the bow and flipped the powerboat as if it was a toy in a child's bath.

Elias took a deep breath and closed his eyes. Andrea. He

had to get to her. That was his last thought before the water was everywhere and he was in total darkness. It took many long, disorienting seconds before he managed to figure out which way was up.

He broke the surface of the water and looked around. The boat was capsized and sinking about twenty feet to his left.

"Andrea!" His voice was a curious cocktail of hoarse and terrified.

He spun in a circle looking for her, but the waves kept coming. He started to swim toward the boat. He wasn't going to lose her. Not again. He'd wasted all those years without her. All that time they could have been together. He swam as hard as he could, desperately pulling himself through the water.

Suddenly, there was light everywhere. "This is the United States Coast Guard. *Seas the Day,* stay where you are and prepared to be boarded."

Engines roared, and as a wave lifted him up, he saw the cutters moving in and the yacht leaving. He looked back toward the capsized powerboat, but it was gone.

"Andrea!" he screamed.

No. He couldn't think. Couldn't breathe. She just couldn't be gone.

"Elias!" He heard his name and spun in the water. It was Santiago. He was holding on desperately to one of the cushions from the powerboat. "Elias, help me!"

"Just hold on to the cushion," he yelled back and then he lost sight of Santiago as the swell of a wave came between them. He yelled for Andrea again, but nothing. "Please God," he prayed, "don't let her die."

Santiago was yelling again. He seemed to be struggling. Elias ignored him and kept searching the surface of the water for Andrea. He heard a motor and recognized it as the sound of a RHIB. He turned to see one coming in his direction. They were going slowly and using the spotlight to search the surface.

Andrea had to be alive. She had to be. He tried to scan the sea for her, but the salt was making his eyes sting. But then, a bolt of lightning lit up the sky and, in the flash, he saw her. She was at the top of a wave about thirty feet away.

He struck out for her, swimming as fast as he could. After about a minute, he looked up, but he hadn't gotten any closer. His leg was killing him, and it was only going to get worse. The adrenaline was helping now. Later it would be a nightmare.

He stopped and waved his hands in the air until the spotlight on the RHIB lit him up. Then he pointed to where he'd seen Andrea last. It took a few seconds, but the light swung around. They did slow sweeps of the area back and forth over the waves, but there was only water.

Lightning flashed again. There! She was swimming toward the RHIB, but they were just missing her with the light. Elias started yelling and waving his arms. He knew one of them would have binoculars trained on him so they didn't lose him. They also knew he was trained for this, and as long as the rain held off, they'd keep looking for Andrea while they slowly made their way to him. The light swung back in his direction, and he pointed behind them.

The light swung around and again started a slow back and forth tour of the waves. It made two passes before it stopped and zeroed in on Andrea. They swiftly turned and went to get her. Elias treaded his arms and legs, fighting to keep his head above water for the next few minutes until they pulled her from the waves.

Relief flooded his body. He could breathe again. He saw them help her up into the boat and wrap her in blankets. At that point of relief, he also became aware of the fact that he was cold and his leg was killing him. He started to raise his arms above his head again to call them over when he heard Santiago screaming.

He turned and saw the man bobbing in the waves about twenty feet away, still holding the cushion but struggling with something. Elias was having a hard time seeing what Santiago was doing, but then he realized. "Let go of the backpack!" he yelled. The asshole had the backpack with money over one shoulder, and he was desperately trying to get it on his back without losing the cushion.

He started to swim toward Santiago. The ocean was with him this time, and he reached the other man quickly. "Santiago, stop fighting with the backpack. You'll drown!" When Elias reached out to grab the backpack, Santiago went nuts.

"Leave it alone! You asshole, this is all your fault!" Santiago reached out and tried to hit Elias.

"What the hell? I'm trying to help you!"

"You are trying to take me down! Just like that motherfucking Russian. Just like Jasper. No one is going to take me down!" he screamed.

There was a sound, a kind of a muffled roar, and Elias knew instantly what it was. The rain had arrived. Within seconds, they were in the middle of a deluge. Elias reached out for Santiago again. "You need to stop fighting with the backpack!" he yelled. "I'll help you stay afloat."

"No!" Santiago screamed and tried to swim away from Elias.

Elias held on to him. "You'll drown," he bellowed but Santiago continued to fight him. He hit Elias on the jaw and Elias let him go. It was too dangerous if Santiago didn't want his help. He would drown the two of them. "Okay, I won't touch you but stay here. Help is coming!" He gestured to the RHIB that was advancing on their position. He turned and watched as the boat approached, but when he turned back,

Santiago was gone. Where the fuck did he go? Then the boat cushion appeared on the swell of the wave. Santiago was beneath it. Elias swam toward it. He reached out and turned Santiago over. The backpack was still tangled around his arm, but Santiago was staring sightlessly up at the sky.

"Elias," Nick called.

Elias turned. The RHIB was only a few feet away.

"We'll get him. You get in the boat," Nick said as he offered a hand.

Elias nodded. He reached out and grabbed Nick's hand and tried to push out of the water, but his leg was killing him and he didn't have any energy left. Finn reached over and grabbed Elias's other hand. Both pulled hard until Elias was half out of the water and laying over the inflated side of the boat, then they reached down and grabbed his belt. They pulled him the rest of the way into the boat. He lay on the floor of the RHIB, rain pounding on his face and body, and sucked in oxygen. He was just so happy to be out of the water.

A second later, Andrea was there beside him. She sat down and helped Finn cover him with a blanket. Then she rearranged hers over her shoulders and leaned down and kissed him. Her fingers were ice cold as she cupped his face. "I am so fucking happy you are alive," she said and then kissed him again.

"Yeah, me too," he mumbled through frozen lips.

Cain stood over him. "Seriously." He shook his head then bent down and grabbed Elias under his arm. He pulled him into a sitting position and then helped him shift so he was sitting on the floor and leaning against the side of the boat. Andrea moved over and snuggled up next to him.

"Santiago?" Elias croaked as pain seared through his thigh.

Cain shook his head.

"Peter and Jacobo?"

"On the other RHIB with Axe and some other Coasties."

Elias raised his arm enough so Andrea could put her head on his chest. He dropped his arm around her shoulders and leaned his head back. Then he promptly passed out.

CHAPTER TWENTY-FIVE

"You know, I'm kind of tired of being wet," Andrea said as she looked down at Elias. He was busy soaping her leg and obviously hadn't heard a word she said.

"Earth to Elias!" She tapped him on the shoulder.

"Sorry," he murmured, "I was in heaven."

She laughed as she made him stand and then gave him a quick kiss on his way up. They stood under the hot spray, wrapped in each other's arms. He was not wrong. It was heaven. She sighed as she broke off the kiss. They were going to have to discuss things at some point.

A cell phone rang. "Yours?" she asked. They had the same ring.

He shook his head. "Nope, that one is yours."

"Shit." She tilted her head back into the spray to block out the sound. A minute later, she leaned out of the spray. "I guess I'm going to have to go in today. I have to tell them what happened. Or at least a version of events."

He nodded as he started soaping her back. "But not before breakfast. I'll grab some eggs and bacon from the deli around the corner once we're finished here. As to what to say,

Nick is going to tell the truth to Bertrand and then the higher-ups will decide what to tell everyone else. My guess is they'll advise you to tell the truth except about the Russians. As long as you call them Cubans, it will be fine."

She tilted her head. Part of her wanted to protest. She should tell her people the truth, but on the other hand, she understood the need for secrecy. "So, what will happen now?"

Elias ran his hands down over her back, rubbing in a circular motion. It felt good. Really good. Like panty-melting good; if she were wearing panties.

He kissed her shoulder blade "Well, Captain Myers using the cutter to capture the yacht was a big deal. There will be denials from the Russians, of course, that they knew anything about it. They will say it was a single actor, doing it all on his own. We all know that's not true, but that's what they'll say. And they know that we know it's not true, but it won't matter."

He went lower and started to rub circles on the small of her back. "The blond guy who shot the other two will go to some deep dark hole somewhere, and the yacht will be confiscated. The FBI will investigate the Sons of Freedom. They'll keep an eye out to see if any Russians show up to train them. If they manage to catch a Russian when he arrives, then they'll try and flip him. Get him to fill them in on the bigger picture like how many groups are being trained and who is involved in the Russian government."

He started going wider, so he was now soaping her butt and her thighs. "The FBI will be extra vigilant since all of this has come to light and try their best to nail down the extremist groups involved and get guys on the inside. Either way, this all just got a lot harder for the Russians." His voice was gravelly, stimulating.

She made a sound deep in her throat. How could she want him again so soon? She just had him. Twice.

He moved his hands around to the front of her body. He washed her stomach and then moved up to her breasts. He started kissing her neck. She moaned. "What about Peter and Jacobo and the rest?"

"Hmm. They'll all be questioned and charged with various crimes. Peter admitted that Santiago killed Mark Waters because Waters realized that Santiago had crawled into bed with the Russians. Peter admitted helping to load the body into the boat but denied being involved in the murder."

His hands went back down over her belly to the spot between her legs. His hard cock was rubbing between her ass cheeks. "Santiago's empire is dead. They will dismantle it piece by piece and see where everything leads."

She moaned again as his fingers entered her. She opened her legs wider. "So, it's over," she breathed.

"It's over," he agreed as he moved his fingers deeper inside her. His other hand held her hip as he rubbed himself faster along her ass.

"Elias," she hissed as he added a second finger deep inside her. Her hips rocked faster and faster until she crashed over the edge. He rubbed a few strokes more and then joined her in oblivion.

They leaned against the shower wall for a minute until her phone went off yet again. She turned to face him and frowned.

"Someone is in a hurry to reach you," he said as he dropped a kiss on her nose.

"Yeah. I guess it's time to go back to reality." She closed her eyes and then gave her hair a final rinse. She stepped out of the spray. "Duty calls."

He kissed her again before she got out of the shower. She

toweled off and then towel-dried her hair. She brushed it out and pulled it into a ponytail.

She really did have to go into work today. Sighing, she opened the bathroom door and walked down the hall to the bedroom. She chose navy dress pants and a white blouse, then pulled on the matching navy blazer. She added a touch of makeup using the bedroom mirror and then put on her socks.

Her shoes were out by the door. She left the bedroom and passed Elias in the hallway. "You're going to get food right? I'm starving."

He grinned. "Two minutes." He disappeared into the bedroom.

She finished walking down the hallway as her phone rang. She answered, "Peña. How are you?"

"I'm downstairs. Let me in."

"You're here? Great. Give me a sec."

"I'll let him in," Elias said. He was dressed in faded jeans and a black t-shirt. His still-damp hair fell over his forehead. He still looked sexy as hell. She sighed as he pulled on his sneakers and then hit the buzzer. Then he dropped another kiss on her nose and opened the door. "Back shortly."

She waited by the open door. "Peña," she said as she gave him a quick hug when he reached the open doorway. "So good to see you. How are you doing? What's going on at work?"

She turned and went back to the kitchen area to pour herself a cup of coffee. "You want some?" she asked.

Peña swung the door closed. "No thanks."

She frowned. Peña always drank coffee. He never turned down a cup. They'd made jokes about caffeine, instead of blood, running through his veins.

She finished pouring her own cup and then turned

around, cup in her right hand, to find Peña standing there, pointing a gun at her.

"What the fuck? What are you doing?" she yelled.

"I tried calling. I tried to get you to come in and talk to me, but you refused. I don't have a choice."

"Riccardo, what are you talking about?" she tried to keep her voice steady and maintain eye contact. She fell back on an old hostage negotiating trick of using his first name to build a rapport with him. It was then that she noticed how bad he looked. His skin looked sallow, and his eyes were bloodshot. His breathing was rapid, too. "What's wrong? Are you sick?"

"Andy, why couldn't you just tell me what was going on? Robins was always an asshole. I didn't really expect him to tell me anything. You know how he was all smug when he knew something we didn't."

"You killed Robins," she murmured. Her stomach knotted. Her hand holding the coffee mug started to sweat. "Why?"

"He was an asshole. Look how he hung you out to dry at the exchange. He only thought of himself. Stupid. I asked him to tell me what was going on. I begged him, but he kept saying it was a matter of national security. It wasn't until after I burned him with the cigarillos that I realized he truly didn't know anything. He was bluffing." Peña started to laugh, the sound high-pitched and harsh. "Oh, the irony of it all. Him lording it over us, saying he was read in when he was just as clueless as the rest of us. If only he'd been honest, he'd still be alive." He cackled some more.

Sweat trickled down Andy's spine. She took a step forward, put her mug down on the counter, and then grabbed the edge to steady herself. This was crazy.

Peña raised his gun. She noticed it had a suppressor on. He could shoot her and no one would hear especially since half the people in the building were elderly and had their televisions turned up very loud. "Now you're going to tell me what's going on. I don't want to have to torture you, too."

Her mind scrambled. How could she let Elias know what was going on? She didn't want Peña to even think about Elias.

"Don't worry, I passed your boyfriend on the stairs, so I know you're here alone. "Now talk."

"Riccardo, I don't know what it is you want to know, so how can I tell you?"

His face clouded over. "I need to know what Santiago was up to."

"Santiago is dead."

He let out a long sigh. "I'm aware of that, but I need to know what he was doing. Who he was working with? Are they going to take over his business?"

"Why are you so interested, Riccardo?" Andy was trying to stall for time. She knew the moment Peña had pulled the gun on her that he was going to kill her. He was an ATF agent. He couldn't pull a gun on another agent and talk his way out of it.

Peña glared at her. "I don't have time for this. Just tell me."

Suddenly, the weird pieces of the puzzle clicked into place. Pieces she hadn't even realized were part of the puzzle. "You work for Jasper. He's been spying on Santiago for a while now, trying to figure out how Santiago managed to make him lose all those shipments and trying to find out who the new partner is."

Peña's face hardened. "Just tell me what I want to know."

"It's Izzy's medical bills, isn't it? That's what made you do it. You can't keep up. You want to give your daughter the best help possible, but it's costly and you can't afford it."

"Goddamn insurance keeps turning me down. I had no

choice and now…" He paused. "Just tell me Andy. I promise I'll make it quick. If you keep drawing this out, I will be forced to torture you just like Robins, and I won't enjoy it nearly as much."

Andy's stomach rolled. "Okay," she said, "but tell me one thing: Are you sick?"

He nodded once. "Pancreatic cancer. I got maybe six weeks left. Jasper promised me that if I can find out what's going on, he'll give me enough money to take care of my family after I'm gone."

Andy's heart broke just a little for Peña. He was a desperate man in a truly desperate situation. It didn't excuse what he did, but she understood. "Jasper will have free rein now. No one, at least no one I know, will be stepping in to take Santiago's place. Jasper can duke it out with the normal contenders. You can also tell him his shipments will no longer go missing. At least not because of Santiago."

Peña's eyes narrowed. "Why are you suddenly telling me this?"

"It's what you wanted, isn't it?" She did her best hold her rising panic at bay. She needed to drag this out until Elias got back. She had to give Peña something so he didn't shoot her.

Peña raised the gun, pointing directly at the middle of her chest. "Who was ripping off Jasper?"

She frowned. "I can't tell you that. It's not important."

"It is to Jasper. He has a reputation to uphold. He can't let someone get away with stealing from him. He has to show everyone that he's the boss. Send a message. Santiago was humiliating him. He needs to make sure everyone knows he got his revenge so no one else tries what Santiago did."

"I get it, but he can't get revenge on these people. Just tell him that the people who had been ripping him off and making it difficult for him are gone and they aren't coming back. Santiago is dead."

"I need details," Peña shouted. "I'll shoot you in the shoulder and work my way down your body if you want. I've had practice recently in the art of torture. I know how to make it hurt."

She blinked. What could she do? There was no way for her to reach a knife and even if she did, he would shoot her. Her gun was still in the bedroom. "Okay, it was the Russians."

Peña frowned and the barrel of his gun lowered a smidge. "What game are you trying to play?" His lips flattened into a hard line as he brought the gun back up to aim at her chest. "I don't want to hurt you Andy, but I will."

"I am being truthful, Riccardo. It was the Russians. Santiago made a deal with them. They helped him with his Jasper problem, and he helped them connect with various extremist groups across the country." Using his name didn't seem to have the effect she'd hoped for.

He poked the gun into her flesh. "The Russians?"

"Yeah. They supplied all the muscle and helped Santiago with his cash flow problem in return for selling guns and training militias in the US."

Peña frowned then cocked his head. "I guess that makes some sort of sense." He raised the gun. "Sorry, Andy."

The apartment door opened, and Peña whirled around letting off two shots in rapid succession. Elias disappeared from sight. Peña was turning back towards her, so she ducked down behind the island.

Oh, please, God no. Do not let Elias be hurt. Do not let us die here. There were another two shots and then a *thunk*. Andy peeked over the top of the counter. Elias stood leaning against the door, his gun down by his side.

He looked over at her. "He's dead. You're safe." The relief in his voice was profound. She found herself swallowing hard to get rid of the lump in her throat. She walked around the counter and directly into his arms as the tears started to roll down her cheeks.

Then she noticed. "You're hit." Blood streamed down his arm.

"Just a graze. Nothing to worry about. I did drop breakfast though so it's going to be a bit longer for food."

She glanced down at the brown bag on the floor and started to giggle. Then she looked up into his eyes and kissed him. Hard.

CHAPTER TWENTY-SIX

Sun streamed down on the top of a picnic table where they were sitting. The ocean waves washed up on the beach with a muted roar. The day was beautiful with light glistening off the water. A light breeze that brought the smell of the salt air and pizza to her nose. "Miguel, are the pizzas almost done? I'm starving," she yelled.

Inside his pizza truck, Miguel shook his head. A few weeks ago, Elias had offered Miguel the money he'd won at the poker game to start his own pizza truck business and, judging by the line outside waiting for some pizza, it was a raging success.

Elias was sitting next to her, staring out at the water. "You know, hassling him is not helpful. You're going to make all those people think he's slow at making their pizzas. They won't be happy."

"The only thing people in line are thinking right now is, 'When am I going to get my pizza? I'm starving.'"

Elias laughed. "Fair point."

Her cell phone pinged, and she glanced at it.

"Do you need to go?"

She shook her head. "No. They're just keeping me in the loop. If the situation goes hot, I'll get the call to come in."

"Are you liking the new job? Is it a big change?"

Elias hadn't asked her much in the six weeks since the whole Santiago/Peña debacle, and she appreciated it. They hadn't seen each other much either. She needed time to wrap her brain around everything. How could she have been so wrong about Peña? They'd all been wrong about him. She felt really bad for Jay. Peña was his best friend. He was really struggling.

Anyway, after endless debriefs where she could only say so much, she finally quit. She called a former teacher at Quantico who said if she ever wanted a job to let him know. He'd come through for her. She was now an FBI agent. It was taking some getting used to, but she was enjoying it.

She'd finally gotten to tell her aunt the truth. Her aunt had shifted between crying and hugging her for almost an hour, sometimes doing both, but it had been cathartic for them both. Things were finally looking up.

When Elias turned to look at her, she realized she hadn't answered his question. "Yes, I am enjoying the new job."

"Are they going to let you stay in Miami?" He frowned. "Do you *want* to stay in Miami?"

She sighed. "It's a tough one. I want to put the past behind me, and that's easier to do if I leave here. On the other hand, my family, such as it is, is here. I would like to be close to my aunt."

"I see." He stood up and turned to face her. "In case I haven't said it yet, I would very much like it if you stayed. I've been trying to give you space. What you went through is…a lot. It takes time to get right with it."

She nodded.

"But Andrea…"

The tone of his voice was serious. She looked up at his

face, searching for whatever clues she could find to what he was thinking. It was so hard to fathom him sometimes. "What is it?"

"I still love you."

Her heart slammed against her ribs at his words.

He grabbed one of her hands and wound his fingers through hers, his gaze dropping to the ground. "When the boat went over, my only thought was to get to you. All that time we wasted because I was an out of control, cruel asshole to you. Everything became crystal clear to me. Then I almost lost you again to Peña. I just can't imagine my life without you in it now. I love you and want to be with you."

He looked up at her finally, and their gazes locked. She opened her mouth but then closed it again. What could she say? "Elias, I...love you, too. I don't think I ever stopped loving you, but you hurt me really bad. I get it now and I understand it, but I don't think I would survive it if I had to go through that kind of agony again. I am just a bit...gun shy."

He nodded. "I understand. We can take it slow. You choose the speed. You tell me what you want, but Andrea, know that I am willing to do whatever it takes to make you mine again."

"Elias," she breathed as she wrapped her arms around his neck, "I'm already yours."

SNEAK PEEK: BREAK AND ENTER
CALLAHAN SECURITY BOOK 1

Callahan Security is on the brink of disaster. Mitch Callahan pushed his brothers to expand the family business into private security, and their first major client is a complete pain in the ass. It's no wonder the man has a target on his back, but nothing could prepare Mitch for how seductive his adversary is.

Love hurts. No one knows that better than Alexandra Buchannan, so she uses her talents as a thief to equalize the scales of romantic justice. Your ex still has your favorite painting? Not for long. Alex's latest job is her biggest challenge yet. Her target just hired a new security company, and the team leader is as smart as he is sexy.

Mitch knows he's jeopardizing not only this job but the future of Callahan Security. If only he didn't find Alex so damn irresistible. Soon their game of cat and mouse explodes into a million pieces. Unbeknownst to them, there's another player in the game, and his intentions are far deadlier.

BREAK AND ENTER

Chapter 1

Sweat trickled along Alexandra Buchanan's hairline under her wig. Her heart thudded in her chest. She was minutes from her goal, mere seconds from obtaining her objective. She had been planning for months. Her fingertips tingled as the seconds ticked by slowly. She itched under her red velvet Venetian mask. Its feathers tickled her face.

The humid air hung heavy in the grand ballroom. The smell of women's perfumes and men's colognes mixed with sweet scent of the dozens of flowers that were on tables stationed around the room. But none of it could mask the funk of body odor or the even stronger stench of money.

The room was filled with the elite of Venice, of Italy and beyond. Women wore eye-catching costumes. Sequins and jewels glittered in the light from the ornate chandeliers. Men wearing masks and capes flashed jewels of their own on their fingers and their wrists. The room was a swirl of color and sound. Everyone who was anyone was invited to the Santini's spring ball. And this year it was a masquerade. She smiled to herself. She couldn't have asked for a better cover. It was as if the stars had aligned perfectly just for her.

She glanced at her watch. Only another twenty seconds, and the song would be over. And then it was time. As always happened at this moment, her senses heightened. She could hear every voice distinctly, see every small movement. Time slowed down to a crawl.

Finally, the orchestra was playing the last few notes of the song. This was it, the moment she lived for, the moment when she either conquered her goal or she failed miserably. Adrenaline roared through her body. Excitement exploded in her chest.

Alex moved across the floor as dancers mingled, looking for their next partner. She had her target in sight. He was passing his partner from the previous song to another man. He turned and smiled at the woman standing next to him. He took his new partner's hand in his.

She increased her pace slightly so that she was directly beside her target as he swung his other hand around to clasp the woman. She didn't look at him as she jostled him slightly. It was expected in this crowded space. Her fingers deftly performed the task they had done many times before. Quickly, silently she had her prize. She made her way across the floor, smiling as she went. She slid her hand into a hidden pocket, depositing her bounty.

This was it—the worst and, yet, the best moment. Would he notice? Would he yell? Would he point her out?

She kept her head up and her steady pace as she broke free of the dancers and started up the stairs to the mezzanine. Sweat was a fine sheen across her body. She had a fixed smile on her face and nodded to several of the partygoers as she crested the top of the stairs. Walking across the floor, she made her way toward the restrooms but glanced around quickly. No one was close. No one was paying attention. She passed the restrooms and made for the hallway on her left.

She moved down the corridor and made it to the doors that led to the terrace, but she kept walking. The security plan she'd gotten a hold of indicated they were tied to an alarm that would be on tonight. She went a few steps farther.

After making sure the hallway was clear, she did a little dance and slid her crinoline off. She wouldn't need it anymore, and it would just be in her way. She'd bought it from an online shop using a fake account and had it delivered to an office building. She hadn't touched it without her gloves so there were no prints, or at least not hers.

Glancing around she spotted a chair a little farther down the hallway. She put the crinoline on the far side of the chair, so it wouldn't be immediately seen by anyone walking down the hall.

Alex went back to a window at the far end of the balcony and unlocked it. Lifting it silently, she was once again amazed at how many people didn't alarm their windows above the ground floor. Tugging her costume up around the tops of her thighs so she could move her legs freely, she put one foot through the window, ducked under, and brought the rest of her body through onto the balcony. She lowered the window again from the outside.

"Where the hell did you come from?" a voice demanded from the darkness. She froze. No one should be on the balcony. She had planned this heist meticulously, and nowhere in the Santini security arrangements was there any indication that someone would be on the balcony.

A guest then? As she slowly turned in the direction the voice had come, a man dressed in a tuxedo emerged from the shadows. Damn. Security. They were wearing tuxes instead of costumes. But not Santini security. He didn't have the same type of ill-fitting tux as the Santini security guys. His fit him like a glove, like he was born to wear it. Someone else's security. A private bodyguard. Great. She'd been fifty-three seconds from freedom, and she runs into James Bond.

Her mind reeled as she tried to figure out a different escape route. The weight of the watch hidden in her skirt was a thousand pounds heavier. *Don't panic.* She smiled and moved forward a couple of steps, letting him take a long look at her.

The trick was to keep as much space between them as she could without seeming reluctant. She thanked her lucky stars once again that the party was a masquerade ball. For a thief, it was like hitting the jackpot. An *Asset Repossession Specialist Extraordinaire*, she mentally corrected herself.

Her duchess costume, which she'd had made especially for this job, not only showed off her assets but had a few hidden surprises. The security guy's gaze lingered for a moment on her "girls" as she called them. Not her norm to display them so blatantly, but she'd wanted to be sure anyone looking at her would be distracted, even the women. Better to show too much tit than too much of her face.

She took a deep breath. If she was careful, maybe she could still get away unscathed. After all, the mask she wore covered most of her face except for the lower part of her jaw, and the voluminous brown wig hid the rest of her head. Her heart rate started to come back down to earth. She could do this. The fine sheen of sweat had turned into a small river making its way down her back.

"What are you doing here? This area is off limits. No one is supposed to be up here." He walked closer to her, his stance showing easy confidence. They were about twelve feet apart, separated by an area bathed in shadow. The breeze ruffled the feathers of her mask, but it also brought his scent to her. He smelled of soap and citrus and something wholly male that had her taking notice.

"*You're* here," she said in her most sultry voice. She prayed he wouldn't come any closer. He was bigger than most men, much bigger than her diminutive 5'5". At least six feet, she figured, which wasn't necessarily a problem, but his shoulders were wide. Why couldn't he have been one of the doughy types she had seen earlier? The guys who'd gone to seed years ago. She could have handled one of those guys no problem. Years of kick boxing, Tae Kwon Do, Krav Maga, and general self-defense training meant she could have rendered one of them unconscious soundlessly.

But she had to get the keener who looked to be in fabulous shape. All narrow hips, broad shoulders, and solid muscle. One of the major lessons she had learned was how to assess her opponent, and this one would be tough. Her stomach roiled. A fight with this guy would be loud and painful. Fighting was off the table.

She smiled as she studied him. His hair was a light brown with blond highlights. He wasn't wearing a mask, but it was hard to determine his eye color. There was no mistaking his square jaw though, especially since it appeared to be clenched. He was also drop-dead gorgeous and sexy as hell.

His eyes narrowed and focused on her after casing the rest of the balcony. "Who are you?"

She ignored the question. So, throwing him over the balcony was not going to work. Physically impossible, and besides, she wanted to avoid a scene. The water in the canals would catch his fall, yes, but everyone would rush to see as soon as they heard the splash.

"Who are you?" he repeated as he stepped closer. The Venice breeze ruffled a lock of his hair so that it fell over his forehead.

She gave a girlish giggle while mentally rolling her eyes. Men loved that crap. "Well, doesn't that defeat the whole purpose of a masquerade ball? I can't tell you who I am. It would ruin the mystery."

"Then why don't you tell me how you got onto this balcony? Like I said, no one is supposed to be out here."

She pouted. "Well, *you're* here." Then she closed the gap between them with a sexy stroll. She smiled up at him while caressing the pleats of his tux shirt with her gloved fingers. She needed him to stop asking questions. "All by yourself, I might add." Yes, all muscle. She could feel it through his shirt. Warmth spread through her insides as she peered up into his startlingly gray eyes. She had never seen eyes that gray before. They were like polished steel.

If circumstances were different...she still wouldn't touch him with a ten-foot pole. She'd been down that road before. If she'd learned nothing else in life, it was that the best-looking men were the ones that couldn't be trusted. Not ever. Not even if they were family.

He grabbed her fingers and held them fast. It sent an electric charge skittering up her arm. Startled, she tried to pull her hand back, but he held on. Her plan wasn't working. *He* was the one who was supposed to be distracted, not her.

"You need to leave. Now." There was no sign that he was remotely affected by her presence, unlike her who was totally suffering from their closeness. Her pulse skyrocketed. She was surprised he couldn't see it with her chest on display. Maybe he could. Sweat was now running down her legs as well as her back. This man was sexy as hell, but he was like kryptonite. She needed a new plan and fast.

"Uh..."

"Go for Callahan," the man said as he pressed his earpiece. He dropped her hand. Then, turning around, he walked over to the railing and looked down.

Recognizing her chance, she quickly and silently moved the fifty feet to the other end of the balcony. She took off her shoes and stuffed them into the hidden pockets of her dress. Then she hoisted herself onto the railing. With a quick glance back, she saw the man was still on the other side of the balcony looking down. She quickly stepped onto the small decorative ledge running along the front of the building and, hugging the wall, slid her way carefully to the corner.

She reached up and grabbed the edge of the roof and swung herself around the corner. Regaining her balance, she took a second to breathe and rest her cheek against the building. She took one hand off the wall slowly and wiped it on her dress. Then did the same with the other. After she lifted her cheek, she carefully removed her mask and pushed it into the pocket next to her shoes. She put her hand back on the wall.

She loved Venice. The buildings were so close together here, and in her line of work, that was a big plus.

ALSO BY LORI MATTHEWS

Callahan Security
Break and Enter
Smash And Grab
Hit And Run
Evade and Capture
Catch and Release (Coming Soon)

Coast Guard Recon
Diverted
Incinerated
Conflicted

Brotherhood Protectors World
Justified Misfortune
Justified Burden

Free with Newsletter Sign Up
Falling For The Witness
Visit my website to sign up for my newsletter

ABOUT LORI MATTHEWS

I grew up in a house filled with books and readers. Some of my fondest memories are of reading in the same room with my mother and sisters, arguing about whose turn it was to make tea. No one wanted to put their book down!

I was introduced to romance because of my mom's habit of leaving books all over the house. One day I picked one up. I still remember the cover. It was a Harlequin by Janet Daily. Little did I know at the time that it would set the stage for my future. I went on to discover mystery novels. Agatha Christie was my favorite. And then suspense with Wilber Smith and Ian Fleming.

I loved the thought of combining my favorite genres, and during high school, I attempted to write my first romantic suspense novel. I wrote the first four chapters and then exams happened and that was the end of that. I desperately hope that book died a quiet death somewhere in a computer recycling facility.

A few years later, (okay, quite a few) after two degrees, a husband and two kids, I attended a workshop in Tuscany that lit that spark for writing again. I have been pounding the keyboard ever since here in New Jersey, where I live with my children—who are thrilled with my writing as it means they get to eat more pizza—and my very supportive husband.

Please visit my webpage at https://lorimatthewsbooks.com to keep up on my news.

Made in the USA
Coppell, TX
28 May 2022

78226884R00184